TO BE SUNG
on the WATER

TO BE SUNG
on the WATER

A Novel by

MEREDITH STEINBACH

HOUSE OF REMINGTON
PUBLISHING

Published in the United States by House of Remington Publishing, Bristol, Rhode Island. No part of this book may be used or reproduced in any manner whatsoever without written permission from the publisher. For information, contact House of Remington Publishing, P.O. Box 1045, Bristol, Rhode Island 02809.

Printed in the United States

ISBN: 978-0-9882836-3-3

Cover art: *"Girl on the Beach, 1896"* by Edvard Munch
Book and cover design: Mary Tiegreen
Author photo credit: Zach S. Hartman

Parts of this novel have been published previously in *TriQuarterly Magazine, Southwest Review, Ploughshares, Reliable Light,* and in *The Long Meanwhile, An Hourglass Anthology of Fiction.*

With many thanks to Jacqueline Russom for the use of her excellent editorial skills.

Grateful acknowledgement is made to the authors of the following works which have been used for reference: *In The Deserts of This Earth* by Uwe George, *Illustrated Encyclopedia of Plants and Animals* (Bisacre, Carlisle, Robertson, Ruck, and George, editors), *The Complete Works of Herodotus, Desert* by Miranda Macquitty, *Complete Mediterranean Wildlife* (Paul Sterry, editor)

With continuing gratitude
to the exquisitely talented and delightful
Mary Tiegreen

—◊◊◊—

Happy. Happier then. Snug little room that was with the red wallpaper, Dockrell's one and nine pence a dozen. Milly's tubbing night. American soap I bought: elderflower. Cosy smell of her bathwater. Funny she looked soaped all over. Shapely too. Now photography. Poor papa's daguerreotype atelier he told me of. Hereditary taste.

He walked along the curbstone.
Stream of life.

Ulysses
James Joyce

CHAPTER I

THESE THEN ARE THE BEASTS OF THE DESERT that I managed to see: aardvarks, blister beetles, wasps, scorpions, wood lice, termites, scarabs, mites and ticks, orb-weavers, wolf spiders, ant mimics, other hunting spiders, wild cats, cheetah, addax and oryx, gazelles, patas monkeys, grasshoppers, the melon ladybird, aoudad, three species of frog, six toads, reptiles, camels, men... Some are confined to erratic watercourses, ditches, some inspired by the occasional ten-year rain. Did I say owls?

No you did not say owls, my increasingly overheated wife Isabella says. And snakes. Do not forget snakes.

At night we freeze, shaking under metallic blankets. By day the heat passes 120, yesterday pressing 130 degrees. We have ceased to sweat. And with each sandstorm, the static electricity is so great; our heads are ready to burst. Isabella claims she has stopped her headaches finally. With an umbrella. She goes everywhere creating shade and then driving the metal shaft into the sand, grounding herself.

"Wear your high heels, too," I try to laugh. "They must have metal in them."

"You laugh," she says. "Go on and laugh, Birdy. But you're the one going round and round with a seismic eruption in your brain stem."

"Don't talk so loudly, Iz," I say, clutching at my temples. "Now I know why that ostrich did his weird act."

Iz drives her umbrella into the ground again and out comes a fierce rattle like a snake. She jumps nearly half a foot and runs the rest of the way back to me. I jump, too, for pity's sake.

"Jesus, Birdy," she says. "I nearly skewered a rattlesnake."

"Or, got skewered," I say. "Tapped and suckered by a rattler." But it is not a rattler Iz finds when she goes to dig him out, wearing the bite proof gloves, a helmet, and other amulets. It's amazing she doesn't collapse with all that stuff on. "Temperature control, temperature control," I remind.

"Here, Birdy," she says. She holds out in her palms a set of baby owls and there at the back of their fearful beaks is the rattling sound. After everyone has seen and photographed them, she puts them safely back.

The crew trudges doggedly by, sneering toward the end of another exhausted day, dragging the metal scanners to and fro. The upper crusts of all our skins seem to be peeling back to reveal a uniform, fleshy pink interior, irrespective of race or temperament. The sand is so hot now that even in the early evening, we can hardly walk on it. It's as if we have no shoes on at all. Now the sun plunges down behind the earth, and the stars are everything. We rock back and forth under all creation. You can barely hear the wind coming up for all the clacking of teeth. We are like wind-up party skeletons.

Men crossed this moonstruck terrain with nicknamed camels, wives, lovers, children, wagons, water. A caravan stretched out for miles under these stars, traveling by night for energy and relief. Or, I say to myself, maybe they didn't need to hide from sun. In the end, all of them were lost to a shift in sand and wind, without one trace. Soon we start working under the floodlight of our own time. How many days and months have passed?

It's impossible to say, but perhaps Rose can conjure its tympanic memory. Was it as long ago as yesterday? Perhaps during breakfast the throbbing was already with her. She goes into the airy chamber and stares at it. It is a slow bead that wells up at the end of the spout and then drops into the sound it will soon make. The Husband is away. Who knows where the Lover is. Fully clothed she lies down in the bath. She will not get wet. She lies looking at it welling up. It is long ago, far away.

—⁂—

The two little girls nestle on the porch swing beside Grandmother, thinking they may be able to see that house where their six cousins, their Aunt Polly, and their mother's adamant brother Uncle Gideon live. Just two miles up the road! Their favorite Giddy! Uncle, Uncle Giddy! Uncle Giblet! The little girls kick their shoes together fondly. The swing soars back and forth. If they could see it from here, Rosie thinks, it would only be the slightest lemon drop anyway; it is such a very small house.

No, her sister Georgie says, from here their cousins' house would look like a bright kernel of corn with its green roof like a leaf laid over the top.

Then, too, the windbreak is in the way, off to the right, mysterious and dense, one thick line of trees in all this flat wilderness. Something frightening and unknown must live in the tangle of old wires at the center of Grandmother's grove. A horse cart has crumpled to bones in there, the leather seat and bonnet disintegrated to something like the shoelaces of boots. Their gentle mother has explained that the pony itself must have died long ago—even before their mother's time. Surely Grandmother remembers it? No. No one will ask her. Surely they will all be crying if anyone says a word about it.

No one looks in the direction of Uncle Giddy's house. Perhaps the Cousins will appear at any joyful moment, or perhaps the Cousins are at home begging even now to come here, so jubilant to annoy the little girls. Grandmother hums a melody, with glossy-haired Georgia on one side and under the other great fleshy arm, Rosie like a brown-headed puppy. Even when they are completely grown, Rosie will think of their grandmother as immense—although Grandmother will be tiny really for the last quarter of the century. The little girls don't say a word, just squirm in tight. They are all three looking at Mother who sits on the porch rail with her back to one white pillar.

No, nothing at all can describe the brilliance of their mother's azure eyes. Their mother's cheeks are flushed into peonies with her zany laughter; her straight white teeth sparkle as she smiles at them; and around her shoulders floats a cloud of chestnut hair. Mother's new canvas shoes perch together on top of the rail. Mother's turquoise skirt is tucked up around the backs of her thighs. In the front it cascades over her knees and calves, then pours off between the spindles of porch and a flourish of pink *Rosa rugosa*.

Rosie and Georgia have been saying it, over and over all afternoon, *Rosa rugosa,* with a laughter bubbling out of them like many silver bells. They take turns calling one another by it. Georgia walks by indifferently, limping only slightly when she tries on that name: Georgia Rugosa.

They are watching her talk from time to time, long periods of it perhaps. Rose forgets to listen, just watching her sister laugh at something Grandmother has said. Everyone says it: their mother has a nice figure. Her white blouse dips in small at the waist. But Rose will always be smaller, it seems. They look so very like one another.

Because she is oldest, Rosie knows, that is the reason people say it to her most: "Your mother is so young." What is it to come from such beautiful women? What is the sweet powdery scent of it? Rosie asks herself now. What is the silken texture of women when you put it onto a linen canvas with vivid colors and a brush?

The little girls live in town, hours from here. Too far. The distance from Grandmother's house is a small grey stone of aching, thrust somewhere deep in Rosie's ribcage.

The girls kick off their shoes and Grandmother pushes off again, as the three of them on the swing move toward Mother on the railing. The fuzzy caterpillar weed is in Mother's fingertips. With it she tickles in turn their toes when they approach her on the rail. Mother and Grandmother are murmuring between themselves all the while the girls are swinging through the dreamy scene. When the girls decide to listen they can know their mother and their mother's mother's verity. Words drift on currents between them. Words chart what must happen, how the press must act toward each one of them—even the little girls can hear their own names mentioned from time to time—and who must be where at which diaphanous moment in order to insure the plan. Their mother actually says it.

Strategy and success is pleasant in a drone among them.

Rosie nearly leaps out of the swing at the thought of it. "Diaphanous!" Diaphanous! A big and shimmering word!

"Silly Billy," Georgia says.

"Don't start up, little girls—" Grandmother says. "Let a pleasant moment live its life now."

—⁂—

Beyond their mother, the little girls will always see it: the patchy green lawn, the rusty old pump like an arm rising up for greeting, the way the lane winds off as though mesmerized by swaying grain. But the little girls will not for a moment deign to look toward the chalk-white barn where their grandfather, cousins, brother, and father have gone to do uninteresting things. They would not think of it. Once a work of sustenance, the farm has become a hobby for their grandparents. The hired men will do the work now that the grandparents did for so many years when they were younger—after their own years in college, after the teaching in the one-room schoolhouse. Oh! Those glorious days! The farm years! Will they never come again?

In front of the large, pink, country roses, their mother is so still, so radiant, both girls will all their lives be awestruck at the thought. When their mother is in a room, even strangers stare at her with soft eyes.

Grandmother runs her finger over Rose's shoulder, in and around the sleeveless arm of Rose's blouse in a motherly fashion. Air drifts back and forth over Rose's face as the porch swing sings out, as Grandmother's legs touch down, push off again. Grandmother wears a perfume that is subtle and warm. It seems to float in and around them like a sun-struck cloud.

Now the men are hailing from the drive in front of the barn—Grandfather and Father, great hard men, tall with wide shoulders and keen intelligence. The little girls' twin cousins, their brother Fred, and the other boys scream past, going on about the election, whether Grandfather should run for governor. Even the little girls know what it means. Georgia leans around Grandmother's minty cotton dress, toward Rose, as they swoop nearer Mother and away. Georgia rolls her eyes back, and Rose turns her own in toward the burnt sienna of her freckles disappearing just there at the bridge of her nose. Why even discuss the election? Everyone knows Grandfather will run, and if he runs he will win. Or else he would not have decided at dinner last night to give up his state senatorial seat. Every one of them knows that.

"Now, now," Grandmother says, catching them at it. She pats both their arms. "Your Grandfather needs every reassurance he can get, especially from his boys." Whether Uncle Gideon is included in this, the girls cannot make out; all their male cousins certainly are. Their father has always been included, even though he—and now these his little girls, too—have been raised in a city, hours from here, in another state. Rose taunts, her thumbs in her ears and her voice veering: "Boys." These two little girls simultaneously poke out their pink tongues. Even Grandmother laughs. Mother cocks her brow, a flickering at the corner of her mouth.

Father and Grandfather and Freddy troop past in their heavy boots toward the mudroom at the back of the large house. Grandfather keeps a pair of such boots here for Father who would never wear them at home where he must live up to his law practice. Father laughs toward Mother alone, bright and knowing, happy yet deep in his chest. At the back door, the little girls can hear their cousins hooting at something Grandfather has said, something about the election.

Rose contorts the end of her nose. "Cock-eyed," Rose says, and Georgia breaks into squeals again.

Then they are quiet. Grandmother waves toward Grandfather, and Grandfather does the same back. Their hands move in almost the same rhythm, side to side. Grandmother will run the campaign, is already running it; everyone knows that by the silence Grandmother makes in its wake.

"Now, now," Grandmother says again. She pats their arms, and with a creak they push off and swing into the future. Because of her, the little girls will never in their lives be truly afraid as many women are. Even in childbirth, some part of them will be held in her arms. In new times, Georgia will be able to speak out in her job; Rosie, although painfully shy, will become a painter respected in her field.

—m—

Rose is waiting for the Lover, back from one of his expeditions, to come to her in her studio. Every week has been filled with him in some way, by telephone, by mail in the sunlit room with the shiny vast floors, where daily she paints.

Today their meeting will be brief but no less poignant. This week the Lover and his wife have had their second child; there is a certain excitement for everyone. Later in the week he will bring the baby here so Rose can meet his first son.

When he saw Rose's own little boy, the Lover kissed Alfie on the side of his soft golden-brown hair, held him high. "You 'member my daddy?" her little boy—aloft and wheeling about the room—asked him as though his father had somehow disappeared.

"I remember about him," Rose's lover said, about the man he had only seen once and that from a distance.

"You 'member my daddy?" her little boy asked the Lover once again. "My daddy has so important work he forgets sometimes. But I remember him."

"Indeed we all do remember him," the Lover said, lifting Alfie up and down in his flyboy corduroys. "Indeed I do, little man," the Lover laughed, spinning Alfie safely through space, making the sounds of a jet plane. A certain sadness enveloped Rose then.

Now he has rung the buzzer, and she has opened the door to her studio. He is smiling as he always does, so brilliantly. It is all part of the fabric. After all, the spouses have had their own unusual lives from the first. Still it is not exactly what Rose would have chosen for herself, but then what is?

—⁂—

Mother is in the family room with her feet up for a minute on the footstool. At the far end of the long room, *Gone With the Wind* is propped up in a stand by the ironing board. Father has gone to the office, is working on a new case. Georgia curls over her toenails on the sofa, painting them so pale a pink you cannot tell which ones she's done except under a bright light. She holds her foot over a piece of cardboard. Even if she did get polish on the sofa, Rose is thinking in the wing chair on the other side of Mother, the spot would only be a rosy petal in among the flowers of the polished cotton cushion. If Georgia were to speckle the frosted coating onto the Sheraton coffee table, now that would be something to make Mother speak up.

Georgia and Mother have read *Gone With the Wind* five times together, so far, passing the book back and forth. To Rose's annoyance, they make jokes: "Tomorrow is another day," constantly. Rose has not read the book once, though she has seen the movie several times. This is something that Rose later will find regrettable.

Rose is bored. It is very hot outside, and she can think of nothing to do in such heat that would not require misery on her bicycle getting to the event. If she offers to iron, Mother will surely tell the exciting story of her trip to the East Coast again, of how she sold salt-water taffy on the beach and met a man who is now a film star. On the other hand, Rose has already heard the story many times. And there is a great deal of ironing.

It's quite true, Rose will only realize when she is grown: Vivien Leigh looks exactly like Mother. When her mother is dead, Rose will remember her mother's face as that of Scarlett O'Hara and, once in a while, as the quiet mask trying to hide behind the Easter lilies in one photograph.

Mother must be caught off guard to have her picture taken, and then she always looks slightly odd—stiff, quite unlike herself. For a long time, Rose tried unsuccessfully to convince her mother to let her paint her portrait.

Mother is almost through with her iced coffee. Soon she will stand up and begin reading while she irons. If Rose doesn't hurry to make up her mind, the moment will have passed.

Now Mother has gone into the bathroom. She is wearing her bright yellow slacks and her white cotton blouse. Mother always brushes her thick hair when she goes into the bathroom. "If you do it each time, it will always be glossy," she says. "Every time, and you will always have exquisite hair."

—⁊⁊—

When the Lover comes into her, he can stay inside forever it seems. Forever stretches out eternally, just as forever is meant to be.

When the Lover is inside her, he sometimes tells her stories. She likes this best on summer afternoons when she turns off her studio air conditioner so that they can slide about in a film of sweat. "Tell me more about the desert, start with the tents—" she says.

"I painted one blue circular stripe on the top of each tent. From the plane—" he breathes into her ear, "all those tents look like your eyes."

"Oh," she sighs. "Such adulation. Graphic, too."

—⁊⁊—

The man owned seven mountains, the man who loved her mother and now is a film star, which is the part Rose remembers most. She has seen the famous scar on his chin many times on late night movies. She imagines her mother putting the tip of her fingernail just there under his smile. Still, no one can ever compete with Daddy.

In that recurrent dream of hers, time is all mixed up: at the funeral of their mother, Rose is already graduated from art school, is just beginning to feel Alfie leaping in her belly. Her husband stands next to her; and there at a distance, as if at another grave entirely, stands the Lover. He wears a dark suit that is infinitely more tasteful than the perfectly fine one her husband has on. Rose is so upset that she cannot get over thinking about the beauty of the Lover's suit. She cannot seem to do anything appropriate about the horrible surprise of the funeral. Her memories seem to go fast forward and reverse until she wakes up. Everything is shaking.

There are things she can remember very well: Monday morning, and her mother stands directly in front of her, insisting: "If you can't even walk to school by yourself without being terrified, Rose, what will happen to you?"

On days when the edict comes down, her best friend takes a ride with Rose's older brother Fred, and so does her sister Georgia. She and her friend will meet in the art room and glower, silently staring out past their easels, through the plate glass windows and over the autumn field that Rose has had to traverse alone just that morning. They gape toward that edge of town where Rose's mother is, no doubt, having mid-morning coffee.

Her mother calls it Loneliness, that which she wishes to expunge from Rose. Rose cannot name it. She stands on such mornings before her mother at the front door. Soon Rose will be outside, then stepping around the corner and going down the long street edged on each side by the excitement of houses and people. But then the town will fall suddenly away. She will try not to think of it until she is directly upon it. And then it will be over, until it happens again.

Only as an adult will Rose think of the possibilities of defiance and trickery that other girls might have used with such a mother. Nor will she explain to her mother what it is exactly that frightens her—having to cross that vast open field alone with no one watching or caring what becomes of her.

In school now, and later in the world, Rose will always be seen as completely confident

—⁓—

The Husband has his hand just beneath her elbow. Perhaps he steadies her lest she might fall straight over, along with their unborn infant, over the edge of the grave onto the gleaming mahogany casket in the steel crypt. There she and the unborn Alfie would lie like a fruit basket on a well-polished table, her belly a sumptuous arrangement, the fabric of her dress swirling around them. And right there surely, below them: her own mother, the mischievous child, on hands and knees, would be crouched under this banquet. Her mother's chestnut hair is down around a face gone pale white; her own mother is laughing wildly. Even in death.

Perhaps Rose is being melodramatic. Her lover holds her with his eyes; her husband's arm is around her. There is an element of jealousy in the Lover's face, seeing her with her husband for the first time, and repeatedly. Both men steady her as she has steadied them for a number of years now. The two men complement one another so entirely that if either were to leave her she would leave the other one also. It is amazing that her husband does not notice her lover over there. How could anyone not see his strong face? At least, she thinks, her lover and her husband have managed not to come here on the same plane.

Inside her now as she stares into the grave, her baby swims, kicking like a frog this way, then that, as he will for many days, oblivious of the fact that he has already lost his one remaining grandmother.

This ancestry is one of the few things she cannot share with her lover, although on this day he has come closest—anonymously standing in the funeral home, looking for the first time onto the dead face of Rose's lost mother. She will never meet the Lover's parents or brothers, nor will her children have knowledge of them.

Now the warmth of the Husband's body carries the sweet perfume of his morning shower toward her. Whenever she is sorrowful around him, she undoes the top buttons of his shirt and rests her face at his throat among the wealth of his soft hairs. It is as if her mouth has filled with a sweet mother's milk. Comfort washes through her whole body. There is no question that she loves him.

Though still at an immense distance, it is the Lover who stands directly in front of her, gazing across the rows of upright stones and the red flowers dripping onto the landscape. Beside her, Georgia's long black hair lifts like a wing on a momentary breeze.

Georgia takes hold of her hand so hard Rose thinks perhaps they are crushing one another's fingers. But then, maybe Georgia is barely touching her arm. Her hand may merely have gone to sleep; there is so much numb acceptance. These changes should come with warnings!

—∽—

Yes, everywhere there seems to be the sound of screeching tires slipping endlessly through water over pavement. If Rose were to look up she would expect to see her mother's umbrella floating there in the dreamed death— disembodied and completely startled. It is so much easier to think of her death as sudden this way.

Grandmother and Grandfather, Aunt Polly and Uncle Gideon, and all their boys and their wives, Aunt Emily and Uncle Arthur, their daughter,

Freddy home from his last year in Vietnam, the whole family has collected, the living and the dead. Many of Grandfather's colleagues and friends. Everyone is here.

Including Mother! Rose conjures wildly. Mother is here somewhere, I feel it. Dashing about the graves. In a turquoise sundress. And, barefooted, she is bare-footed, as anyone can see.

This part is also true now, or as true as anything between the ears when the night has fastened down one's lids: It would be a splendid summer afternoon if it weren't for all of this. The world turns around on its axis, casts a balmy breeze about the whole contorted scene, threatens to cast all of them off, whole seas and continents, by mere centrifugal forces. Black automobiles are parked up and down the winding drive of the graveyard. At the center of the bank of flowers is the loveliest wreath. It is at least four feet across, a mass of golden yellow roses. Tiny and hammered, the sterling silver horse and feminine rider slip almost imperceptibly over the white ribbon. There is no card; even Aunt Emily has looked for it.

Any number of strangers moves through the graveyard. Once in a while, an unknown man looks up as if from a movie screen to stare into her eyes, perhaps by coincidence.

—m—

"Do I have them—do I have the movie star's ears?" Georgia wiggles hers at Mother under her pixie cut. "They don't look a thing like father's."

To their surprise, Mother storms out across the back lawn. The screen door slams shut. "Where is your mother?" their father asks later. Rose and Georgia say nothing. The story of the seven mountains has been to the two girls a secret gift from Mother's life.

Father has not even put down his briefcase. Finally the girls look down at the floor. "Walking," they say.

"Your mother never goes walking right through the dinner hour. What did you two say to her? Tell me!"

The girls each give an adolescent shrug of their shoulders, together, to say it: Not Guilty, Sir, of hurting our Mother. And, we would never ever hurt you, no matter how often you ask.

When Mother comes in later, she goes upstairs and down the hall, cries on her bed and says nothing for a long while. "Close the curtain," she does say. "And go out of this room. Do not bother me once, you traitors, until tomorrow morning."

Father, too, is not to be admitted again. "What is it?" he asks again.

"On second thought," she says to Father, "you come back in an hour or so. These two I don't want to see until Friday."

"Friday!"

"Or Monday after next. And you know what for, you two; so don't go around here saying otherwise. And don't apologize. Nothing will ever make up for it now. You've destroyed it, an entire part of my history."

"What is it?" Father asks, quite alarmed.

"It's between us," Mother says. "Don't ask again."

—⚏—

At the appointed hour, the Lover calls. Sometimes he calls when he says he will, most often he does not; she spends endless hours supposedly waiting. And while she is waiting she paints, without fretting, in the air acrid with the smell of turpentine. Sometimes she cannot be home when she tells him she will be; often she is. Her little boy comes first, of course. That's the way it should be. This is rather an aggravation to the Lover, but nothing compared with their not having one another. When they make a decision to meet, they both show up.

Today the Lover says that he has a cold: "I have water up my nose! Rosie!" She can hear that in his voice; it sounds quite uncomfortable. "I want to come to the studio anyway," he laughs hoarsely. "We'll use face masks! "

"And blotters!" she says.

—w—

Her husband is reading to her while she soaks in the bathtub; they often do this after Alfie has made his way through story time, songs, evening snacks, glasses of water, and many good nights. She listens while she watches the droplets welling up on the end of the faucet. Her husband has barely begun tonight's chapters when the telephone rings. It will not be her lover; he does not call at this time and has no idea what she makes of these moments each night. And, he would never dare to ask.

Her husband hands her the telephone: "It's Georgia," he says. And then he laughs, seeing her wince when she takes the receiver. No matter how many times he has told her, Rose is still afraid that she will be electrocuted—most particularly while taking hold of a telephone, when naked, in a tub of water so frothy it looks like a meringue.

But her husband has stopped laughing, and Rose is listening intently now.

"I have some bad news for us," Georgia says very bravely—or so Rose will see it tomorrow. Her sister Georgia has bravery beyond belief, a mastery of the world. She is like Father and Grandfather; she is what her husband might wish to be.

And what has become of the shyness of Rose? By day, Rose paints vast landscapes of her childhood; some may be abstract, but they still point back toward the same swing. A woman at a gallery in Boston sells them on Newbury Street. Some of the other paintings are put into museums and pictured in beautiful catalogs where Rose is mentioned, sometimes beside a minuscule photograph of her face.

But what of this bad message from her sister? What does it mean?

By tomorrow morning, Rose will find herself elsewhere, back there in Grandmother's country. She and Georgia will have been washed up onto their grandmother's porch. She is not dreaming for once. And besides, her mother is already too long ago dead.

—⁂—

Rose finds herself in her little son's bedroom. He has been calling out in his sleep. She brushes along his damp cheek, through his silky golden hair. His forearm is still round and doughy where it dips in toward the small bones of his wrist. Her boy has taken the shirt off his bear so he can rub its fat tummy while he is going to sleep. She finds herself gently pushing another bear's furry paw through a miniature sleeve, then the next. It is the shirt Alfie appreciates. "Believe what you see in your Alfie," Grandmother said. "Very few babies are so affectionate."

After Alfie has been cuddled and petted, in the last moments before he drops off to sleep, something makes him have to stroke someone else. Rose will never forget her surprise at seeing his tiny newborn hand, smaller than the etching on a sand dollar, his wispy fingers, lift out from under her comforting palm in order to stroke her own skin.

—⁂—

In the State house, Grandmother asks Rosie, who is now nearly old enough for school—her confident one, so Grandmother truly believes—to carry a silver tray around to all the people who have been invited to meet them. Across the vast terrifying emerald green carpet Rose goes, offering the tiny sandwiches. For Grandmother, she will do anything.

Later on the tour of the new fallout shelter, Rosie will cry out, "But Grandfather can't stand up! It's too short. It's not tall enough in here for my Grandfather! Let him out! My Grandfather will have to sit down until they dig him up— or until he dies in here. Let him out!"

Once she speaks, none of the adults will ever have to say it. They have made an unspeakable error in the design of this governmental vault.

—⁊⁊—

Rose will not be able to reach her lover before she leaves the city. When she does she will be standing in her grandmother's kitchen, talking from the black wall phone beside the pail of well water and the familiar family dipper. Out the back door she will see the outbuildings, the barn to which she only once ventured to see the new little chicks, the empty boots on the back porch, and just beyond, in the entryway on a railing in a specially vented bag, Grandmother's long mink coat.

"Hello," she'll say to her lover. "I'm glad I reached you in time."

"Is something the matter? I thought you were meeting me at three."

She buries her face in the fur, in the fragrances that used to grace her grandmother's skin. The crystal bottles still sit upstairs on the vanity. "I had to go home," she says into the mouth of the portable telephone.

In the background her lover's little daughter is chattering; his new baby boy howls on his other shoulder. Soon the babysitter will arrive. "I thought you were meeting me at the studio," he repeats. "You're still at home now?"

"I'm at the country house, Gram's house. My grandfather died yesterday."

"Shush up now, Holly honey, just one second, then I'll fix it for you," the Lover says in the background.

She can hear his warmth turning her way again. "Oh baby," he says. "I'm sorry. Are you O.K.?"

"I don't know." She says it before she realizes it's true, "Suddenly everything seems so very tiny." She can see the kitchen counter where the waffle iron seemed so magical; now it seems like a glinting dime.

"Is your grandmother going to be all right?"

"I don't know yet," she says.

"Oh, you must feel miserable. I want to hold you up close, poor darling."

"Yes," she sighs. "Yes next Tuesday maybe I'll be back."

"I'll see you then." There is a commotion of children in the background. "Oh, fuck," he says. "I forgot all about it. I'm sorry that's the week of the Toronto conference. Are you all right? Oh hold up, love—I have to go. Her car just pulled in the drive. You know how I hate to aggravate."

And then he is gone. Rose is sitting on the mudroom floor, crying hard for her grandfather, for her grandmother's life now shattered, into a fur coat that she would never wear herself, pressed up against her face. So many little droplets to make up a life.

—m—

Grandmother is not only half her former width; she has lost inches in height. She now comes only to Rose's shoulder. It appears that she has been literally drained.

Now she and Georgia sit at the kitchen table while Grandmother stares into the teacup. Then Grandmother announces: "Gideon arranged the whole funeral for Papa!" Grandmother says it proudly, alluding to Uncle Giddy's release and partial recovery.

Rose bursts out on Grandfather's behalf, before she can stop herself: "Not Gideon!"

Something pointed and hard like an anvil has socked Rose under the table. "Oh?" Rose says, backtracking, rubbing at her knee. Georgia's angular face has hardened across the table. "So Gideon has arranged everything?"

It still gives Rose a tight feeling somewhere between her throat and stomach, like having swallowed something way too hot that won't go up or down nearly quickly enough. It is better to think about the little house for a while: the peeling yellow bungalow down the road that housed so many children, a quaint little house really, with the kindly Aunt Polly in the apron that might have been splattered by Miró, the upraised wooden spoon a mid-air declaration of authority.

In Aunt Polly's front yard, for three entire summers, Rose stood at her easel painting the prairie scene. Eventually Rose would discover that, with each work, the golden house shifted further to the left as if intent on moving upstream through a neighboring field of wheat.

—⁜—

There is also the Christmas that Rose and Georgia both like to recall. Gideon stands shirtless on the middle cushion of the sofa, a holly wreath around his neck, in full declamation, reading aloud to all of them and all their cousins: "Selected parts, children! Selected exquisitional party parts for the birthday of Our Great Devisor! Lay on the Christmas cookies! Down the eggnog! Take your places, children, quickly sit yourselves down!" Hour upon hour, by day, from Finnegan's Wake. Grandmother is convincing him to take off his shoes at least: *Gideon! Sit down from time to time; at least let the children take their dinners at the table.* Twelve children take their dinners on the floor beneath him; they will not leave him to come to table. In his dark blue pants, and white shirt with the red Christmas tie leaping about over his pine green suspenders, every waking hour he stands above them with the twelve acolytes around him, mesmerized. Quietly they crack the shells of marbles into one another. No one murmurs, no one shouts for fear of missing a syllable. Silently, the children harvest paper elves and Santas from the classifieds, inking on mustachios. Later, without a word, they will play with the stunningly pigmented pick-up sticks.

The girls are soaring their tuneless paper airplanes around Uncle Giddy's feet, when Freddy makes the merest breach: a sudden and pronounced put-put-put of his twin engines and then a searing whine splits Finnegan's Wake. You should have seen Giddy's face! A barely audible duet of puffs and then Freddy's plane has crashed into the hassock mountaintop.

Uncle Gideon sits down in a daze on the back of the sofa. "Where were we?" he asks. "I can't just now recall where ever we were." He surveys the array beneath him; his head swings back and forth like a folk puppet on a stick. Everywhere the living room scene seems to be sprinkled with red and green sugar like the loveliest holiday cake.

Later, at night, we rise from our beds in our night shifts and drift down to see him in the wee hours, rising from the sagging sofa where his footprints trod the invisible and irreplaceable stuffing underneath. His whole body has begun to go completely rigid as he reads aloud and only to himself the reassuring words of *Fear and Trembling and The Sickness Unto Death.*

"That was one Christmas I didn't like to see come to an end!" Grandmother shook her head, "That day when Giddy stopped reading to you, and then your mother drove off with you girls to the city, that was the day my baby Giddy lost his inner light." So many years later, and about it still their grandmother can cry.

"Life is all the same day, my darlings," she said. "My babies, keep alert, won't you? Don't let life go giving you the slip."

Afterwards, Uncle Giddy grew surly. His shoes sat like firecrackers at the edge of the carpet. In the kitchen and the dining room, grownups could be heard muttering within his earshot. When jumping rope or playing ball, the children mimicked him.

"When is Gid-Gid-Gideon going to pain— going to pain— going to paint—his house? Uncle Gideon! Giddy! Giddy Id-deon! Get off! Grandma's sofa! And go to work?"

"It's not the time, Rose, to think about Uncle Gideon," Georgia interjects gently but firmly.

Rose agrees very quickly. "We have to think about you, Grams."

—w—

As far back as she can remember, there sat on Grandfather's desk a gallon jar of rattlesnake tails a farmer had given him in lieu of payment, a friendly gesture, a symbol of the underlying, if hidden, power of their state.

After Rose had started college and she had come to visit, Grandfather looked her in the eye and tapped the rattlesnake jar with the back of his fingernail until she shifted uncomfortably. Then he laughed out loud. "Be tough," he said. "Grandma says so."

Strolling around the art museum with her on his arm, Grandfather intently listened as she pointed out the spectacular differences in brush strokes and shadings: "I see it, Rose. Yes, my Rose, thank you. It was right there in front of me in the fog until you came along." Up the lane at the farm and in the city between state house and executive mansion, they meandered.

"In this family, Rose," her grandfather said, "reality is not just an allusion to a story by Henry James. If your Grandmother says it's so, it is."

—◈—

No, it cannot be kept out of their thoughts now. Rose and Georgia remembered hearing the story only once—as told to them by their mother. There was a sickness in Gideon, that was certain, but it seemed intentional suddenly when he began waving the barrel of the loaded shotgun about at Aunt Polly and the crying little children. While the deputy took Aunt Polly and the children into town, Giddy's high school friend, the sheriff, was to take him into the pasture and distract him.

The Grandparents were collected by the deputy and put onto a floor of the hotel with the rest of them, under armed guard, until Gideon was arrested.

Later that week after Giddy's escape, they would find him sitting in a daze, still holding his gun with their dead horses in a ring around him.

"It must have pained them so much to put Giddy onto a ward like that," their mother had said to each of them. "Please don't ever mention any of it to either of them."

—◈—

"Do you remember—" Rose asked with incredulity as she and Georgia walked to the funeral home, "what Grams said once about Uncle Gideon as a boy? How he took Mama out to the chicken house and made Mama hold the baby chickens while he cut off their heads with an axe?"

At the thought, Georgia's slender hands winced toward her face.

—m—

On the day of the funeral, Grandmother is sitting at the kitchen table at the farm. Her hand circles her mouth as though a cigarette were still between her first two fingers. This is not senility. Not even despair, though the despair is real enough. She has been circling her mouth this way with her hand, off and on in conversations, since she quit smoking twenty years ago. It was when she quit smoking, oddly enough, that Grandmother lost all her excess weight. "It turns out," she laughs, "I was only eating in preparation for the cigarette—to build up to the taste."

There on the table is the same periwinkle blue Fiesta butter dish. The juice pitcher is yellow as sunflowers with whorls on its flat sides. The little roosters are in perfect formation in the everyday dishes for sauce. In the formal dining room china cabinet wait the stacks of beautifully painted plates, the fine Limoges, the Haviland and crystal. On the bottom of every one is a sticker with a name on it, written in Mother's hand during the time when the girls were adolescent. Each name directs just who Grandmother said would love each piece, or set, appropriately. The same is true for the paintings and the cherry tables.

In the kitchen, suddenly Grandmother is tugging on Rose's arm. "What is it, Grams?"

Aunt Emily is trying to explain: Grandmother is to wear the expensive pink suit Emily has brought for the funeral. It is all quite apparent, Rose is thinking; how could it be clearer to Emily, or anyone? Grandmother has never worn this color in her life and would certainly never wear pink to any funeral. "Grandpa was my best friend," she sobs. "Can't you explain it to her? Please explain it to her, Rose."

Although Rose has seen her cry, her Grandmother very rarely does. "I can't wear it," Grandmother sobs, holding onto Rose's arm.

Rose looks at Aunt Emily, who has grown heavy under the eyes though the rest of her body is still slender. "Well, Mother—" Aunt Emily sneers, "you'll have to wear it. I've sent your other things to the cleaners. They won't be back for a week. I thought I was doing you a favor."

Grandmother sobs, in Rose's arms. "Papa would be ashamed of me in that," she cries. "He was never ashamed of me once, Rose, in his entire life. Not ever. Doesn't anyone understand that? You understand me, don't you, Rosie?"

"Of course, I understand you," Rose says. "I understand it precisely. Pink is not a tribute to Grandpa." Aunt Emily turns on her heel and walks into the downstairs bathroom. For a second, Rose and her grandmother stand listening to the fiercely running water down the hall.

"Grams," Rose says. "Oh, Grams, we're so much alike, Grams, my grandma." They are sitting together in the living room on the sofa,

"It is true about Emmy," Grandmother whispers sadly.

"Yes, Grams," Rose says. "That was worse than thoughtless."

"Yes," Grandmother sniffs. "I had three children. One was thoughtless, one was crazy, and the other one died." And then she is crying again, her face in her hands, her white hair softly curled under Rose's palms.

"Oh, Grams," Rosie says.

"My beautiful, thoughtful, bright, funny one died. And now Grandpapa is gone without me. I never thought he would go without me." She looks up, bewildered. "I mean I considered it, but I never actually thought it would happen. Rosie, Rosie, has it really happened? I thought we would be killed together in an automobile."

—m—

On the morning following the funeral Aunt Emily would be taking Grandmother home with her to live. No, Rose would not be allowed take her home instead. And, as Georgia said, their own plans would be truncated. Georgia and Will and Rose would drive across the state a week earlier than they'd planned, to Georgia's house, and then Rose in a few days, or whenever she was ready, would fly to her own home.

—⁓—

Fifteen minutes later, in a pay phone at the station ten miles from the farm, she is charging the call to her private account. Miraculously, her lover answers. "Hello," he says. "Ah," he whispers, "I can't talk now." He clears his throat. "I'm sorry," he says fairly loudly then. "You must have the wrong number, dear." Then the phone goes dead. It is as if the rows of corn were marching upon the telephone booth at this rural corner. The field is all she sees, and this immense sky. When she can think again, she dials and her husband answers. She can hardly keep from crying.

"How's it going, love?" he asks.

"Not too good," she says, gazing out at the field of stalks and ears. "Soon everything will be gone, the whole thing, everything as a child I ever dreamed." Then she stops to catch her breath; this is the most important thing: "Is Alfie O.K.?" She listens carefully into the telephone for sounds of him. But the television is on in the den; the dishwasher in the kitchen is whirling away.

"He's good," her husband says. "We had a bicycle ride."

"I never thought Georgia would bring Will along; she's staying in a motel with him. I was counting on being able to spend some time with her. Alfie should have come, and you. You should be here, too."

"Yes," her husband says, with what seems like an air of dismissal. "But you know I'm tied up here. About the rest—I guess that's just about the way these things go. I'm sorry you feel bad."

She leans her head back against the glass of the booth.

"Yes," she says, "that is exactly the way these things go. I know that."

Over there is corn, and over there. Her own phone has lost its energy and the power cord must be lying on the front hall table at home. If it weren't for this crummy little gas station there wouldn't have been a phone like this with privacy for hours.

"Rose—" her husband is saying. "Come back. Hello? Are you there?"

He knows very well that she is still on the phone. It's just that she can't seem to get any words to come out of her throat, it is so swollen with tears. Over the years she has explained this fact to him many times. Of necessity, it is after the fact. When upset, she cannot speak.

"Rose—"

Still he cannot recall the nature of it.

"Rose," he says. "Say something right now or I'm going to hang up. Hello?" he says. "Rose, this is costing several limbs."

"An arm and a leg," she mutters finally.

"What did you say?"

"An arm and a leg, that's how your usual saying goes," she says hoarsely.

"I know that," he says angrily.

"I guess I'll go back to Gram's now."

"Good," her husband says. "Keep your head up. Soon you'll be home."

"Is Alfie all right?"

"You already asked that. Of course he's all right. What did you think— I'd lose him in a supermarket the moment you were gone? He's fine."

"What's he doing right now?"

"He's watching *Winnie the Pooh.*"

"Which one? Oh, let me talk to him. Put Alfie on the phone just for a second."

"All right," her husband says impatiently, as if this were an unusual request. But she can tell he has not gone all the way into the television room to ask. It is too much trouble and right now Alfie is engrossed. Right now Owl is reciting the story of his eccentric cousin while Pooh and Piglet are in a flood about to be swept over a waterfall. It is a blustery day, where Alfie is.

"Rosie," her husband says. His tone has changed. "I was thinking about something you said."

"What was that?"

"'Tenderness.' That's what you said when we were married."

"Yes?"

"Last night I finally realized, for some time now we've lost it."

There is no use trying to speak now. She hangs up the phone, leans her head back again, and stares at the smudged gas station windows, the encrusted gas pumps, the long black hoses that snake the broken pavement. Yes, out there, just across the road, across that flowing field, and that one, the horses are running, somewhere, at the edge of a cemetery she hasn't seen for years in another inland state. There the corn rises up against a stone wall, the only one she remembers ever seeing in this part of the country.

—⁂—

Here it takes place, in a cheap funeral home rather than in a church as Uncle Gideon in his recent fantasies has determined. Grandmother, who has always been the picture of elegance, is so small in her pink suited grief that she doesn't truly seem to know where she is. She has never been here before; that is a certainty. A gigantic plastic cross rides the back wall. The music is piped in from a tape machine. But the mahogany casket that Grandmother has chosen is beautiful even in these surroundings. Rose cannot take in the incongruity of it all.

Georgia sits beside Rose. The cousins' dark shoulders are lined up with the other pallbearers in another pew. Here are the aunts and uncles gathered again. All the political chums and even some of the opponents out of respect; Grandfather's successor and the senators are here, too. Georgia's little Will perches alertly beside her in his dark grey summer slacks and jacket, in one of his first ties.

Perhaps Georgia is the only one in the family with her head screwed on straight, she thinks, just as everyone has been saying for a long time. They say it even though Georgia left her first husband in Hawaii when William was three months old. Yes that was certainly something unforeseen; how that very professional man had started uncontrollably to drink and brawl at whatever was in the way—once in a hula skirt—after his son was born.

William is the one bright spot in the entire weekend. If she herself had only decided to bring Alfie, Rose thinks, she would not have felt quite so bad. There would have been two little boys to snuggle up to a bereft Grandmother on the sofa. As it is, they have kept Will away from Grandmother.

The preacher is ungainly, his sable hair slicked back. When he opens his pink lips, out comes a roiling voice that acknowledges no one, something Rose has never seen or heard before in this part of the country. "We are called to the Kingdom but once. And when we are called we have no choice but to give Him the reins." If she is not careful, soon Georgia will poke her with her elbow. She will be whispering, even though Rose's freckles are long gone: *Rose, stop staring at the tip of your nose, your eyes are crossing in your head.*

The music is a tape, Rose keeps thinking. There down the row from

Georgia are Grandfather's friends, bowing their heads. There has been no eulogy. Not one word, so far, has been mentioned about Grandfather's career, not one word about the books he wrote about nonviolence, the peculiar laugh he had, not one word of acknowledgment to Grandmother.

It was not so many summers ago when she heard it on the news. She was in the car with Alfie, driving to the beach. Her husband was at home working. "Sure," he'd said scornfully, "I'll come to the beach, but if I do I plan to sit in the car and read."

Her ears perked up when she'd heard about the prison riots in her grandfather's state. Three guards had been killed, another held by the prisoners. The governor had walked into the fray, they said, unarmed, "accompanied by a pair of Quakers." Three days later, she heard from Grandmother that he'd come out. As Grandmother said, "We came up with a bargain." Certain moneys had been diverted for the housing the prisoners had requested, and to new and mandatory programs. He wore a bandage on his right arm. He said, "It was what I'd been trying to get for them anyway, and would have long ago but for those filibustering heartless clucks I have to work with every day."

—m—

The hired minister stumbles on. We might all be the same, if you were to look at the world through eyes like his. In the end, she thinks, do spirit and generosity and direction not mean a thing? Rose is tapping her fingers on her thigh. The preacher has taken a further turn. He has put on his eyeglasses; he is banging his fist on the pulpit. He steps toward the casket.

Grandmother sitting in the front row leans forward as if speaking to the minister himself. "Not yet!" Grandmother shouts out.

The man looks at her blankly for a moment through his glasses. Rose, two pews back, can hear Aunt Emily curtly whispering, "No, Mother. They won't shut the casket, not until we go. You'll have plenty of time with him."

Will also shouts out loud at this juncture. He leans toward her over his mother. She can smell his hair crème. "Aunt Rosie!"

"Shush shush, dumpling," Rosie says, stroking his hand on the lap of Georgia's cinder gray dress.

"Mama," Will sings in his high voice next to Georgia. "That man is funny. What is that funny man doing?"

"Will," Georgia whispers, smoothing the crease down his little knee. She puts her arm around his shoulders, but he shrugs it off.

"Mama," he whines loudly. "What is that bad man doing up there to our Grandpa?"

Brusquely Georgia stands and makes her way down the row guiding Will ahead of her. For Rose, a chasm opens up just beside her with their loss. The pastor goes on, calling out in singsong tones for wisdom to enter their lives. Grandfather's first name is being used like the squeak in a wheelbarrow.

A brush salesman would have been better, Rose thinks, staring at the back of Uncle Gideon's thick neck. Will she stand up and walk out of her own grandfather's funeral? She shifts in her seat miserably. If only she had left with Will and Georgia.

The hired preacher lifts his arms. No one in the crowded room seems to know him. The people are to join in with the tape and sing a vaguely familiar hymn as written out on a mimeographed sheet. He runs his hands through his hair again, holds them out over the edge of the pulpit, as they are to begin. Even over the top of the recorded music, footsteps clatter through the speakers as Will and Georgia make progress in their departure. Over the pastor's pleading tones again comes Will's high voice, incredulous, "Mommy, what is Grandpa doing in that box anyway?"

Their feet swoosh up the hall, and then the metal lever creaks down. Behind them all, the door whisks open, and then shuts. Through the windows: the more solid sound of feet on the walk, and then off in the distance the melodic chirrup of a swing, a child's high voice describing with certainty the heights and speeds he would like to attain.

The pastor holds his chin in his hands, elbows still on the lectern, staring out over the crowd. He has circles like donut holes around his eyes that she has not noticed before. His hymnal snaps shut. He turns and abruptly sits down in the chair just back of the pulpit. How oddly his body tilts on the gold velvet cushion, and then he is groping awkwardly under his thigh. His face reddens deeply as he maneuvers it out from beneath him, his Bible. When he presses it onto his knee, his eyes pop closed—with a finality that will be the last thing Rose remembers about this service for her grandfather.

—m—

Open fields aren't all bad, her lover said once. I remember one. Yes, she said. He had made love to her once in the middle of a meadow—unshielded for nearly as far as she could see, by even a tree or a coat. She could not close her eyes, pressed like that between sky and earth, the two of them in between, their backs arching in the beautiful landscape. "You have to be more alert to things that flourish. More things are flourishing every day than disintegrate. That's the way it is, Rose."

"Yes," she said.

"And look at us. We haven't gone anywhere bad in all these years. What was the likelihood of that? And your husband—he's been good for you, too—even if he is distant and unpredictable. You have Alfie. You have heaps of goodness all around you. To say nothing of your career."

"No," she says. "I mean, yes."

"Oh, that," he laughs. "I love you more than a little bit. That's all that takes."

"I know," she says. "I know that. Thank goodness."

—∾—

She is in her nightgown now, and here is her grandmother in the hall, looking lost, looking for towels for her Rose.

"It's all right," Rose says, "I got some, Gram. I already sneaked in for a shower; I'm ready to sleep if you are."

"Rose," Grandmother says, small and bewildered. "Where has everybody gone?" Everyone else has gone to motels. Even Emily, who had planned to stay with Grandmother, has thought at the last minute to retreat. Georgia is in her motel with Will so as not to disturb Grams tonight. Rose is glad of this time alone with her. Tomorrow Aunt Emily will take her away from this place, her life-long memories.

"They've gone to motels, Gram. They'll be back tomorrow."

"No," Grandmother says in a high voice. "I don't mean them. Everybody else. You know. You know whom I mean. I don't know how they could be here one minute and be gone the next. I've never understood that. Do you understand it, Rose?"

"No, Grams," Rose says. "I have never understood one terrible thing about it." Her little grandmother has her head on Rose's chest. Rose will never in her life forget the lovely fragrance of her grandmother's skin, especially when her perfume has worn away. When Alfie was born, each time she nuzzled his fuzzy baby hair, she was startled with pleasure: there was the scent of her own grandmother, given to her once again.

She holds her grandmother so tightly. "I'm afraid, Rose," her grandmother says finally, her blue eyes lift up under her snowy hair. What a miracle this brilliant, starry white, after all the color it once held. Already she is a comet about to blaze away from them.

Rose holds her small form against her breasts. "Me, too," she says. This voice is not her adult voice; it startles her and her grandmother also. This is a voice torn straight out of Rose's own childhood. "Me, too, Grams, I'm skeered."

Her grandmother does not, under such stress, forget and say what she always said to her as a child. Still the phrase hangs there as if one of them had spoken it.

"He was never a bear, Gram," Rose says.

"Because I made you all keep quiet, that's why, Rose, when you were 'skeered' and crawled in bed with us."

"Grandpa wasn't mean material," Rose says. "And we were never quiet."

"That's true," Grandmother says, fiddling with the sleeve of Rose's nightgown.

"The little boys jumped on the end of the bed, and Georgia even wet it. Grandpa never once growled."

"That's true enough, my darling."

Tonight Rose will lie in the mahogany bed in her grandfather's place, her eyes looking into the dark, trying to see what her grandmother has seen each time she has waked in the night: the tall bureau, the large round mirror over the vanity where she saw herself change from a great beauty into a beautiful heavy woman into a frail, small, elderly elegance. There needn't be light for Rose to see the tapestry seat of the vanity stool, the sheers lifting on the breeze that sweeps in over a field of corn swaying as far as anyone can see. The crickets sigh themselves to sleep in a land so vast she cannot contain the thought of it.

She holds her grandmother all night, and her grandmother sleeps quietly. Rose strokes her arms, the sides of her face, the beautiful shrinking form, wishing for her grandfather's hands.

In the morning Grandmother is carried away like a portrait, waving there from the window of Aunt Emily's back seat, out of her own life. At this time, Rose thinks and Grandmother thinks it, too, Rose can tell from the way they cannot pull their eyes from one another at the last. They will never see one another again.

—m—

At a roadside café on the way home, in the middle of nowhere, as both of them call it—the absolute middle of the unspoken everything, they have lost track of where they are, after hours of driving out in the open, Rose and Georgia stop for lunch. Will is hungry, is grouchy, is half-asleep, has had his blond little head stuck out from his car seat in a scowl for miles.

In the café, men shoot pool, lean in their undershirts against a bar and make jokes. When the two strangers and the boy come in, every one of them smiles. Dinner is before them so quickly.

But, in the middle of the peaceful moment in the little booth in the country café, "No, no, no," William is crying out. This is what small children do: cry out, again and again, Rose thinks. No matter how many times, no matter the love, it is so burdensome. "No taters," he cries.

"Stop," Georgia states firmly. Rose rolls the edge of the paper tablecloth beneath her thumbs and forefingers. "Stop. You wanted potatoes; you specifically wanted potatoes; that's what you said. Look here's the catsup. We'll make a little face on them."

"No, no, no," he cries, and then he has picked up one and flung it across the room.

Now Georgia has gone out with William kicking under one arm, without lunch, to the car; and Rose sits alone. She can hear her nephew bawling all the way from here, and her sister is talking in a fiercely restrained voice. "You are not going to behave this way in public. This is not the way to behave."

"Go away," Will yells. The sun is a fireball on top of the tin roof, she is sure. Soon it will melt down the outside of the windows like a slice of orange cheddar in this cornfield. A queasiness reels over her.

"It's been a long, long day. You did so well, Will, and now can't you just hold on a little bit longer." Will is crying and yelling. "William, you are driving me absolutely mad."

"Go away," Will screams. "Go away, Mommy, go away."

"If you don't stop screaming that—"

To the background music of passing tractors and semis, Georgia stops mid-sentence, then begins again, very slowly. "Don't ever say that to me again, William, don't you ever, ever say that to Mommy again."

"Go away, go away from here, Mommy. Go away."

There is a long silence. Rose can almost imagine Georgia grinding her teeth. Then Georgia laughs. "I'll have you arrested, William. The sheriff will come and lock us both up." She laughs a little wildly. "I think they might lock us up *today*, for that matter." William shrieks with delight. But her voice is dropping. Will giggles and then is quiet; Georgia is talking to him, but mostly she is speaking to herself.

When Rose goes back to the car, she has packages of food wrapped up for them. Will eats his fried potatoes, soggy with catsup, smearing them onto his car seat and singing at the same time. Rose sits on the trunk and studies what she thought at first to be a mosquito stuck onto the far horizon; but it is a windmill. "Oh yes," she sighs out loud

"Don't sing, Will," Georgia says, staring back from the passenger seat at his red-smudged face in the center of the back seat. "For Christ's sake, you might choke. Don't sing while you eat, Will, please."

"Let him sing, for God's sake," Rose says, pulling onto the long flat road unreeling before them. "If he chokes, we'll get it out of him, I swear."

"Right, you're right," Georgia says. "I hope."

"He probably won't choke. Will he?" Rosie whispers, looking briefly back at him.

In the back seat, Will looks wide-eyed at them, a French fry lifted into the air, his mouth open wide enough for an artichoke.

"It's ok," Georgia says. "Will, eat. And then, sing! Be happy. It's O.K. Aunt Rose is here with us after so long away. And we are going, thank god, straight home."

"It looks like fierce rain," Rose says, "let's drive carefully."

And then William is asleep. The radio plays music they both have loved in college, while the windshield wipers whisk back and forth.

—m—

All Rose can think of now is the story of the seven mountains. Between the two of them, Georgia and Rose piece it together. Mother must have been very young. She could not have been more than sixteen, and he was perhaps seventeen. The sand swept out and out along a vast open sea, the likes of which their mother had never seen. Bright blue umbrellas arched like tents over the beach. When she opened her mouth that first time under saltwater, the brine of it startled her enough to make her gasp and exclaim—

Oddly, neither of them remembers much about the location of the seven mountains. Once Mother went to dinner at the young man's house, the young man who became a film star. A man met them at the door, clearly a servant.

Both of them remember one particular conversation in the same way:

"And did he— Did he—"

"Yes," Mother says finally. "It was the most beautiful summer of my life."

"You made love to him?"

"Well, almost. In those days you didn't have to. You must never tell Daddy any of this," she says.

"Why didn't you stay with him?"

"I was only sixteen. It didn't seem like it could be right already, a decision like that so early in my life. And, I wanted to go to school."

"But Daddy."

"Yes, Daddy," she says. "He started flying his plane over the house, training for war. Figure eights, all of that. I had pretty much given up on my theatrical friend. He seemed like a failure, especially to himself, he said in his letters; he could never ask me, after all this time. He could not even get a part as a bellhop, he said."

"Not really!" they exclaim in astonishment—not yet knowing the disappointment upon which fine successes are made.

"And don't feel sorry for Daddy," Mother insists. "All his life he's been mourning for his old Louisiana beauty."

"*Daddy* had a girlfriend in Louisiana?" one of them had asked her. "He flew an airplane over Grandma's house?"

"But of course! He picked me up from college and flew me home in it. You didn't think we had a boring life, did you?"

The land has begun a bit to rise and fall under the heavy clouded sky. In the back seat, Will stirs a little, and the two of them lower their voices. "Think of it," Rose says. "She had one of the best moments of her life at sixteen."

"At least she had that one," Georgia says. "That's more than I can say."

"Oh, Georgia, your husband had quite a few redeeming features, you said. And, you are the recipient of a law degree."

"Right," Georgia says sardonically.

"Right," Rose goes on, returning to what can safely be said.

"But, Georgia, at sixteen Mother couldn't have even known what best was."

"And after that, except for us, she had no one. She didn't have a job," Georgia says. "She never really went anywhere. All she did was read. I guess already she was in a lot of pain. And Daddy, poor Daddy," Georgia says.

"Oh, Daddy," Rose says. "Daddy was so wonderful."

"Oh yes," Georgia says. "Daddy isn't cold, not Daddy."

"This is not charm we're thinking about."

Georgia looks over from behind the wheel of her new car. "He had great stamina. But did he 'light up'?"

"Obviously he lit for somebody, eventually. Who knows?"

"Good God," Georgia gasps. "I never once thought of that in my life. He was so warm to me."

"Different sort of warmth entirely."

"Oh my God," Georgia says. "I've been looking for the wrong thing."

"Ha!" Rose laughs. "And I found it. Daddy exactly, that's what I've got."

"At least you've got someone. Two! You've got what's-his-name. Lawrence of Arabia. You could have told me when I could at least have had one look at him."

"Are you kidding?" she laughs. "At Mama's funeral? In front of the family?"

"Henry Miller," Georgia says then, with incredulity, staring into the rain-drenched road.

"Henry Miller?"

"Fitzgerald and Henry Miller were her favorite authors; she told me after I got to college. And did you know she wrote to Aunt Eleanor?"

"Henry Miller!"

"My goodness," Georgia says. "Was that supposed to be a secret?"

—⁂—

It occurred to Rose once while holding to the strap of a subway car. It seemed so obvious: Andrew Wyeth was surely the only living being to have understood that moment when she stood at the edge of the field and felt the top of her head fly off like a rocket and whirl into the sky, how it happened each time, just when her foot touched down on the abyss that stretched out between the edge of town and the distant school. He had surely understood the boundless distance between two points. And now he had come out with them: his portraits of Helga. Two points seemed always to demand a third—to make a reverberating plain.

—⁂—

The Lover, newly home from his most recent expedition into Sahara: "They understand the concept of water, but they cannot grasp 'lack of water.' Can you believe that?"

—⁂—

But they have stopped the car, here where they have not been in so long. After all, it was on the way, nearly. Will is awake in the back seat and anxious to get out. Here is the road to the cemetery where their mother is buried. When last Rose saw it, it was an open stretch of land from the highway on the border of town, all the way out through pastures and tillage to imaginary outposts. Still now the horses run in the pasture off at the end of the little stone wall, the intervening picket fence. The ground has been broken in patches for more graves. They will get out of the car; and over there, soon, they will stand at her grave and be swept back.

It has truly begun to rain now. The windshield wipers go back and forth as the car moves through the curving paved lanes. They have opened their doors; Will is released to run among gravestones and exercise his lungs. Over there the small trees have grown up. Vast white heads of tree hydrangea hang down in the rain over her stone that lies flat to the ground. Even from here, they can feel her name even if they can't see it as they approach. "My God," Georgia says. In an instant, a red rash has gone up over her throat. Rose cannot say a word. She stands with her hand somewhere in the air near her face, staring at the watery reflection of clouds and bushes in the grave.

"What is it?" Rose says before she can realize what she has seen. A rectangle of water sits where the mound of grass should be. Their mother's grave has sunk completely into the earth, and in it water has its way.

Georgia's voice scratches with her anger, "They are responsible for keeping this place up! We pay them an annual fee!"

"It's actually sunk." Rose has gone hoarse. "It's completely sunken. How long can it have been this way?"

To say that she is crying is an understatement. She has even raised both fists into the air as she walks away. She is so outraged she cannot even see herself in her grief. There are so few graves.

But at the grave of their mother, her sister has not moved. Georgia stands over there, aghast.

Why am I on my knees here in the middle of this cemetery? Rose thinks. Surely her sister asks this question about Rose as she glances over toward her. There Georgia stands, a rash growing up over her chest as it has since they were little, whenever she's been terribly distraught. Red specks cross her sternum, each one her way of releasing tears, there are so many that Rose can see them clear over here. So much love goes between the two sisters that they do not need to say a word. And there is Georgia's son, Rose's nephew in his yellow slicker at the grave of his unseen grandmother. Georgia has made him put on his boots.

"Mommy," Will says. "Why is your mama sleeping in that little lake?"

And then she is speaking very softly to him, leading him the other way.

—∞—

In the beginning she used to ask her lover quite frequently, "Why do you need me? Why me?"

"Why do you need me?" he would say, smiling at her. "Have a little faith in something earthbound, won't you, please?"

—∞—

This grave belongs to a young man who had lived not far from them, a boy not ten years older than Rose and Georgia were. Only a year later he had come to this place, maybe a little more, so long ago now. According to the date it was one of the first to have gone in after her mother.

She remembered a face only for this dead one, who had lived there just on the edge of the vacant lot where the earth dropped off into field and flatland, the autumn remnant of grain already harvested. Perhaps her mother was right after all; perhaps it was loneliness. Still she thinks it only an horrific fear of those open, unending spaces: that field. And on it, among the dirt clods and stubble she moved, feeling like an upright stick, a pencil in progress across an asbestos world. My god, how stringent her mother used to be. And how rarely this fact had occurred to her in all these years.

Georgia is speaking again as she walks William back and forth through the rows. Rain is glancing down over them all. Oblivious, Georgia runs her hand through her own wet hair. Her dress is soaked through, but the air remains warm. On Rose, the rain feels good. She can hear Georgia speaking to Will: "That's a place where many people from many religions go after they die. Their spirits go there, I guess. It's very hard to explain."

"What's a 'sprit, ' Mommy?" William asks.

"Oh, I don't really know, Will," Georgia says with weariness in her voice. "It's time to get some exercise now. Let's do some running while we can."

"What's a 'sprit,' Mommy?"

"Oh, Will, it's something you can't really see. It's who you are in your deepest sense. You'll understand it better when you get older."

If only these revelations could be spoken from generation to generation. If only her mother had tried to help her see what she'd come to know.

Here was this boy for instance after all this time coming back to her as if actually seen: his clean hair slicked back to one side, his sharp knowing eyes. Why couldn't her mother do that? At least, she could have remained a memorable face, not something replaceable by photographs. This boy's was a face that did not smile but that looked on with a certain interest. He was not beautiful, not really hard or handsome. He was vivid, a sort of young movie star on a motorcycle, the sort her own mother might have noticed when she was younger and not already devoted to their father.

Yes, in her mind, he was not unlike the movie star who had grown up owning seven mountains. This boy had had one, too, a very shining chrome and black leather mount, a motorcycle that would take him to his death. Vaguely she remembered hearing, by letter perhaps, from an old friend. Oddly enough, she had seen him so frequently, yet never once had she heard his voice.

Her mother had only one friend, Rose thinks now. And that friend had lived across the street from this boy. Perhaps her mother's friend had actually watched her cross the field. It seemed unlikely though, didn't it? Did her mother know in that small town—only as a child had it seemed like a city—that the boy stood there every day carefully polishing those long silver tubules? For Rose, he was just as much a part of that ritual her mother had imposed upon her as the field had been—although until now she had never realized it.

There the boy stands, very tall at the house at the edge of the field, much older than she was—a senior perhaps at the college. She would have been too young, too intellectual for him—in just those few years difference, too much another generation, her wire glasses not at all like his leather jacket as he polished the chrome each morning as if he had nowhere to go but here in the driveway at the edge of the world.

Perhaps her mother and her friend had designed the whole thing, an intended meeting between the boy and herself. It was her mother made her wear such a daring bikini to the pool all the summer before, rather an embarrassment. "Don't be so shy. You have such a good figure."

All she had seen was the great open space of her trepidation. There he stands. Still she can see him polishing the already—why did she never notice it—they were *already* gleaming: the exhaust pipes at the side of his bike. It was not ostentatious, nor was he—not radical in his appearance. A clean face, not really boyish perhaps. That is what set him apart; perhaps she, so much younger, intimidated him already known for her drawings in the school, a peculiar play she'd written. Who recalls? On those days she went by him, blinded, thinking hateful things about her mother, the arch enemy who would have her daughter separated from her friends for her own experiments in loneliness.

And then inexplicably, her mother had sent her away to college, to summer school, on the very afternoon of her graduation. An absurd command, even her father had thought it so. Her former boyfriend Peter had already been gone to college two years, had gone away chaste. Why had her mother done such a thing? The young are so easily inflicted with wounds.

If she had stayed for the celebrating night she might have fallen into someone's arms, been held away from that loneliness, that edict, that she would go away from that town on the very day of her graduation with no parties, no lying down in a nakedness for the first time in bare arms in a blanket in a field, under terrible unforeseen stars, in the balm of departures. Perhaps her whole character would have been different. Perhaps that's what her mother had imagined. Perhaps she herself would have married a different man.

But brief kisses only it would be for her then, on that night, and then her friends falling away as she looked once through the automobile's windows at her hometown receding never again to reappear.

Even before that, her father would move into a practice in another town, hours away; then Freddy would be drafted; Georgia would start off to law school; Rose would marry a man from the East and go there to finish her own college education. Two men she would meet from the East, one already married. Their mother would be buried in a grave so heavy that it would sink right out from under her. Yet here was this boy, brought to stare each day over this flatland, somehow nearly an acquaintance, a reassurance to Rose finally, perhaps as he was, all along, meant to be. Why has she never known who his mother was?

Rain washed down through Rose's hair, through the lone tree at her mother's graveside, seemed to cloud up the sky in reverse. Why had she, Rose herself, never even tried to share in her mother's little occupations?

When she and Georgia were little and even the Cousins had not yet been born, her mother had confided in them: she had tried to leave their father, riding by train one night with the two of them tucked in at her sides, reading books about painters to them whenever they woke up. Pointing at the red and blue images. It was so long ago that Grandmother had sent them all home; Grandpa was running for his senate seat. Not only would it have created a scandal for the family, after all, but also Mother had admitted that she loved him, she would always love their Daddy—even after he had found someone else.

Their father had told them, "Your mother, you can't know what she put up with for me."

When Georgia pressed him, he said it. "There were rats," he said. "You were little, I was in school, and there were rats."

"We had rats in our house!" they had cried out together.

"I was so busy," he said, "I forget it myself."

Had her mother's friend known all these stories from her mother's life? When her mother died and the young man at the edge of the earth was riding toward his own later death a year after that, what had her mother's friend known then that her own daughters didn't know?

Sitting here on his grave, she sees this boy for the first time. In these dead dark eyes is manliness, indifferent, yet engaged. She can almost see life's short fall from his shoulders, the spray of young hair between upper arm and chest wall, the curls that must have grown across his nipples, his face, and then her chin on his shoulder, pressed up against the moist side of his neck. Perhaps he was her mother's dream. Was that what her mother had wanted? What did it mean?

Still it rains, falling down over the flattest, most beautiful empty dark black land you have ever seen. Her mother's grave is sunken into the earth. When the sun rises, nothing anywhere in sight can conceal it. Only the silhouettes of horses will cut the horizon. And there, the broken arch of a town. Rain comes down, does not cease. The grave is so sunken even now that perhaps the coffin has dropped out underneath and been swept into some vault of the underground, carried on an unearthly current through rapids and infested streams.

She had forgotten what rain was like in this country, the sky breaking open, a sulfurous lightning burning its way through loam-scented air. Sound drives down the soil as much as the rain. Everywhere is water in rivulets. Filling even her mother's casket, hair and limbs waterlogged and floating. Is there no sanctity anywhere?

The word floats up over the tiny people wandering among insignificant tombs. Someone is crying it out, hoarsely in the distance. She looks up, startled, her own mouth open, hollering. The cry wends its way from the depths of her chest, burns out of her throat. What was her mother's greatest fear? "Water!" Water in every cell bursts. She could not go out on open water, even in a covered boat.

Her sister's brow is furrowed, almost in terror, as she looks back at this stranger. Her sister's body does not turn from the grave yet her face cannot stop staring at Rose who cannot stop screaming the word.

Her whole body has begun somewhere to hurt. "Water!"

Tiny splashings lift in the background. "Water!" Rose screams.

"Water!" a high, lovely voice lilts.

Then she has truly startled herself. Maybe her mother did have something for herself. Perhaps that boy, that young man, was sleeping with her mother, just as she herself sleeps with her own lover. That was something so invaluable in her life that, even to her sister, it could not be explained. She had tried to assume such things of her mother before, and in the end she'd found only innocence. It was more likely that her mother had asked that boy with the motorcycle to watch over her each time she crossed that field. Maybe she had asked him to watch over her awkward, frightened daughter Rose. Maybe she hoped he would ask Rose out; the boy seemed rather lonely. Then again perhaps the boy and her mother had never met, were destined to lie together, not six feet from one another for an eternity with only Rose to cross between them on her trajectory—as always, over the expanding open earth.

Then Rose hears it, quietly at first, and then again. On the winding road in the rain, hanging off the hand pump at the well, running up and down the aisles of stonework now, Will dances. He spins circles in his black rubber boots and yellow slicker, set loose from the intensity of the airtight and grown-up automobile. His eyes are full of fortune as he shifts it with his feet, this beautiful substance, shimmering in reflection of his golden coat. "Water!" the nephew sings in a grandmother's grave. He leaps and kicks it up: God's great gift in this long, long weekend of inexplicable occurrences. Here it is: a splendid summer afternoon of moats and boots during Aunt Rose's unexpected visit from the East.

CHAPTER II

Rose Reynolds insisted that her mother have a color TV; but Freddy, who would be leaving the country again almost immediately, won out on the issue of expense. Her sister Georgia had not returned but once from studying to get into law school. She was in Hawaii after all—too far away to be of help.

It was true that the house was modest, blue, wooden, a replica of every other house on the street, and her brother when he would come home for the final time from Vietnam would spend nearly all of every month driving from small town to small town selling vinyl mattress covers to hospitals. "Well," Freddy said then, "it's better than delivering body bags."

"Well," her mother said in return, supposedly about the television, "it can't be helped."

Her mother had never had a color television in her life anyway, she said. She might not like all the colors leaping about; it might have made her even more nauseous. That was something the mother of Rose Reynolds feared above many other things. We mustn't be greedy, she said. It was 1968.

During the year Rose cared for her mother, her mother had three experiences in the way of visitors. A lady came around to see her mother, who was new to the neighborhood after all and whom she had heard was ill. Her mother looked at the woman from her bed.

"Ill?" her mother smiled mischievously. "Where did you hear such a thing? I lie here by choice."

"My daughter had Hodgkin's Disease," the slightly plump woman said, ignoring her mother's joke entirely.

"Oh my," Irene Reynolds said sadly as Rose brought in the tea tray. "Hodgkin's Disease. Rosie, did you hear?" Rose preferred not to speak.

"Yes," the woman said, quietly, "she died last year. She was just nineteen."

"Oh my," her mother said again.

Rose Reynolds looked around the form towering over the bed and smiled at her mother reassuringly. I'm right here, the smile said, if you're too tired and want me to throw this woman out. "Sugar?" she said handing the woman her cup and pointing toward the chair before the bed. "Mother doesn't allow many callers."

"Yes," her mother said. "It gets in the way of my serenity."

"Yes," the woman said. "I know what you mean. It's hard to achieve a penetrating serenity."

"Yes," her mother replied. "It certainly is. What do you do now that you're without her, without your daughter after such a long struggle? I can't imagine being without my Rose. Your daughter struggled five years? And, from such an early age—"

"Oh, I don't do much," the woman said. "Well, frankly, I've been trying to lose weight. I've joined a club. The ladies get together and refuse to eat. It isn't much fun."

"Oh," piped up Rose Reynolds, sitting down behind her mother on the bed, automatically beginning to stroke her mother's whitening hair. "Eating isn't everything."

"No," the woman said. "Eating is nothing at all. Unless you haven't enough food. I also work for a group sending packages to boys in Vietnam. My two boys are over there."

"Oh! No!" Rose Reynolds and her mother cried almost simultaneously.

"Our Freddy just went back!"

"Your sons were *both* drafted?" Rose asked, regaining herself.

"No," the woman said. "They are good boys, they wanted to go."

"Oh how tragic," Rose's mother whispered. "They've both gone. And after your daughter's death. My other daughter's gone off to Hawaii. I'd hoped she'd seen her Dad again since we split up. But not much has been heard of him. I guess he has a new family, I hear he has another infant."

"Couldn't your sons have gotten out of it?" Rose asked, "since your family is bereaved? We tried to get Freddy out because of Mama's illness, but it didn't work. But two boys, surely there must have been some way—"

"Their father thought it a good idea, to take their minds off their sister, and to see the world. He thought it would be good for them. I only wish I didn't worry so—"

"I've never thought much of war myself as a way of seeing the world," Rose Reynolds' mother gently replied. "I wouldn't want my own brother, even now, in a war in order to forget about my trouble. My daughter Georgia has gone off to preliminary law school, and our Freddy—" She stopped suddenly as though she were repeating herself again and again, and realized she was. Then it was to her as though she had spoken Freddy's precious name carelessly in front of someone who had never cared about him once. It seemed a sacrilege.

"It must be quite hard for you," Rose Reynolds interrupted, seeing the visitor's bracing face.

The woman plumped herself up like a bird and stared back at her with tiny eyes. "Yes," she said finally. "Their father and I are alone for now. We are waiting every day; every day is another eternity."

"Yes," said Rose Reynolds' mother. "We know a few other boys over there. Some boys who grew up with Rose are there right now, too. Rose writes to them. It gives her something to do, so she doesn't have to always think about me."

"That's good," the woman said. "It's hard to be the caretaker."

"Rose is my reliable girl," Irene Reynolds said. "I'm afraid she has to bear an awful lot. It would do her good to get out once in a while—if only we could figure a way."

"It's not so awfully hard," Rose said defensively. "We enjoy ourselves together, don't we, Mama. We try to find ways to enjoy ourselves."

Shortly after, the woman got up to go; and Rose went to see her out. "Why don't you ask her?" Rose's mother said as Rose trailed behind.

For the first time in two months the young woman imagined herself out of the house. She stood at the front entryway, looking into the snowy suburban streets, seeing their visitor out. "Oh please," she blurted at the door. "Do you think I could come along?" Snow was actually falling through the light from the street lamp outside into what she had thought to be a summer world.

The woman looked at her lean frame. "Oh heaven's no," she said, "you don't need us. Look at you, you're so thin."

"Maybe I could just come along," Rose Reynolds pleaded with unconcealed eagerness. "It's hard being the caretaker, as you yourself said."

"We're just a bunch of fat middle-aged ladies," the woman said. "You'd find us boring."

"No, really I wouldn't—" Rose said. "I would so much like to get out of the house just once, even once a month would be O.K. I don't know anyone else in this town. My mother just moved here. And my brother and sister are gone. Really, I've been afraid I'd gain weight here, all the time in the house." And furthermore, she wanted to say, you can't believe how much I miss my father, my wonderful father has gone away—"Maybe it would help me not to gain weight—going with you. I wouldn't stay long or bother anyone—"

"Well, really you would," the woman said after a moment. "You'd make everyone in the group self-conscious. You're just too thin," the woman said. "I'm glad to have met you," she said. "I took care of my daughter for five years. But of course she wasn't bedridden like your mother is. Your mother's spirit will always remember you for this." And she pulled the door closed behind her in a rush of dead air.

"I didn't like that woman," Rose Reynolds' mother said. "I hope she doesn't come again. If she does, don't let her in."

"Neither did I," Rose sighed. "Anyway, I don't think she will come back."

—w—

Irene Reynolds turned on the television set—poking the button with a long thin dowel like an arm that Rose had found in her brother's deserted basement workshop. The news was on the television with all the usual fighting. In black and white, children were running in terror through a flat field of rice; and grenades were going off. Young boys, with helmets on, crouched and ran around huts. Napalm blazed from side to side. Martin Luther King was making his speech about dreams again.

"I like that man," her mother said.

"So do I. I'd vote for him for President if I had the chance."

"If it weren't for Bobby Kennedy," her mother smiled, reminding her.

"Yes, I'd vote for both of them."

"You have my proxy," Irene said.

Rose Reynolds had been having dreams about Bobby Kennedy now for several weeks. She had dreamed him with wings, without wings, and elected President. She had dreamed him the substitute for her former boyfriend Peter who was older and had taken her to his high school prom just a few years before. In the intermittent moments of their sleep, Bobby Kennedy wore a tuxedo, and he played rock music on the bandstand. The sounds of Jimi Hendrix came out of his instrument.

"How's your dream man?" her mother would say in the morning, or maybe in the middle of the night. Time meant nothing to them now, not day or night, not winter, or fall. Bobby Kennedy's bushy hair stood up straight on his head to think about Rose Reynolds' bizarre dreams. Often her mother laughed until she cried. And then they turned on the television set to see the image of the real man striding through South Dakota fields near where her mother had been born and one of her grandmothers still lived. On every channel and in the newspaper, a Native American child held Bobby Kennedy's hand.

—ᴍ—

In the mail a square blue envelope with the address of a school friend arrived. There was no way of telling from it where the friend really was or would later go; it was a military address.

"Go on," her mother said. "You may as well send your photograph. It will warm him up to see a friendly face. Who knows how soon he might be sent into the thick of things." It was the only one she had; and it showed her off nicely, her mother said. Her hair was long and dark brown in the photograph, and she was wearing a pink cotton t-shirt with a v-neck, though of course none of the color showed in the black-and-white photograph. She was smiling nicely, they agreed, in a friendly and reassuring way. "You were like a sister to him, I think," her mother said. "Poor thing. He never had a sister like you. He must have needed one the way he carried home so many of your books." Jon's girl friend had been younger by two years, a pretty girl who resembled Rose Reynolds very much in the hair and face.

He had been on the basketball team; but her own boyfriend, Peter, was an intellectual against the war. "Your thrilling firebrand," her mother always called him with a spark in her eyes.

"Many people have it worse than we have had it," her mother said, holding out her emaciated arm.

"Yes," Rose Reynolds almost agreed.

"Our country has never been bombed except in Pearl Harbor. I will never forget that day." But her mother would not speak more about it. "I can't," her mother said. "I lost someone. Sometimes mourning never goes away. You'd think it would after all these years."

At six o'clock every night they watched the news; and at the end of it, the rolls of the dead ran up the screen. Like credits in a movie for annihilation, so her mother said. "Why don't they stop?" her mother said. "Why don't they just stop and think? It isn't doing anyone any good."

*

Bobby Kennedy was singing now at night, protest songs. He had a beautiful tenor voice and he carried a tune quite well. Sometimes he was the lead singer, sometimes the backup voice for a vision where rubble turned miraculously into high-rise apartments for the poor. At the end of the dream, people rushed out of the buildings cheering. In real life, Martin Luther King had moved into a ghetto in Chicago; he was preaching non-violence.

—⁓—

One night after a very long siege of sickness and crying and comforting, Rose finally had her mother's permission to call the doctor—only to ask a question of him, something they had sworn they would never do once her mother had come home from the hospital. Was there anything stronger her mother might take for the pain? Rose asked him. But there was nothing short of morphine and Rose Reynolds' mother refused to take morphine. She said it was 'on principle.' Also she was saving it for the last, she said, the last hard days. The doctor had never visited them, but now after the call he insisted that he come. He only lived around the block anyway, he said.

When he arrived, Rose Reynolds had an uncanny hopefulness that things might be made better for them.

"Indeed they might," the doctor said. "They have found something at the University. It could change everything—for you!"

Her mother lay stunned, listening in her bed, as they talked about her in the same room. Tears streamed down her horror-stricken face, as she looked at herself in the mirror beside the bed, for even her bones had twisted by then.

"Let's go out now," Rose said to the doctor; her mother was gesturing for him to leave. "Let's let mother alone to rest." At the front door Rose asked him, "Is it true? Is it true about the cure? Can we get it for her?"

"No," the doctor blithely said. "I just said that. I think it's always better to hold out hope so close to the end, don't you?"

When Rose returned to the room, her mother was weeping: "Now I don't know what to do. Now I don't know what to do. Even with a cure, there won't be walking or moving about anymore!"

—⁓—

In this way, Rose Reynolds understood again why the two of them had instinctively refused for so long to have a doctor in the house. The young woman asked herself repeatedly why she had let down her resolve and let him enter their peacefulness. That night she had had to tell her mother about another aspect of falseness in humanity.

—⁂—

To try to cheer her mother up, they had made popcorn—or rather, Rose Reynolds had made it in the modernized kitchen. There the pine cupboard opened between rooms onto the small dining area barely big enough for the round oak table. It was one of the pieces of furniture her mother had refinished several years earlier in her search for making beautiful old things new again.

"Lots of butter!" her mother called, because today she could eat again. And when she could eat she ate her favorite things. Life moved along very pleasantly.

Today there would be no more running back and forth for Rose between the bathroom and the bedroom with basins and towels. Today there would be no desperate rubbings of inflamed muscles and bones, no heating pads and cold compresses, no ice cubes in the swollen mouth. There was no need for quiet humming and crying and breathing exercises that they had picked up from a childbirth show on TV. Today there were only the usual precautions and medicaments, the creams to avoid more sores. Today, as on some days, her mother was lovely and soft again, almost painless in the face.

They leaned together around the bowl on the double bed against the pillows, listening to Joan Baez on their record player, and then to Bob Dylan. Her mother felt well enough that day even for Hendrix and Janis Joplin. Then the usual shows went by on the television, and it seemed forever until he appeared: Bobby Kennedy going through the crowd, shaking hands. "I will never forget this moment," Rose said.

"We are together now, " Rose Reynolds' mother said. "In this one moment in time, we are together—here with each other, in this peculiar little house. Together," she said. Her mother reached over and pressed her hand.

—⚏—

Heavy seas, the Lover says and laughs. Isabella laughs, too. Her eyes are sparkling like agates in her head. Ramon laughs back, his body tight as a male tiger's. Physique, the Lover thinks. The scanners go back and forth over dunes looking for metallic finds. They will work early morning and evening, rest in the afternoon. Today is the worst of it so far. Already the heat is undulating off the grit in horizontal snakes that smack them in the face. Piers wears a dishtowel around his face, tucked under his baseball cap. It flies about his significant shoulders, turns up striped on the ends as in a painting of a little Dutch girl's locks.

Piers turns up his radio. Piers taunts even the radio. "I will follow you!"

"I like it," Allan teases in return. "My favorite. That guy's got a voice I don't mind following."

"Go back," Anne says. "What was that other one? No, the English, for once."

Iz looks up. Everyone has grown a little thin, Iz especially.

"*Tea in the Sahara*—With You!" Richardson shouts out from where he is scratching and brushing.

Ramon bares his teeth.

"*Brothers in Arms!*" Piers cranks it up. "Now this is my favorite!"

It is as if the song, not the heat, levels Iz. Iz is a lump in a hummock of fine dirt; dirt frosts her arms and legs, her chin and lips, the end of her nose. The first tear tracks down her cheek like a small animal heading toward cooler parts. I think 'water' first, not 'tears.' Other tears are not far behind. I can see her but I am digging here. I am digging toward a small fleck showing on our screen. How odd, I think. Whenever Isabella cries, I think of Rose. When Rose cries, I think of Iz. Or so I did until Rose's sister Georgia stepped along, for some relief from the two of them. Then the tears come. It will not be the last time I will hear Isabella cry on this expedition. It's so hot that I've seen tears on all of them. And now the quavering. I almost don't hear it anymore, her tears for him. Iz is really crying now. The lost brother in the war has come into our little humdrum life once again. Ramon takes full advantage. It is all I can do not to kill him some days. I look up to see what stage it is. Weeping, Stage 3. I haven't heard her sob like this for six or seven years. Her voice shudders like an electrified rod is pressing intermittently against her throat. She gasps and sniffs. Ramon ventures his arm around her again. Gerard has come out of his tent to stare. He comes across with his prize cookie tin. Now I am digging to the bottom of this pit. *Brothers in Arms* wails out over the complete endless earth, egging her on. "Turn that damned thing off!" I shout but it is too late. Now she has begun to relive it all. In a Meltdown. Stage 4.

"That stupid fucking war. He was sweet and smart and my father made him go." The others gape at her. All our emotions are frayed. Truly everyone understands. Still it's embarrassing to see Isabella blubbering that way, her legs crossed up under her like she's gone to meditate, her piquant face down in her hands, her shoulders skittering about under her shirt. "For the Honor of it!"

Ramon squats down again, puts his arm around. Annie sits down next to her and strokes back the side of her hair, pats her cheek. She moves round in front of her. Puts her hands on her knees.

"Oh what the fuck," Piers says. "Let's all have a good cry. At least we've got a reason this time." He sits to the other side of my wife. Puts his arm around her, too. Piers and Ramon's arms make a kind of snake across her shaking spine. No one looks toward me although I send up a rain of it:

burial dust.

"Everything all right over there?" I call.

There is a remarkable lack of movement in response. This turtle pulls in his head and digs in.

"Hey, guys," I say. "I could use some help when Isabella gets it back together again. Something's turned up on the scanner over here."

"I always cry when I hear that song," Isabella sniffs. "I'm sorry, I can't help myself from doing it—" She sniffs again.

Only Iz, I think, only Iz.

"My brother. Under a flag, As if by then he mattered to any of them—" She sniffs again.

"Maybe it did matter to him." Ramon kisses the side of her face, turns her head to meet his elegant one. "Of course it mattered."

"Hey, Ramon," I say. "Maybe we've got a button here. Maybe we've actually got it."

It's my Isabella who finally turns. "O.K., O.K.," she says. "Just O.K. won't you?"

—⁂—

It was the third visitor in that year who surprised them both. One day a man selling Bibles rang the front bell. It might have been morning or afternoon, it made little difference to them now. "No no," Rose Reynolds said politely to him. "We already have one, even two or three around here somewhere."

But her mother insisted from the back bedroom, "Rose—let him in. For heaven's sake, let the poor man in. He has to make a living, you know."

And so the hollow-core wooden door to the blue house swung open for him. Rose was surprised to see that it was summer outside, and that the stranger had sandals on and wore no coat. Light fell in around him where he carried his duffel bag. Greenery fringed his earnest, clean-shaven face like a beard.

"Bring him back here," her mother called, "but first come help me rearrange myself." When Irene had had her nightgown adjusted and the covers drawn up over her—"To the chin," her mother insisted. "We wouldn't want to frighten the poor man"—and all the signs of sickness had been quickly put away: the bandage scissors and sanitary pads, the toilet paper and towels, the plastic basins for nausea, even the cigarettes—then Rose brought him in to sit in the straight-backed chair beside the bed. He had almost yellow blond hair, very pleasant, that came down behind, clean and long, tied in a brief ponytail at the back of his head. His nose was, as her mother would have said, a serious nose, long enough to be dignified, with a bony structure to it. It gave a serious masculinity to his face.

"I understand you might want to look at a Bible," he said.

"Are you from Missouri?" Rose Reynolds' mother asked impetuously. "Or, from a nearby southern state?"

"Why yes, I am," he said. "How did you know that? My accent gives me away. Everywhere I go I'm stuck in the history of a region I don't respect."

"You don't respect it?" Rose Reynolds' mother exclaimed, perking up, staring straight at him. "Is that right?"

"No, I don't, ma'am," he said. "I don't expect I'll ever respect that region again."

"Is it because of the racism? Is that why you don't respect it?"

"No, ma'am, that is part but not entirely it."

"What is it then, son?" Rose Reynolds' mother said.

"Well," he said, and his ponytail switched one way and then the next. "I guess I'm not much of this earth, as they say. Wherever I've been I never much want to go again."

Rose Reynolds sat dumbfounded behind her mother on the bed. 'Son?' she thought. Her mother had not let the local minister call on her, nor the doctor but for once, nor even Rose's own grandparents; and now her mother had let in a Bible salesman off the street, one not much older than she herself was.

"Well, my littlest mama—You don't mind if I call you that, do you?"

"Not at all," she said. "I started it."

"Indeed you did, Mama. And it had a warm quality to it, even though you look much too young to be my mama, sickness not withstanding. I can see with humbleness that you are much closer to God than I am. I can see that with my eyes, though your beauty is still very great."

Rose Reynolds' mama laughed suddenly and with warmth: "Are you trying to sell single Bibles or whole crates?"

"Oh no," he said in horror. "I'm not selling these Bibles. I'm giving them away!"

"Oh no!" Rose Reynolds' mama said with equal horror, leaning back stiffly against her pillows again. "You're not going to try to recruit me now, are you? You're not one of those Army for God recruiters? I can't stand armies of any kind."

"I expect you are the one recruiting me," the young man said.

"How old are you then?" Rose Reynolds' mother asked. "How many years has it taken you to find me here?"

"Oh not so many," he said. "Twenty-six."

"Twenty six," Rose Reynolds' mother pondered. "I would have taken you for thirty-four around the eyes."

"No, big mama," he said, then beaming fully. "I'd like to lie to you and say I was thirty-four last week, in order for you to take me more seriously, but I'm as straight as an arrow and as bright as the day—forgive the clichéd speech."

"Once I'll forgive you," her mother smiled. "I'll forgive it just this once." The color had come back into her face. "Did you want to talk about God?" she asked.

Rose Reynolds fiddled with the corner of her mother's sheet, sitting cross-legged on the double bed.

"If you like," he said. "I'm never likely to turn the subject away. I can talk about whatever you like though. I'm not in any hurry; I'm not really going anywhere fast in my life. I just stand here and the world turns under me. It was turning a moment ago when it whipped me in through your front door. You can imagine my surprise."

Rose Reynolds was staring at the handsome young man now sitting beside her mother. He was not that much older than she was herself. Perhaps she had imagined how breathily her mother spoke. But no, the young man *had* taken her mother's breath away.

"I'm so—" her mother said, looking into his face with her sapphire eyes, "I'm so—surprised, too."

"Would you like me to read to you?" the young man offered.

"Yes," her mother said. "I'd like that very much."

"Would you like to put your head on my knee?" he asked—"while I read to you?"

"Yes," she said, "if you don't mind."

"No," he said, "I don't mind at all." And then they were just like that, the man where her mother's pillow had been with his legs crossed and her mother's head on his lap. And Rose had risen now, awkwardly, and started to gather the misplaced things around the room. But neither seemed much to notice her.

"You probably do this wherever you go—" her mother said to her visitor who sat with a stack of burgundy-colored Bibles beside him.

"No, Mary," he said, "I don't. You don't mind if I call you that, even if

Mary is not your true name?"

"No, I don't mind," her mother said.

"I'm sorry, Mary, to say that this is the first time anything like this has ever happened in my life. I'd like to think I had had it happen before now. I'd like to say I see my life unfolding like this all the time. But I see you before me now as a unique experience."

"It doesn't matter if you don't see it as unique," Rose Reynolds' mother offered seriously. "Tell me now, what will you read to me?"

"I am going to read you a part of the Bible you have probably never thought about much before. I am going to read you the table of contents on page 4."

Beside the bureau, opposite the bed, Rose Reynolds gave a startled laugh.

"Rose," her mother said abruptly, looking up. Her mother's face was flushed with its former beauty. "Rose, you haven't been for a walk in a long time—Why, I can't remember when you were out of the house last. Good Lord, I can't remember it. Why don't you take this chance to go down to the movies and rest yourself—I'm sure this man can take care of me if I have a bad turn. If I stop breathing, I expect he can start me up again."

"I would be delighted," the young man said.

And so Rose Reynolds walked around the block one brisk turn—thinking about unknown strangers in the house—and came back to sit in the garden with her back against the blue wall. She leaned under the windows the young man had opened for her mother, listening still, in case her mother might have any need of her.

"I'll read it to you in a minute," he said. "But—I had the feeling there was something you wanted to say to me."

Her mother's throaty voice came out between the white ruffled curtains in a puff. "Yes." Her mother laughed. "I have had the most uncontrollable urge to ask you a childhood joke that is absolutely inane. Why can't I get this asinine joke out of my head?"

"What is it then? You have to tell me now."

"I can't," her mother's voice said. "It's just too dumb."

"Ho. I can take it."

"No," she said. "You won't believe how dumb it is. And you might think it's offensive. I don't mean it to be offensive. I just don't know why I can't get it out of my head. I've been thinking it over and over again since you came in the door. Please don't get me wrong."

"I guess it's meant to be then. Lay it on me in a strong full voice. No matter how dumb it is." Then he said more quietly, "I'm sorry," he said, "I didn't realize how painful that part of your back must be."

"Rose uses the cream over there," her mother said. "That's wonderful. Rose is such a good girl to me. She is the angel of my life."

"Yes," he said. "I could see that the moment I laid eyes on the two of you. God has been truly good to you."

"Yes," her mother said. "Yes, it's true."

"Now," he said, "now tell me the joke."

"It isn't even a joke really. It's a riddle with an obvious, completely obvious answer."

"O.K.," he said. "Hit me with it."

"What," she said, "what is dog spelled backwards?"

"Oh don't ask me," he laughed. "I only got through Yale law school."

"No!" she cried.

"Well, it wasn't Yale really but I hate to say what I did before I turned to God. Wouldn't want to demean the alma mater of the South in the face of a good joke. So dog spelled backwards is God? And that's it."

Rose leaned as if arrested against the summer hot wall, listening, embarrassed to the hub for her mother who was saying such foolish things.

"I'm sorry I said it now. Now you're offended. It's the stupidest thing I've ever said in my life. I've never had much truck with religion, but I'm not against it. I just couldn't get it out of my head."

"It isn't stupid," he said. "Well—it's completely stupid, as you said. But there must be a reason for this phrase coming into your life, don't you expect? Otherwise, why would you be thinking it again and again? I can only tell you what lurches into my head when I hear you say it to me. I don't know that it will do you good, but I'll try to think about it out loud if you like."

"I wish you would," her mother said, in a room which lay right behind Rose Reynolds' back and seemingly far away. A complete stranger was rubbing her mother's back in there with the pink cream Rose always used on the now very thin back. And her mother was telling a completely stupid, pointless joke to him. Rose could feel that her own face had gone completely red.

"Do you mind?" he said very softly.

"No," she said. "It feels very good."

"It seems to me that the word God is the word dog turned inside out, as if you had turned a sock inside around. The dog is like that—mouth end inside out, with all the animal guts hanging out all the way to the puckered-up butt end of it."

"Not really?" her mother said with interest.

"Yes," he said. "God is a dog inside out. "

"Really," her mother said again, incredulous.

"Yes," he said. "I think the message in this joke is that God is very ugly."

"No!"

"Yes," he said. "God is guts and grime and pus and cells. He comes out of the soil like plants and germs. And fungi. Do you know the word 'fungi'?" he asked.

"Yes, of course," Rose Reynolds' mother said, matter-of-factly. "I'm turning into one."

"Well, now that you mention it," he laughed, "I hadn't been going in that direction, but now that you mention it, I guess we are. You much less than most," he said warmly. "Look at your beauty. Of course the Creator is beautiful, too."

"But—" Rose Reynolds' mother challenged him. "In your theory, how does God come out of the soil?"

"In pain and agony," he said quietly. "You can imagine the agony of a dog being turned inside out."

"Yes," she said. "I feel it every day. That is the precise feeling of what is happening to me."

"I'd say I'm sorry," he said, "but I wouldn't truly mean it."

Her mother was silent for a time, and the stranger, too. "I'm sorry your beauty is going into something else," he said. "Because I'm still attached to this world, I can say I am sorry for that. I can say I'm sorry it's gone painful for you, because I have fear of pain and I have a liking for you. I can say I'm sorry for Rose because her pain is most immense, but I'm not sorry you are going through it. The dog would rather be God, I think, in the end— afterwards anyway—Are many of your bones broken?" he asked.

"No," she said, "only a few. The disease takes me this way."

"I know," he said. "I can see it in your face that you have broken bones."

"Can you?" she said.

Rose Reynolds leaned back against the hot boards of the blue house among the flowering peonies and felt the sun on her face for the first time since Christmas. Her brother had arranged before his departure to Vietnam to have the groceries and pharmacy items sent over regularly here. There had been no need to leave the house, and anyway she knew no one; and her mother not only needed her but also liked her genuinely. And all their filial differences had fallen away.

"What else can you see?" her mother's voice asked after a time.

"I can see a bad bruise here on your knee. I am going to put my hand on it now and see if it will go away."

"Do you think it will?" she asked.

"I don't know. I never thought to try this kind of thing before, but I have heard of it. This moment is isolated for me from anything else I've ever known. Let me just try it now. Maybe it will turn into a very bad joke, a truly bad one, but then maybe it might turn around on us, gut side out. I don't want to hurt you though."

"You won't. In any case," she said, "pain is all the same to me."

Outside, Rose Reynolds heard the short gasp that came from her mother and leapt to her feet. Through the window she could see the man leaning over her mother's knee and the back of her mother's head against the pillow beatifically, all her radiant hair flung out over the blue nightgown, and the sheet pulled down to her calves, below and beyond the soft length of her back.

"No," he said. "The bruise, it's still there."

"No," her mother said, "it's not."

"Yes," he said. "I can see it. Can you lift up enough to see the back of your leg?"

"I don't need to see it. It's like a black hole now. In a universe of pain. The bruise is sucking everything in—I can't tell you what I feel."

"It's enough you feel it," he said. "You don't have to tell it to me."

"Could you?" she said. "Could you—"

"Yes," he said, "you don't have to say it to me. I will be very, very gentle; I will be like a gentle, penetrating wind. I will not hurt any part of you. You know," he said, "usually I stay so much to myself."

Rose Reynolds sat down on the ground then with the heat up full in her face and heard her mother sighing. In horror, she heard him reciting in a clear soft voice, all the books of the Bible from the table of contents. Then as she looked in through the summer screen again, into her mother's room where the two of them had lived relentlessly for six months, she saw him rubbing her mother's forehead and kissing it, brushing back her hair, long and full against the pillowcase, all the way to the ends of their beautiful, dead strands. She saw the man's face cradled against her mother's chest and she sank back down again.

"Think of it this way, Mary," the stranger said inside their room. "These are all who have gone before." And then he was reciting them backwards, and her mother was laughing. "And inside out, Mary," he said, "from the middle little squiggly parts, alternating toward the ends." And then it was quiet again for a long time but for a creaking and sighing not unlike the voice of wind until Rose couldn't stand it anymore and jumped back up again.

There she saw two things. In the mirror that they used to show her mother their garden growing splendidly beyond her reach, Rose saw her own shocked face. She also saw her mother in the young man's arms, wrapped tightly in a winding sheet, while the young man in a pair of old black shoes jumped squarely in the middle of the mussed up, creaking bed.

"Higher," her mother was crying joyously, while Rose was transfixed at the window screen, "higher, higher—" Gently after a time he laid her mother down and continued innocently to stroke her head. Rose sat back down against the new blue wall ashamed of herself at what she had thought.

"Sleep, beauty, sleep," she heard the stranger softly sigh. "Let beauty sleep when it is done." She heard the door to their bedroom opening. "Now, Mary, let your long, clean rest begin."

When Rose came into the house, the man was gone; and they never saw him again. After a day or two, Rose discovered in the closet the inexplicable thick black shoes, something cobbled out of a country perhaps the world had never known. Several times she meant to mention them to her mother; but somehow she could never manage it. As the weeks wore on and her mother grew yet more frail, Rose thought her mother must look for him; but when finally she questioned her, her mother replied dreamily, "No, no, my darling, don't worry yourself. It's not a repeat thing."

—⁓—

Everyone gathers around me at Iz's signal. Ramon jumps in the ditch we've dug, nearly on top of me, and if we did not have to be so careful we would dig like dogs. Together we shift aside our ignorance. "Eeee-ha!" Ramon shouts in my ear, just to irritate, in his recurrent America joke. But this time I believe he means it. "Eeee-ha?" he asks looking up at the scanner. Iz stands at the edge, staring down the pit in awe and disbelief. In my rage against him, I am not beyond noticing this: She is not closer to him than she is to me.

Piers lowers the machine again. "You dropped your watch down there again, you kids?" But for our tools, we are completely undetectable. Piers has come up with many jokes on that score, that if I were to be lost in the sand at night on one of my wanderings there would be no way to find me again even with these. "Go a little more to the right. It's dropping into an air pocket! A little more, you're almost on it now. Go on, slip it under. You'd better use your brushes now. Brush it down." I whisk away at it. Rose sent this her brush with me for luck. No, another one.

A glint comes up at us, and as if stunned by it I start to cough.

I don't know whether it's a joke or not, but Piers starts to cough as well. "Swing low sweet chariot," he coughs. "I'm booking my flight right now."

"Just find the sucker," Anne breathes. "And let's get out of this fucking hellhole. Right now."

Piers steadies himself and fires up his camera. "Send down another spatula, we've got us some over easy eggs."

Ramon reaches in to assist while I hack away.

Tears fire down my cheeks between coughs and gags. I am doubled over in the pit in front of all of them. They could not have a better vantage point for my fit. I am surprised to hear how high my voice can go in ratcheting—caught this way by some kind of persistent god-like grip around my throat and ribs. Ramon draws back. "It's the Curse of the Mummy!" Piers shouts. I take the handkerchief from my vest and cover my mouth, and then for just one second everyone leaning over me sees it as I see it, for the first time, too. For the very first time it's on a rag: a red shiny spider of my pneumatic blood. It is as if someone has thrown my blood onto a windowpane in front of us all. There's a splash of red wherever I look, sprinklings of my own red mottled soul. Even in the pit, there is a sparkle in futuristic phlegmatic red. Everyone has stepped slightly back. Iz's eyes are wide with fear. I cram the future into my pocket, but everyone has seen. She turns aside and I take up the brush. She does not bawl about her brother again. Like the air that hovers next to the earth in the shadows here—everything seems slightly cooler now. Shadows are well worth hunting here. We are all looking past my existence at the find, whatever it will prove to be.

Ten thousand years, I hope. Annie has drawn it in its position; Piers has photographed it and all of us. Ten thousand years have passed between the time when I have seen the handkerchief and when I have to pull it up. More than seeing it, I can feel the fragment's weathered surface, between my thumb and forefinger, almost smooth on the upper side, the other patterned against my thumb as I lift it out.

—⁂—

It was the 10 o'clock news that brought them the name of someone they knew, finally, who had been killed in Vietnam.

"I didn't know," Rose Reynolds cried in disbelief. "I didn't know Peter had gone over there. He was against the war."

"How could you have known—stranded here like this with me?" her mother sadly said. "I liked him oh so much. He was so nice to you—and to me. Even if I was just your mother."

"How could a boy like Peter have gone to Vietnam? I would have heard if he was drafted, wouldn't I?" Rose asked again. Maybe he had gotten so depressed in college that he had flunked out—because of her, she thought. And been drafted.

"You don't know these things," Rose Reynolds' mother said, stroking her daughter's tear-stained face. "Two whole years have passed between the time you saw him last and now. So many things can happen in a year or two, my darling. During that same amount of time Freddy might come home to us."

"But I thought Peter was working away in college somewhere on his degree! He wanted to go to Stanford. I thought he would be with some other girl. I thought he had another girlfriend by now."

"There there," her mother said. "There there, my little sweetie. I only wish it didn't have to be like this."

That same year they would see many people's names on the rolls, names they thought they recognized, but it was the second one, the boy she had briefly dated in college before she came home to care for her mother, it was his name that hurt her so, this second death among the close friends she had had—in that other world where people lived. This second death had amplified the other one, brought it home. "Let's not talk about it anymore," she said.

—⋘—

One day her mother had begun again, "Planning for the future," she blithely said. She declared that she refused to have a tombstone that stood up from the ground. "Promise me that," she said.

"But why?" Rose Reynolds asked.

Her grandfather in the depression had bought up a lot of farms, her mother said. It was all gone now, the boys had squandered it; but when she was little her grandfather had made himself very rich by buying up the neighbors' farms. Rose Reynolds tried to picture it. As a little girl, Rose's mother had been forced to go into Marshall Fields and parade in front of her grandfather. The grandfather pointed from a big stuffed chair, picking them out—the new dresses of the season—beside a mirror where the little girl was reflected in triplicate: Irene's short bobbed hair and innocent face. He picked out the ones she would be forced to wear to the one room schoolhouse where all the other children were wearing burlap bags.

"There isn't a difference," Rose Reynolds' mother said, "between people. There shouldn't be. Everyone should have the same chance. I refuse to have my death made a monument to the rich—even if we aren't rich now, even if we were rich once. Rose, I don't need a gigantic stone. I will always know that you love me, Rose, in my soul."

Rose promised her then that she would not have a monument that wasn't flush with the ground. And the ground was level anyway, all the way to the horizon, where they lived overlooking the flatlands.

If Rose looked out the square window through the small glass panes of the bedroom where she and her mother lived, she could see across the field all the way to New York City, it seemed. And if someday she thought about going as far as the living room windows and throwing back those curtains, she would see, she was sure, Los Angeles.

"When I'm gone," her mother said late one night, and then she hesitated. "When I'm gone," she said again, but then they were staring at the television set where a blast had gone off. Bobby Kennedy was down, people were screaming, the cameras were swinging round and round.

—⁓—

"Time is a terrible thing," her mother said, breaking down in that early morning. "Time is so terrible to me. That I should live to see this atrocity."

That week the two of them were stunned into silence to see the funeral train going to Washington, and all the ordinary people, like themselves, lined up along the railroad tracks, their hats like beating human organs on their chests, rubber curlers in their hair, tears flooding down their cheeks.

It was not a good time for Rose to help her mother to die, but her mother had decided it. She could not take it anymore, she said, watching all the dying going before her—Rose's friends, Martin Luther King, Bobby Kennedy, and who knew what else would happen now—to Freddy and to other people, too—and not one bit of relief for herself. And not one thing she could do for anyone else in this world.

"But you do do something for me," Rose Reynolds tried not to whine. "You do everything for me. The important things. You talk to me, you laugh, you cry."

"I can't take it anymore," her mother said. And it was true that in the days before, her mother had ground her teeth with a pain that would not stop. "When I go, you'll be free. You can go on and live your life. You can work for these things you care about. And, if you want, you can have a baby, maybe a baby who looks like me. It gives you joy," she said. "And besides," she said. "I'm not ready for living anymore. You have to be ready," she said.

"You are ready," Rose Reynolds insisted. "And I need you," she said.

"You need your own life. You need to live. And, I'm sorry, sweetie. I can't take it anymore. I didn't know it could be so bad. I didn't know it could go on so long like this."

"I'm not ready," Rose Reynolds said to herself. "I'm not ready." But for her mother's sake she kept these words to herself. "I'll never be ready," she said in a chant to herself.

Quietly Rose Reynolds held the bottle over her mother's hand and dropped the pills in, two or three at a time, maybe forty times, watching her mother trying to swallow them. In the end, she only threw up a few into the basin beside the bed. And then the two of them lay down and watched the funeral of Bobby Kennedy.

"I'm the first person to ever attend her own funeral," her mother said.

—◊—

Rose had promised her mother one more thing in the end—that she would not submit her mother's body to a church ceremony. Even though Rose herself had wanted one, it was her mother's wish, after all. But her sister and then her brother had returned on leave to overrule the living and the dead. In the end, Rose had relinquished it in order to make the monument decision stick. "Choose the more important thing, the lasting thing," her mother had said so many times in her young life. And besides, her mother had had her funeral earlier. "This is the funeral that counts," her mother had said anyway. "Nothing else matters after this. You've given me everything I could ever have wanted, darling girl. You are my darling, darling girl," she said. "And you must never feel guilty for helping me. And you have helped me so much."

—◊—

CHAPTER III

They are ill discoverers that think there is no land,
when they can see nothing but sea.

— Francis Bacon.

THE SHIMMY OF IT, THE GLORIOUS CACOPHONY OF IT, at the corner of California and Nebraska Streets: light pouring down through trees, the free movement of air, motion of cars, and behind it all: the nearly silent helicopter winds of repetitive hushed-up things going on far away, thousands of miles. On top of it, the permeating songs: guitars—Gibsons, Martins, Strats, and all the little consequential strivings of unnamable stringed melodic instruments from Sears & Roebuck, Harmony, from the Classic Music Discount Store—that made background for the raspy young would-be voices of the sweet mandolins, hand-made zither, someone's Selmer saxophone that had the year before played with unspent emotion at the funeral of yet another Kennedy boy. Clothes hangers squeaked and sang under wind-borne tie-dyed t-shirts on the wrought iron college gate; long-haired poets sang simultaneous San Francisco/Berkeley exegeses to the constant woodpecker jabber of tack hammers and staple guns as the information went up:

BRING MY LITTLE . . ., sing-in with Dave on the corner stoop, sit-in in front of Harris Hall, American Friends Service Committee, Campus Christian Groups Against the War, Students for Democratic this and that, meetings, meetings, meet-me, have you seen my small black dog?, Martin-12 string, needs slight fret work, great guitar . . .a little brown triangle flying back and forth and then the finger picks like frantic earth-turned beaks, and over it a cascade of silky yet suede, rust-colored, leather-jacket fringe, frenzied and good, yes good. Even possibly great! Getting great! Anyway! One day, Man! Surely going to be great—certainly without one doubt, truly great, Man, that cascade all over the place! And that amplitude of sheer acoustical gone-electric sound! WOW! Zithers, horns, harmonicas, placards, hair picks, combs, penny whistles, placards, drums, bongos, placards, flutes, tables with the fold out metal legs—A.F.S.: Avoid the Draft—personal placards: BRING MY LITTLE...

Janis Joplin wailin' it: WAH-WAH-WAH-WAH-WAH-WANT out the windows of one fifty dollar, blue and silver-streaked renegade Buick, 1953, a relic, electronic windows, scratchy bench seats and a couple of rusted portholes drilled into the sides. Fumes pouring out the top like smoke from a trout freshly turned; bad, bad fumes out the top, exhaust system dragging on the ground; Never Ever Drive Without Those Windows Down, Girl; intense music out the sides: WAH-WAH-WAH-WAH-WAH-WANT YOU! A passel of young women wailing it,

WA-WA-WA-WANT YOU! Taking their shirts off. And their bras. Atop Daddy's green World War II army blanket, looking straight at the poster of Uncle Sam and his pointy finger I WANT YOU placards: BRING MY LITTLE BROTHER

On the big sweeping green and yellow, over-hung with massive oaks and maples right there in the middle of the beloved prairie, bedecked with ionic columns, on the river-side, undulating, living, breathing, fulminating, herbaceous, college lawn. And right here on the corner sitting on the black metal railing, many languages. BRING MY LITTLE . . .

Rose!

BRING MY LITTLE BROTHER HOME! The placard says. AND I MEAN ALIVE! YOU MOTHER FUCKERS!

...accumulated the year before, Bobby Kennedy, Martin Luther King, Rose's former high school boy friend, Rose's former college boy friend—both in Vietnam—, her own beautiful little mother who had been younger than Kennedy, nearly as young as Reverend King—by a few graced months. Not the only one reeling inside.

Janis Joplin, Jimi Hendrix, that fellow who lived in the attic who looked like Neil Young, unnamed heroes in Southeast Asia who were related to everyone we knew, a lot of Southeast Asians.

Rose Reynolds' brother had drawn his draft number, Number 19, and had already gone to Vietnam.

Pumping out the windows with the curtains on the breeze from every radio and record player. Coming up with the grass.

It really did start with a bathroom window.

In the bathtub with your elbows propped up on the sides and the pages of HOWL held well away from the bubble bath and the window flung wide open, the background birds pumping in some hard-core music to which you can already recite the words.

A bag of chocolate brownies wouldn't hurt. And a glass of milk with a teaspoon of nutmeg and a banana whipped into it. You must put on some weight.

After a good run with your dog in the park, a hot bath is good.

College men will not be in the women's dormitories after midnight, or at any other time outside of regular visiting hours.

Leroi Jones and Allen Ginsberg, while looking at gross anatomy diagrams.

Her brother, Freddy, had occasionally danced, too, he said, in Vietnam and in Thailand before the 'mishap' as he called it, would happen when he stepped onto the tripwire that sent him catapulting into a tree. After hearing two or three hours of poetry and then Greek philosophy and then assorted quips from medical texts, Rose did not wish to return to a dorm anyway. If she went back there, even five minutes late, she could be expelled from school—for being out when she was actually trying to get in. Better to spend the night. It was a big thing for a woman to lose her education because she had missed curfew; for a college man it might mean death by way of Vietnam. Just a bit of the serious penalty, they often joked, for being late. White rabbit, and all of that.

And then, too, she had to remember that eventually they had brought her own brother, if injured, permanently home. Again and again in his mind, and in hers, there was that bit of good luck. That was one thing anyway to be grateful for on the home front, during the unbearably long, illicit war.

—m—

Even Piers says nothing. And we all look at it as I turn it in my palm. Piers doesn't have to say it. No one has to say it but he does: "Is anyone homesick yet?" He goes on taunting in his brain. I can hear him; he doesn't have to say it. He knows it, and he doesn't know it.

Isabella flops backward on the dunes from where she kneels, her legs twisted under her, denouncing the concept of earth.

—⁕—

Up through her brother's sloping lower lawns, Rose Reynolds ascends through all the wooded terraces cut in and defined by beds of pink and yellow flowers, precarious walls of stone. Wrought iron fences graduate the sight of the spindled porches and pale wooden exteriors from cliff to cobalt sky. And there, descending from the widow's walk, looking out toward the crest of sea, jumpsuit yellow as a finch, leaps the spectacle: her only brother's new wife. By the time Rose has reached the house, her sister-in-law has donned her bright white tennis shoes. "Freddy, Freddy," the sister-in-law calls toward the house. "Your sister's here. And I've got you both the biggest surprise you've ever seen. Freddy, aren't you there?"

"Oh absolutely please—!" the sister-in-law whines, already taking Rose's hand. "Absolutely don't look yet!" Rose shuts her eyes and opens them at once. "But oh! Of course you must. And now! That naughty Freddy's gone off to the office. I can't find him anywhere just now."

It is the absurdly beautiful sculpture that rises up and looms over both their heads—erected by what numbers of men?—that makes Rose Reynolds want to laugh, or cry, she doesn't know which. A large round table, made entirely of polished cemetery marble, stands dead center of the uppermost patio. And from its core, exploding into a fervent early summer foliage, bursts a tall, pink, marble edifice—nine feet tall—thighs buried in the naturally slit, dark stone. The statue's carved male body rises lean and striated with elegant musculature, the shoulders broad, the long, masculine hair swung into the wind, his arms cast above his head in unremitting, dark dismay. It is as though these arms were caught off guard, warding off, if not its own fiercely beating hair, well then something very near to it.

Rose sits down abruptly on a wicker chair at the base of it and stares.

The sculpture's softly rounded buttocks and undermost parts shine above the table, ever so softly, and yet again in the near mirror of the polished black tabletop.

"You don't have to say anything," her sister-in-law says. "I know it's an amazing work."

"But what does it mean?" Rose asks quietly.

In the finely beaten face of the man, an abject pity lives. In his pupilless eyes, a notion of terror resides—also in and around his mouth. But for the wings, Rose thinks, her sister-in-law might have imported the statue directly from the leavings of the ancient Greeks. Three carved, black, marble benches kneel around his large salmon-colored human feet.

The sister-in-law sits down now beside Rose, beneath the sculpture's shadow and takes Rose's hand. Gently she presses each of Rose's young fingernails. "It's a tribute to my husband," she says quietly, "my first husband who died just before, just before your brother, you know, came along—" Freddy has already informed her of the circumstances: Ginny's first husband shot himself after returning from the war. "Also," Ginny adds pensively, studying the younger Rose's lovely, ringless hands, "it's a tribute to your and Freddy's mother, because of the wings, I mean. I know you took such good care of her while Fred was gone—. Well, I feel that I've known her all this time since I met you both. Her presence is always with us, besides—"

Ginny manages a quick squeeze of Rose's wrists. "It's good luck, isn't it?" she says lightly, "to have a sculpture in your garden to ward off bad experience?"

"Yes, of course," Rose agrees with her, quite perplexed already. "But now I think I'm a little tired—after the bus."

"Oh, of course," Ginny echoes her. "You must be beaten sick." She slides aside the patio door, hesitating on the way into their living room.

It was a small, yet nearly tangible, emotional manifestation, already a feeling like a gerbil, or perhaps something like a ferret, Rose thought, that moved through her chest as the nearly new acquaintance, Ginny the sister-in-law, held her hand. And just now—too late actually—Rose considered that perhaps she might as well have stayed just this one additional summer at the University where she had been learning to paint and sculpt. Even though her friends had graduated and gone on to other more personal and promising things, her old lover was still there for yet another month or so, and with him a feeling of her impending accomplishment. Even so, she had decided to leave him behind especially after so much of the last semester had been spent trying not to lose his baby. This was something she would not discuss with Freddy or this Ginny, she was sure.

Ginny carried on about her now in a low-pitched voice as Rose Reynolds leaned against the living room door, silently begging admittance to the interior where finally she might lie down. Her sister-in-law was saying that the name was actually Genevieve—as Rose might not have known—though no one had ever called her that, the sister-in-law sadly pointed out. Yes, Ginny had been thinking about her own name, Ginny said, when she saw Rose coming up from the bus along the garden path. She had always been called Ginny, she rattled on, as though her name had been Virginia instead. It was one of those great disappointments in life, Ginny said, waving her one leg over the other where she flung herself back. The slender legs crossed over the arm of the lime-green stuffed chair. It was so disappointing, Ginny said, to be given a completely beautiful name at birth and then never having had anyone, in all her life, call her that. She held her lemonade glass in its knitted yellow sweater aloft. "If you see what I mean?"

Rose Reynolds considered, looking wide-eyed herself into the stone eyes of the statue just outside the windowpane, and then into each of her sister-in-law's pupils where her plastic contacts had been tinted such a light and penetrating green. "Genevieve?" Rose Reynolds politely smiled. "I'm sorry to join the enemy ranks. But Ginny is a very good name, don't you think?"

"Ah well," said the sister-in-law with disappointment, drawing down her pinched face nearly into the mouth of her drink.

"What if I called you Vivien?" Rose asked hastily.

"Ah yes!" the slender new sister-in-law said eagerly. "That would be a help. Then everyone would know when I corrected you that Genevieve is really my name!"

"Yes, indeed," Rose Reynolds cajoled, rolling her mahogany hair up into a knot at the back of her head and repinning its clasp. It was as though in these last moments she had been caught and immobilized in a queue of ceaseless standup comedians, and now by association or self-preservation she'd become one herself. For a moment she went on, weak-kneed, humoring the slightly older woman in the yellow jumpsuit as best she could.

Rose Reynolds with difficulty fought off the impulse to roll her eyes. "It is a little odd, Ginny, but I suppose it might work . . . if you said and did the things a Genevieve might do, then, I suppose—"

"Oh yes!" the sister-in-law cried. "What a notion! 'Vivien, '" she tried the name on herself. "I actually like that name!"

"What utter irrelevance," Rose thought, taking pity on her brother who had been nearly lost at war and healed again against all odds, only to come home to this. Rose Reynolds leaned over and picked up her bags. A Genevieve would not have bought such a statue, Rose Reynolds thought. And a Vivien would have admired it in a museum and left it at that, instead of trying to pretend it was a tribute.

"Exactly," the new sister-in-law announced. "Vivien will be just fine."

Rose Reynolds nodded again, indicating the way in. "Do you mind, Vivien, if I go in for a moment now and rest? It's been a rather exhausting week. I'm feeling rather urgent, if you see what I mean."

On the ascent through the house to the room where she would sleep and another where she would paint, Rose Reynolds could not help but notice that the sister-in-law had had other effects on the stately home since the only other time Rose had visited it.

In the beginning of that summer then, the air was filled with a presumed pleasantness. Her brother was home from the war now and recovered, her mother was dead, her father gone now for years and years, never to return. Yes, life had moved on rapidly for them. Only a few years before, they had been riding bicycles on family outings, their mother radiant at the front, and now both her parents were gone entirely. Instead, here the tall, lightly freckled Vivien stood, in perpetual helpfulness and intended charm.

After a few days of awkwardness then, it began to seem not at all abominable for Rose to sit in Vivien's company in the suburbs on the back terrace near the angel Vivien had installed. Rose stretched out politely alongside her sister-in-law on their padded chairs overlooking the pool. She grew accustomed even to the unusually sweet and blended drinks her sister-in-law made for the two of them during their innocuous discussions of things like cooking and flowers. And if anything else might come up, about her brother's wartime experiences, or her mother's death, or anything about Ginny's past at all, "Let's think pleasant thoughts," Ginny, the new Vivien, said. "Let's not think of anything past, not right now." The neighborhood was sweet for walks when she could not get the next portion of her painting, and her brother's large hairy dog was always eager to bound along in a rather intimidating and friendly way, much as their old dog

Rascal had.

Beyond the colonial cemetery and down the hill lay the grassy volleyball court her brother had carved out with a chain saw for the neighborhood. Down the street lived Vivien's best friend Mirth who had recently given up being a doctor in order to marry a ponderous podiatrist, Vivien said.

In the fading light each night, the fireflies began to come out—first low in the sea grasses and Queen Anne's lace, then rising in among the beach roses and stone walls, a chorus of light. Rose Reynolds did not like to play volleyball with the older people from the neighborhood. She preferred to continue in her room at that hour, reading and drawing with the image of her mother in mind and the image of her brother's new happiness leaping in and out, a yellow flame, a cheerleader at the edge of the window frame. At all hours, Rose Reynolds painted in the room where her sister-in-law's bare photographs walked up the wall with her brother's larger ones next to the cherry sewing table her mother had used to make so many beautiful dresses for her only a few years before. She was painting a tribute to her mother.

Framed by maples and apricot-colored squirrels swinging from tree to tree, the local ferry came and went. Often, far below, her older brother stood handsome and tan, smiling up at her. She didn't have to summon him to be reassured; he didn't have to repeat his memories of combat in order to be comforted. Down there he would be building one of his projects of nails and wood in the early morning before he went to work. On the weekend, her brother and the sister-in-law would invariably leave her to her peace and go down to their boat.

In serenity she went down to the town's small stone library to check out books. For a dollar and a half, a full-sized pointillist print of fully clothed people, sunbathing in a previous time, was hers. On the blue flocked wall of her bedroom, over the sister-in-law's king-sized waterbed from her previous marriage, the print dwarfed the modern furniture and gave Rose the certainty of its parading populace under opened parasols.

In that waterbed Rose Reynolds could wash about even at night and see the distance of her life, even between the dots of human activity on her wall. Rose Reynolds had come to her brother's house for refuge, to rest and work in solitude. And that was what, in the beginning, she found.

One day, however, when Rose was sitting very quietly, relishing the summer heat and silence, feeling at home, if not with her own mother, well then with this would-be sister who was not all that much older than Rose Reynolds was anyway— On that day, Rose Reynolds received a shock when, so suddenly!, her sister-in-law pushed open Rose's studio door with a look of torment distorting her face.

"Oh, I can't forgive myself," Vivien sobbed, sitting down on the edge of the twin-sized bed. "I can't forgive myself for leaving you up here all alone almost every day all these weeks. Here you are—pining away all by yourself up here."

"But no!" Rose Reynolds tried to reassure her. "There's nothing at all to worry about! Vivien! It's quite all right! I like it—" she tried to explain.

"I've been so selfish, I just didn't think! You must come down now and spend time with us at the boat—every weekend, even every day. You and I could go out, even when Freddy is at work!"

Rose looked at her and was mortified. Certainly Ginny, or rather Vivien, could understand, she began to plead as politely as she could, that she, Rose Reynolds, did not wish to leave the peacefulness of the house to sit among motor boat people who were "very friendly! to be sure!" when she had painting here to do. It was true, really, just as Vivien had guessed, Rose wished only to finish her paintings this summer.

"Are you certain you refuse to join us then?" the one called Vivien, or Genevieve asked again. "You won't think we're neglecting you?"

"Don't you worry," Rose said, relieved. "You go along now and have a very good time."

The sister-in-law crept uncertainly away, her pert face hanging. And the college girl sat down in exasperation to stare at her sketchbook with a sense of wariness.

Early yet in her stay, a few days later, a small hand-written note came gliding out from under the closed door, almost on its own, moving silently over the tarp she had laid down to protect the white carpeting. By Wednesday, another note like a long thin animal, or a pool of liquid, slid toward her from under the door. By Thursday evening, the quiet Freddy himself stood awkwardly in the entrance, conveying the scribbled messages to her:

Rose! Vivien wrote. *There will be a barbecue on South Beach if you can make it downstairs by the time Frederic and I depart. I implore you! Do this for yourself!*

—⁃ℳ⁃—

Reading aloud from Ginny's next note, Freddy rolled back his eyes momentarily, as once he had done so annoyingly and just in time for the photograph depicting his departure for Vietnam. *It is your sister-in-law's expressed wish* . . . Freddy cleared his throat and went on from his carefully penned cue card.

Most precious Rose! Please come downstairs immediately! And 'be sociable' in . . . *your sister-in-law's new house* . . . *where she feels you are now a guest* . . *. and then* . . . *'without fail'* . . . *later, put in an appearance on the boat.*

97

Yr. delighted brother and honor-bound courier, Frederic

With which, her elder brother Freddy with the scars beginning like glassy minnows on his legs and under his shirt disappeared again.

That Friday evening in the dining room, Rose and her brother cast about for conversation until gleefully they began recalling one old time after another when they themselves had sailed together or alone—or with Georgia who rarely liked to leave her mother long enough to join them. An awkward clatter of fork and knife sprang up at the new sister-in-law's place setting. It seemed to Rose that in that one long moment her older brother's hair had given way all of a sudden to streak lightning down the center of his head. His lower lip thickened into a permanent pout above his beautifully appointed clothes. Small jowls had begun to form. Vivien cleared her throat.

"Clever," Freddy called his wife then, smiling enigmatically at her in a most pointed way. "Gin-gin, you are so extraordinarily clever!" Freddy hastened to describe his new wife's recent restorative projects around what he affectionately called their 'building site.'

It was her sister-in-law's *repetitious hope!* So her brother would ever more humbly convey later in the week, that Rose Reynolds might become less inward—as Vivien imagined her to be—and come with them to *socialize.* Freddy shrugged sympathetically, and Rose arched one eyebrow toward a luxuriously loaded palette. The childhood tattoo artist in him could not help but approve that salad of remarkable color sparkling on the palm of her hand before the window.

Freddy had never been gregarious, had never offered up much other than an atmosphere of comfort and strength—but that was all that had ever been wanted anyway from his little sister. "Yes, Rose!" Freddy nearly shouted at breakfast, "Ginny and I steamed her down-river—past the shoals out to the littlest islands just as well! It might have been the Delta!"

Rose for a moment shut the lashes over her hazel eyes, but Freddy had improved, perhaps he had even finally recovered from the beating the war had given him. "Oh Fred, don't you wish we still had *Fair Dinkum?* That was our old dinghy, Vivien. But I guess you wouldn't need a dinghy now."

Vivien laid down her fork, and in it reflected her lightly sun-streaked hair. "Even boats are not all-important in my house. That is not the point," Vivien snapped. "We will not have anyone pining away in this home."

"Well, it's hardly a 'home' in that way, Ginny," Freddy said. "I mean, it's a 'home' but not an institution, Gin. We don't have to have recreational requirements here. Besides, Ginny," Freddy mildly pointed out, "we are talking about our favorite boats. No one is pining away."

"All day long up there in despair!" she cried over her untouched plate. "Your sister is doing that—to my house. And you so recently recovered from the war!" It looked as though the fragile bones in the sister-in-law's face were about to evaporate or, even worse, to shatter.

"No, no," Rose jumped in. "I'm sorry if you've the wrong impression! I'm so happy here!"

"Yes, Ginny," Freddy proclaimed. "Rose's paintings have received a very good response at the University. You know that's why she came to us. So she could have time to paint. Painters have to be in one place a very long time. That's how they do it. They can't be out and about socializing night and day with the likes of us."

"Really truly," Rose offered the red-faced sister-in-law, "I'd love to come with you on your boat sometime, but I—right now, I'd rather finish this painting. Besides, I'm feeling a tad tired. It was a long semester, grueling really."

"I myself find it nearly impossible—" her sister-in-law pronounced, "to mourn on a boat."

"Here here," Freddy agreed, and he lifted up his glass. "There is no one who will agree with you on that subject more than the two of us old salty dogs, isn't that so, Rose-girl?"

"Why, it is!" Rose nearly jumped up to say it in time, before another tear might clatter down onto the new bride's mottled cheek. "It is certainly the truest thing you can say about us, except," she said, "for one thing."

"What's that?" the married couple asked hesitantly.

"I find it impossible to mourn when I paint, I find it even more elevating than water, if you see what I mean."

At which point, her brother who loved water more than anything, other perhaps than his brand new bride, stared at her uncomprehendingly. "Better than water?" he pondered. "Better than water indeed?" Rose could see him rubbing the spot on his belly now with one fingertip. That would be the one, Rose was thinking, where the piece of shrapnel had entered in and left a glossy starfish.

"I don't think it would hurt Rose to be sociable once or twice a day," Vivien sniffed, tipping her spoon into the depths of her cup, ladling up a bit of tea, and staring at it meaninglessly. "It is our house, isn't it? Freddy, well, isn't it?"

"But, Gin," her brother said, "Rose is socializing now. She socializes with us at least three times a day."

To the siblings' astonishment then, the one regularly called Ginny put her freckled face down into her pastel flowered napkin and cried, "That is not socializing! That is not socializing!"

"All right! All right!" her brother's big bass tones erupted then, as much in trepidation as anything. But to all three of them, especially to Freddy himself, surely it sounded more like anger had erupted from his throat. "I'm certain that Rose will agree, Ginny! To coming to the boat—even today! If you insist. Won't you, Rose? Won't you please come to the boat today to make Ginny happy just this once?"

"Of course!" Rose announced immediately. "I had no idea it was such an issue. I can't see quite what it might mean." With which, she excused herself and went immediately to her room and lay steaming and ridiculously afloat in her sister-in-law's former marriage bed.

Just then, Freddy popped his puppy dog head in again, feeling even more self-conscious. "There, don't be mad. You don't really love painting better than water, do you? Oh never mind, you always were completely odd. Even when you were a baby. Although, you always were a good sport. I remember some tattoos you managed to wear to school that must have made you somewhat uncomfortable." He laughed then and she couldn't help but join in with him. As he spoke, however, Rose could not help but remember that he had been away from it all, had been to war, had known persons from other lands, with other dialects and ways much as she still wished to do. Even if he had not been able to help her much with her mother, he had had adventure in his life; for that, she admired him.

Certainly there was nothing to make Rose fearful of boating or the sea. Rose Reynolds was a seasoned swimmer and a sailor. She could water-ski and row quite adequately, and she could paddle a canoe. Her father and then her older brother had seen to that, pleasantly, while Rose Reynolds was growing up. In fact, there was nothing Rose Reynolds loved more than to be on or in water, other than to paint, of course. And that was what Rose Reynolds had come to her brother's home to do, to paint and to try, for once, to avoid thinking about the all too compelling company of one particular man and the consequences to which it had led while she was at the University.

In another season and some years earlier, Rose Reynolds had come home from the University—to a much smaller and plainer house in another part of the world. There in a small wooden house, because of her brother's extended tour of duty in Vietnam and her sister's studies in another tropical world, Rose Reynolds had been her mother's only assistant in death.

In her brother's house now, in strange company, she was painting portraits of her mother. Her mother had been, at her death, still stunning in her beauty and intelligence; Rose Reynolds had been nineteen and it was her first experience with such things. Until that time Rose Reynolds had never seen a human, or even an animal, truly cry in pain. But now, she had already given her mother many gifts in her imagination as she painted that she had not been able to give her in life. She had given her an image that might be said to be singing, something which her mother had in life never much done. She had laughed a great deal, but she had never sung. As for Rose Reynolds she had never been allowed to sing, until her mother's illness, in the presence of her mother. This was something that astounded the sister-in-law one day, when Rose Reynolds confided in her, and Rose had been surprised to enjoy her sister-in-law's sincerest sympathy. The sister-in-law had practically brayed at the thought of such a restriction.

In her sun-struck studio, with a tarp thrown down over the carpet, Rose Reynolds had set up her easel. She was learning now that she could paint more than beautiful scenery. She could create a truly beautiful portrait and she could venture into the abstract. She could turn her brush into whimsical or wrenching things that almost equaled the delight and horror of her own experience. In retrospect each day, Rose felt that she had almost known intimate and understanding company—while painting.

"Wouldn't you like a rest on the water?" her sister-in-law was saying from the doorway.

"A rest on the water?" Rose rolled over and felt the bed slosh beneath what now seemed the painfully colorless Seurat she had brought home from the library. She looked into the merciless insistence of her sister-in-law's face. Yes, Rose Reynolds finally thought. Yes, she sighed, she would go to their boat for a little peace and quiet, she said to herself. Especially she now required peace and quiet, having been interrupted so very many times in the middle of achieving a height in her talents that she had never before known possible. Yes, she said coldly, out loud, she would go if it would make her sister-in-law feel more content with the world.

"Wonderful!" her sister-in-law exclaimed, her little eyebrows perking up like two typographical accents in her comical face. "You won't believe your good fortune on the docks. There are a number of absolutely stunning men down there. In fact, there is one man who has the boat down the dock from us that you might really like. We don't know him well, but he is very friendly with us."

Rose Reynolds hung her head in silent despair.

"It's O.K.," her sister-in-law put in hurriedly. "Really it is, you don't have to be with him, if you don't want to. Well—actually, he usually has two girls with him. I don't know if you could get him—since you don't seem to spend that much time with men. But, he seems very nice. He's certainly good looking—"

"I'm just going out with you," Rose Reynolds made as if to explain—without going into her own personal history. "Let's just have a pleasant time—as a family."

"Oh don't worry," the new sister-in-law chirruped. "He may have a funny name; but he's all right. That Johnny Alaska—Jacky, they call him Jack—usually has two girls with him. Oh, I said that didn't I?"

"Jacky Alaska?" Rose smiled generously. "Vivien. You do invent such interesting names."

103

"It seems unlikely anyway," Vivien hurried on, "that Jacky would leave two gorgeous girls for you, now that I think about it, well doesn't it?"

"It's never seemed unlikely before—in my life anyway, Genevieve," Rose would have said out loud, but then she was too perturbed. The one called Vivien would have been completely astonished.

It was there again: the feeling of the small animal falling into her gut from somewhere near the top of her throat.

Her sister-in-law's sunny head popped in and out and in again at the study door. "Here now! Let's rush!" She was laden with a pile of bright towels. "We've just got time for a round of black jack before Freddy comes and we have to head down to the boat."

Rose Reynolds had always liked the sound of human feet knocking upon the docks where the wooden slats were laid out in layers over air. It was a natural xylophone casting its harmonics into the water beneath, and into all the living in that water, and far below in rock and sand. She loved the tenor, then the pulsating soprano of the stays clacking and the halyards. It was a pleasure to hear the flags and windsocks flapping and the low creaking of all the lines in perfect overlapping and multiple figure eights on boats and docking cleats. Yes! Yes! She was glad she had been pried out of the house to come down here!

But her brother that year had been convinced to sell the handmade family 'sloop' and rent a sleek cabin cruiser, not a yacht exactly, but a motor boat all the same with a cabin in which it was apparent they could all sleep quite comfortably and not have to rely, as Vivien said dramatically, 'On the nonchalance of wind!' Sometimes, Rose saw now, this Vivien could be quite surprising.

Just the same, her brother enjoyed taking them up and down the coast, pointing out all the gigantic bins for oil. Mention was made of their father who had first taught them to fish and sail, of course. But it seemed like a story in someone else's storybook as the bow of the boat cut through a mildly rippled surface, heading out. The older brother remembered it better. Yes, that had been her brother Fred's first tragedy, the loss of their father, before their mother had begun the long trek toward death. His latest ones had occurred on foreign soil.

In chalkily painted, crenellated cones and barrels, the oil canisters and grain bins towered over the landscape—"just like space ships, as you say, Vivvy," Rose agreed.

By now it had become almost a ritual: first the now timid knock and then the insistent and agonized face of Vivien poking in at the door. If Rose would decline to go, almost instantaneously upon her refusal, the house became a vault. The canvas before Rose iced and then the intended image for the day altered like a too cold lettuce leaf. It was true: although she could not paint on the water, once she was on it, all her life was set into idyll. Her sister-in-law, though closer in the boat, seemed very comfortably far away.

—w—

It was on one of their early afternoon returns that Jacky Alaska made his presence known. Indeed, two young women accompanied him, just as the sister-in-law had predicted. The brunette clung to his arm as though they were strutting on the cover of a movie magazine. On the other side, the strawberry blonde managed also to hold to him—while juggling a bag of groceries toward the oversized motorboat.

The man himself was dark with longish hair swept back on both sides in the style that had become current then in the business world. His cheekbones were strong and dominant as if two lemon wedges had been sewn beneath his flawless skin. The man's eyes and their smoldering unknown quality sought Rose's attention, not unlike the eyes of the lover—the one she had left behind at the University, about which she would, could, not speak.

Well now, it seemed to her, against the backdrop of sky and water where it swept out from the river and into the sea, that a quiet alliance might release her from the awkwardness rampaging about in her brother's house. It occurred to her that she might on the stranger's boat even be able to paint. His occupation was, Vivien said, selling stocks, or diverting money! "And what does it matter," Vivien suggested, "for a brief summer contact anyway? It might release you from your grief. Grief is something not to be ignored! That is something I certainly know about!"

Rose did not bother to object again. If it made Vivien happy to think Rose sad, so be it.

—⁂—

Oh to be on actual waves and not on the waterbed, listening to her brother's lovemaking to the squeaky attractive sister-in-law, while weighed down by the stifling heat. On the cabin cruiser then, in the deck chair, quietly sipping the drink the new man had made for her, she endured the ten minute introduction, and then the long obligatory lunch the women had packed, and then the final, brief farewells and also the promises from the man himself to the two departing female friends.

A certain hardness had come over her, in the face of her sister-in-law's insistence. The new man poured a little more wine into her glass. He was pleasant to look at after all, and he liked to laugh, or so she found out that day. In the decision-making—as the day stretched into evening and beyond—there had been the constellations overhead, not surprisingly, and then the brilliant pinpoint stars over his shoulder and finally a few weeks later the stars again beside his ear as he had come laughing and crashing with finesse down on top of her.

It had never been of much interest to Rose Reynolds, this thing about automobiles, but still it amused her when on the next day, quite ludicrously in the driveway, Vivien actually jumped up and down, thrilling at the sight of Rose Reynolds pulling up to the house in the green sports car the man had lent to her. "Oh it's so cute, isn't it adorable?" Vivien cried, leaping into the passenger seat. And it could not be helped if Vivien had to ride around the block twice, right before the podiatrist's house so that she might call out embarrassing things to all the neighbors about Rose's new car. At first she had tried to explain and afterwards she had merely inwardly rolled her eyes yet again and chewed her nails. It wasn't exactly a gift, she said. And the new man had his other car anyway— So Rose Reynolds reported as her sister-in-law pumped her for information that she couldn't care less about, in every private moment Rose and Vivien had.

Yes, yes, Rose admitted, she only knew that the other car was very sleek, black, and low to the ground with shuttered eyes bulging out like a bug's on the front end. It could go 180 M.P.H. on the interstate, which was true or nearly so. She had seen the speedometer, and then she had been forced by vertigo to close her eyes.

"Was it an Italian name?" Vivien leered. "The name of the car?"

"Yes," Rose recalled for the enthralled sister-in-law: "Italian," she thought. Yes, she supposed Vivien was right to gain so much happiness from little things, why not? And so she had remembered it for her after a time, and finally had spoken into Vivien's sweetened face the sound of the automobile's name. She felt the warm motherly hand on her forearm and the delighted little squeeze, and had to laugh out loud. Her own mother had been all too possessive of her, had tried rather often to stop any kind of serious friendships she might have thought about with men.

Still, neither mother nor daughter would have cared much for Jacky Alaska, nor his cars, this Rose already knew, but it was neither his clothes nor his looks that set him apart.

It was true the new man, Jacky Alaska, wore always the same kind of clothing. On his tall, lean frame he wore a slightly worn pair of very clean jeans, an expensive deep blue, knit shirt, loose over his belt, and in cold weather a long, hand-knit, grey Irish sweater with wooden buttons fastened down the front. When he went to work he wore one of several dark grey very well tailored yet loosely fitting suits. His shoes were like small grey mirrors on his feet. His ties and rather long vests, also each one pale grey, were so lovely they were nondescript.

—m—

Rose Reynolds froze, first in the living room, trying to remain motionless as Vivien showed her newest forays into redecorating the elegant Tudor house. "You see I've put these carpet tiles on in a kind of pattern. I didn't have enough of either color so I've made a sort of quilt on the top of each chest. It's all very mod. What do you think?"

All the words drained out of Rose in disbelief as the blood rushed in a fury to her face. Vivien had affixed, with a fast-drying permanent glue, pieces of red and black shag-carpeting to the tops of the three fine antique walnut and cherry bureaus her mother had refinished with Rose's help not that many years before.

Abruptly Rose closed her mouth and crossed her arms over her chest as if she'd been trussed. The sister-in-law took hold of her and led her into another of the large high-ceilinged rooms, now to witness another of her works. "You see," Vivien was saying, "you're not the only creative person here."

Actual tears were forming at the back of Rose Reynolds' throat and a few were moving toward her eyes, for there stood the small, perfect, handmade, wooden chest, their favorite, that she and her mother had labored over so long, sanding the top and all the wooden key holes with fine papers and tooth brushes, and then applying the many coats of protection to it. There stood the perfect chest with the red and black shag carpeting standing like frightened cartoon hair straight up on the top of it.

Vivien put her arm around her now, emanating warmth. "I'm so glad you're happy these days," she said. "You deserve to be happy, you know. You've done so much for everyone. And you're so much fun when you come out of your cave."

In a daze, Rose Reynolds felt the freckled sister-in-law link her arm through hers; and then they were going down into the living room for a soothing drink before dinner. "You know," Vivien said, "I think I'm beginning to understand you and your brother. You're both such silent types."

Just then Freddy came through the room, laughing and smiling at the sister-in-law, in triumph it seemed. "So how're my girls?" he asked. "So how are my happy, happy girls today?"

—ɯ—

Jacky Alaska's house was a contemporary model with large square rooms and expensive if uninteresting modern grey leather furniture. A white brick fireplace in the living room helped a little to break up the stern ambiance as the whole room seemed to go into shadow and the firelight flickered against the walls. In the bathrooms, small gold fixtures perched above the replicated white marble basins like voiceless messengers. The bedroom was hung in black, the coverlet and curtains, the matching sheets. And on each, as she wrote in her little notebook, a small white pattern of slashes like lightning penetrated the surfaces so frequently it was as if they represented a dead god. She had laughed at herself when she wrote that and then she had drawn him throwing his minuscule lightning bolts all over the room.

It was in this room then where the new man made gentle and seemingly endless love to her, looking deeply into her eyes, touching her with a tenderness and respect she had never known. Ironically, every moment she felt as though she were being carried, for the first time since her father had left, in reliable, protective arms.

It was at the big butcher's table in his kitchen where Rose tried to sketch, staring out the window toward the flat and uneventful lawn. It was there while looking for a pen one day to make a sketch that Rose came upon the tiny eye of a man in a colored photograph peering out at her from behind the black telephone. When she picked the paper up she saw that he had a smiling face, and also a hat not unlike the one her brother owned. An address had been written on the back, presumably his own.

That evening, she asked the new man about it, presenting it innocently to him. Most suddenly Jacky Alaska went silent and even white with anger in the face. "Don't go through my things!" he shouted, taking her by the shoulder and shaking her. The rough grey cardigan, that he wore whenever it rained, flapped like the wings of an alien bat against her leg. The slightly silver streak seemed to darken in his hair with rage.

"I wasn't!" she cried out at him. "It fell out from beside the telephone! Why would you leave it out, if you didn't mean for me to see it?"

Jacky Alaska stroked her hair, very gently then, placing a long strand of it in her mouth with his fingertips and running it between her teeth and over her wet lips. This he did again and again then wiped her eyes with his slightly roughened hands. He put the photograph into his breast pocket. "It's all right," he said, offering her a glass of water. He crouched down in front of her where she sat in the kitchen window seat beneath the large open wooden shutters. "I'm sorry; I'm a little jumpy now. We have a meeting coming up. Just business, but it always makes me worry when we have a new account. Maybe we should go down to the boat and cool off for tonight." That night they slept again in his boat, rocking ever so peacefully against a different shoal.

When the two weeks until the meeting had passed, she asked him about it again. "Oh," he said, "it went fine. Nothing to it. Easy as pie. Let's go down to the club." She never again asked him about the man who had reminded her of her own brother, and soon the incident had passed from her mind.

—⁘—

There was such a feeling of acceptance in the household now with her sister-in-law's camaraderie and intense interest in everything Rose Reynolds had done and said. It was almost as if Georgia were back again. Her brother smiled to see them so happy together now. "Less is sometimes more," the brother said, whatever that was supposed to mean.

The house vibrated with the pair of women, chattering together, and planning small encounters in the clothing stores in preparation for summer parties and rendezvous. Rose Reynolds had never felt so ratified in a family life, even if it was an entirely different Rose Reynolds being supported here. She was doing very little drawing or painting now. Every night she was sitting at the bow of Jacky's boat, knees drawn up, arms wrapped around her slacks, the sea breeze sweeping her long dark hair back from her face. Life tingled up and down her arms, and the spiked stars shone as if they always would at the crown of her head.

It was the dancing she loved the most, after the water, of course. In the club, he had swept her along to the beat, and there she rubbed the bright red sweater that her sister-in-law had given her to wear for color against his chest.

She would never love anything more than water, she thought. There was a small crowd of friends now who beached their boats on the sandbar several nights a week, laughing and singing around the driftwood fire. And Rose Reynolds was singing for the first time in her life, openly, if in a crowd, without fear of being told to stop.

—⁂—

In the early August heat, Rose Reynolds grew irritable with the predictability of him. Even the manner with which the lover ate annoyed her now, and how he deleted certain syllables when he spoke, how he patted her endlessly when other men tried to engage them in conversation. To make it worse, he ate what Rose Reynolds considered to be junk food. And most offensive of all things: he insisted on throwing his beer cans overboard. That was reprehensible, she thought. She had chided him more than once; but the next morning after a particularly difficult encounter, finally she had acquiesced and agreed to make up with him and go to the fast food place as a kind of compromise. She was very hungry and there was a fondness for the familiar tastes of the hamburgers, the French fries and particularly the chocolate shakes from when she with her family had traveled across the plains. She was telling him about a concert of computer music she had heard at the University with a young doctor the autumn before, when Jacky Alaska pulled them into the parking lot of the franchise shop with all its golden flashing lights.

"People felt the same way about the synthesizer and the organ before that," she said. "Even the harpsichord, with its remote plucking of strings must have seemed bizarre after the lute."

"I've nothing against the computer," Jacky said, getting out of the low black car and walking with her across the parking lot. "Makes things easier for me. I plan to learn all the tricks. Here," the lover said, "put this in your purse," with which he pulled from beneath his shirt a revolver where it had been tucked against the skin of his abdomen and into his belt. Stunned, Rose opened the top of her bag, just as he had said to do, and felt the weight of the instrument falling between her thumbs. When it hit the bottom of her purse she felt it bounce against her belly, rebounding rather naturally against her womb.

There the gun must have rested all day, for she didn't care to think of it until she was home again, safely in her brother's house and lying in the waterbed, reliving the moments of the day. And no! She must have dreamed it—had he put an actual gun in her purse? At once she rose up and looked into the bag where it rested harmlessly on the chair at the foot of those painted waters Seurat had punctured again and again into the canvas overhead within the boundaries of the cheap library frame. The day had seemed so like a dream, hadn't it? But Vivien was nowhere to be found and she was not sure how she would react anyway if she'd been told.

He must have taken it back, the gun, for there was no way that such a heavy item might have fallen from such a deep leather satchel with the drawstring at the top pulled tight around her makeup and her notebook and drawing things. And, what, she asked herself, was it for? And, how had she walked into a public place like that, just like that, with the thing in her own purse? It had all happened so quickly and unexpectedly. Never in her life had she expected such a thing to occur. Tomorrow she told herself she would take back the little green car he had lent to her and be done with him.

—⁄⁄⁄—

"Come into my study," Jacky Alaska said the next day upon her arrival at his house, taking her by the wrist and leading her into the den to sit beside the large mahogany desk. He sat down behind it, resting his elbows on the blotter, looking at her intently as if over a pair of half-glasses. She sat down and stared at him. He had begun to look much older to her now. "You've lost my gun," he said gravely.

"But how could I?" she asked. "I never took it out. I thought you had."

"No," he said, looking very seriously at her. "What are you up to?" he asked.

"Up to?" she said in alarm.

"Yes," he said. "What are you up to here?"

—⁄⁄⁄—

Jacky Alaska took her to a windowless cement building and signed her in. There they put large protective earphones over their ears and a man handed her a gun similar to the one she'd lost. "Now," Jacky said, "now you're going to learn to shoot a gun."

"I don't need to learn to shoot a gun," Rose Reynolds said.

"Be quiet," he said coolly, "and do what I tell you. If you can lose my gun," he said, "you can learn to shoot one."

"I don't need to learn," she said again. "I didn't lose your gun."

Resolutely he pushed her then up against the place where she would stand. "When you see the target through this site," he said, "aim for the little dot at the center. Try to line them up, one on one."

She stared at him coldly then, and shot her rounds.

When the target came back to them, Jacky Alaska looked at her.

"I told you I didn't have to learn," she said.

"Who taught you to fire a gun?" he demanded, as if someone had stolen something from him.

"My mother," Rose Reynolds said. "My mother was an excellent shot with a rifle, and a revolver. Her grandfather taught her." Still he stared at her.

"It's not such a big deal, you know." She glared at him, in more ways than one. "I think I'd like you to give me a ride home now," she said. "I'd rather not take your car."

He took hold of her chin and looked deep into her eyes. "I don't think I'd like that terribly much," he said. "Besides I've promised us to Al."

"You've promised *us?*"

"Yes," he said. "You'll see."

Later that day they took the cabin cruiser out to meet his friends at the island beach. The boat, plowing through the waves, seemed both small and large at once. On shore, while he had his meetings, she gathered driftwood for the fire, and then she spread out the blanket and fell asleep. For many nights now she had been unable to sleep, even before the incident in the hamburger joint, she had been having peculiar dreams about him. She woke, startled, to find his fingers running up and down the sides of her legs. His fingers meandered into her mouth, as he liked to do whenever she tried to speak, his head over her face. Beyond his head the rosehips flowered profusely in a thorny, soft-lipped pink. "I'd like to go home soon," she said. He shook his head and smiled at her, kissing her firmly on the mouth.

"What are you thinking?" he whispered again and again in the almost stifling heat.

But she was thinking of the gun she knew she hadn't lost and another one. Of the cold barrel of it pressed into the back of a young man's throat, a young man her delightful sister-in-law had known quite well, had even married once.

"What are you thinking about me now, my sleepy head?" His weight was heavy on her as he fingered aside the crotch of her swimming suit, and then falling upon her with a single thrust he had lodged himself between her legs. Involuntarily she felt a heat rise up in her chest.

"I asked you what you were thinking?" he said again.

For a moment she grappled with the thought that lay somewhere behind the vision of the two microscopic targets in the balls of his eyes. In and out he went, driving her from deep sleep into a speechlessness. "What are you thinking, sweetheart?" he asked again and again.

Hoarsely she whispered it then: "Sudden death."

He closed his eyes and laughed, then opened them again. It was as if his spirit were walking into her by way of her eyes, the two of them riveted together by two solid shafts of current at the head. "Sudden death?" he laughed. "Sometimes I think you are the only person who has ever once understood me in my life." She could feel the swimming suit pulling down, against her will, under her breasts, her nipples hardening in his mouth, between his dry lips. Her legs drew up around him, automatically almost, and she could feel him all along her inner thighs and calves, and in the core of her. "There's so much to live for, my Rose," he said. His hair was silky and limp in her hands. He looked down at her like a child. "Don't ever betray me," he said. "Don't ever hurt me, Rose Reynolds. I don't know what I'd do to you. Promise me that one thing." Gingerly she held his cool buttocks in her hands then and felt him coming in and out of her with a smooth confidence that would never destroy itself.

That night she insisted on sleeping at home again and he managed to let her do as she wished. She slept alone in the waterbed. There she dreamed that he demanded she kill a rat for him at the city dump. "I won't," she said, "I won't," until he put his hand over hers and forced her to pull the trigger for him. The animal, badly hit, rolled over screaming in pain and clawed the air with its small pink childlike feet until she wept into her sister-in-law's pillowcase. In the very early morning, before anyone else was up, Jacky called to ask yet again whether or not she had found his gun. "No," she told him, "I haven't found it, nor have I lost it." Abruptly she set the phone down into its cradle again.

"I'll pick you up at six," he had managed to squeeze in.

"No," she'd said. "Don't."

"Yes," he said. "I will."

—⁂—

She had begun to think that she might ask her sister-in-law about it—whether or not Vivien had seen the gun. But every time she contemplated mentioning it, a fear came over her: a fear of the repercussive silliness that might follow such a confession. She could well imagine the reaction her brother and sister-in-law would give to hearing that she had been seeing a man who carried a gun in his belt and that she had carried it herself into such a public fast food place. Her brother, for one, had had enough of guns in his lifetime; he had made a point of that. He had not wanted to go to Vietnam, the whole family had been against it, especially her grandparents, and he was not one for keeping wartime souvenirs.

It mattered very little that it had been Vivien who had engineered Rose's alliance with the stranger on the boat, nor that Vivien had practically insisted upon it. With more and more uneasiness, and rather quickly, Rose found it dawning on her that perhaps the gun, a .38, was not merely for the times when they might drop anchor near any rough unknown town—as she had at first thought, and as he had said to her.

"Vivien, I've something to ask you," Rose finally said after breakfast, after an hour of meandering from room to room.

"Oh? What's that, sweetie?" Vivien rubbed stains ferociously off the front of the pine green refrigerator and stove. Her sun-frizzed hair bounced up out of her scarf.

"Well, it's personal, could you stop cleaning for a moment and talk with me?"

"Why, of course." Vivien blew a curl of hair out of her face. "Why, of course I can. Let's take a drink outside on the terrace."

They sat right down in the late morning sun at the marble table. "You're beginning to lose weight, Rose. I've been noticing that. Aren't you feeling well?"

In the intense heat, Rose Reynolds shrugged and rested her bare feet on the sturdy bones of the table's nearly human ones as her sister-in-law put the tray before them. Already the August cicadas were reeling out their high-pitched whines. The lemonade poured out of the pitcher into each frosted glass with the turquoise knitted sweaters around their waists. Rose held up her hand, but too soon her sister-in-law had already poured gin into it. A jet of cold liquid eased the scene. The ice cubes fell back, and suddenly the sky shone a brilliant blue, and the trees leafed out over the marble man who waved his unexpectedly friendly arms overhead.

"You know," Rose said sincerely, looking at her sister-in-law, leading up to it, the conversation about the gun, seeing her sister-in-law for the first time as perhaps her brother had seen her and was seeing her still. There was rather a glow around everything she said and did, an innocence. An intense and happy freckling, yes that was it. "You know!" she blurted. "You look just like a film star, Vivien! You're so cute."

"Why! I thought you'd think me just old hat," Vivien said brightly. "I'm really touched by that."

"You are, you are just the cutest thing I have ever seen. No wonder Freddy wanted you so badly. Why you're practically Doris Day!"

The sister-in-law looked at her coldly then. "I always wanted to be beautiful rather than cute, but we get what we get."

"I didn't mean—"

"No, no—" Vivien prattled again. "I know what you meant. To Genevieve or Vivien. You meant it as a compliment. And I'm so glad. We really do have a pleasant relationship; I had hoped so much for that. It's hard coming into another family. I was so worried about it, you know, after everything that happened with Davie's death, and everyone blaming me and all."

"Oh, they didn't blame you! Did they?" Rose exclaimed. "That is the most horrible thing I've ever heard. That is absolutely heartless!"

Rose studied the bottom of her drink and the sister-in-law poured her another one. "It is so hot out," Rose said, half-heartedly holding up her hand again. "I can't drink in such heat. Aren't you about to die? Maybe we should have stayed inside."

"He was so young." She put her hand on Rose's arm. "Together," she said, "we were very good. You wouldn't have believed how much we loved one another. Freddy understands it. Your brother understands such things— because of the war, and all."

"Why was he depressed?" Rose asked. "Your first husband. I hope you don't mind my asking such a personal question."

"Oh, no," Vivien said. "You're Freddy's sister. You both understand these things. Why, Freddy and I have gone to decorate your mother's grave. Freddy has told me things that he has never told anyone else."

A wave of jealousy threatened, but Rose pushed it down. How had this woman come to be at her mother's grave? she asked herself. This stranger had been there more often than she had herself. If she hadn't been so far away at school, she could have been there. And with Freddy. She pushed it down. Obviously the woman had also suffered in her life.

"I hope you didn't have to see it happen, Vivien. I can't imagine anything worse."

"Oh no," the older woman sighed. "There's no mistaking the sound of a gun when it goes off inside your own house. There's the shock, and you think to yourself, that was a gun! A cold chill rivets you. It's like when you stick a wet hand by mistake on the ice cube tray. You're stuck there. You know that if you move you're going to rip a chunk of skin right off your hand. And if you don't, your hand is going to freeze. I've heard it in my dreams so many times. The one terrifying sound, and again and again you wake up drilled to the bed and in a cold sweat."

And then Vivien seemed to look at Rose Reynolds peculiarly, as if perhaps Vivien had found the gun in Rose's purse. Perhaps her sister-in-law had actually found the gun and hidden it.

Rose looked down into her drink. "I'm sorry," she said. "About Davie—"

"I don't want you ever to have anything to do with guns in this house," the sister-in-law said then rather harshly, setting down her glass. "Missy! Do you understand that?"

"Oh no," Rose Reynolds cried hurriedly. "I would never have anything to do with guns." For it was true, she could use one, but she would never have one or carry one. She wasn't certain how she had happened to be carrying the one she had conveyed into the fast food shop—it had happened so quickly—nor for that matter did she know how she had lost it, if she had. It seemed almost comic; she was tempted to call her sister the lawyer to rescue her.

"I hope not," Vivien said severely, staring at her still. "Sometimes I think you are sadder about your mother than Davie was sad about whatever it was that took him down, most probably the things he had to see in the war. If I'd only known in time, I could have done something about it. I could have gotten him some help."

Vivien was rolling a straw between her fingertips. "How depressed are you exactly about your mother's death?"

"Why— I don't know—" Rose said. "I'm not sure anyone knows such things."

"That's exactly what I thought," Vivien said. Then pointedly she drew up a little bit of lemonade in it and shot it out, high up, onto the statue's head, the body of which stood not a foot from her hands. The liquid sprang out of the lips above her, down the neck quickly, and onto the ribs of the exquisite man's belly and into his umbilicus.

Rose Reynolds felt a sickness in her own belly and then the human feet of the statue turning cold beneath hers as, simultaneously, the summer heat swelled up around her where she sat on the cold marble bench. Almost unconsciously she was rubbing the bony tops of the stranger's feet with her arches under the black marble disk that held him in place.

"That's why I did this for you," the sister-in-law said.

"Did what?"

"Got you someone to go out with. So you wouldn't sit cooped up in the house. Your sister Georgia is married; she's a lawyer and she's married. She lives on a tropical island and someday, I'll bet anything, we'll all have babies running around this place. I don't know why we never see her. Anyway, you looked much too sad for your own good. I don't want that kind of sadness in my house."

"You know," Rose Reynolds said after a time, "my mother always said whenever something went really wrong that she would blow her brains out but for the one fact that she was certain she would sneeze at the wrong moment and blow the end off her nose instead. It wasn't entirely a joke. She didn't want to be a freak for life."

"Your mother was a very beautiful woman," the sister-in-law said, not without bitterness. "I've seen photographs of her—she was much more beautiful than I am. She had a very hard death."

"You have to stop worrying about me, Ginny. I would never ever commit suicide. My mother always told me the only unforgivable sin was that. There would be no way to ask for forgiveness once you'd done it, she told me that when she had so much pain I couldn't believe it. But she never tried it," Rose Reynolds was lying now to relieve her sister-in-law, trying still to ease the misplaced concern in her sister-in-law's face. "So you see I would never try it myself. I owe that much to my mother. It was something else, actually, that I wanted to talk to you about."

"Yes," Vivien said, standing up resolutely, even angrily, it seemed. "Yes, you do owe that to your mother. And as for the other thing. I think Davie is forgiven for what he's done. I myself completely forgive him, and if there is a God, I doubt my Davie is rotting in some interminable hell." She turned with the lemonade pitcher in her hand. "Now I've got work to do. Remember that I don't allow guns in my house! No matter what you say."

"Vivien—" Rose Reynolds said.

"I don't want to talk about Davie anymore," Vivien trembled underneath the overhanging branches and bird feeders and the entwining pink and yellow roses in the garden lattice work. "I had to clean up that room, where he did it, on my knees. It was everywhere—parts of what he'd thought and been. I couldn't ask anyone else to do it for me . . ."

"No, don't, Vivien," Rose said but Vivien rushed on angrily.

"I know it interests you as an artist how other people feel in circumstances like that, but I won't talk about it. I would if I could. I've come to love you and I would give you anything. Believe me in this, Rose. It's not selfishness, Rose. It's something I just can't do for you—" Her voice began to ascend then, to keen and warble as if not her own. "And Davie—Davie is forgiven, Rose. I know he is. I forgive him every day of my life. I still do." With which, Vivien began to grapple with the heavy sliding door, the pitcher still in her hands, and the lemonade spilling out.

"No no," Rose Reynolds said in a rush. "You don't understand. That wasn't what I wanted to talk about. I don't need to ask people about things like that. I can imagine them for myself."

"How on earth could you possibly imagine it?" Vivien cried with hatred in her voice.

"But that isn't it," Rose Reynolds said again. But the sister-in-law had already turned curtly toward the other door into the house.

"I wanted to ask you," Rose Reynolds said silently, "have you— Have you, Vivien, been going through my purse?"

But Vivien was carrying the tray into the house and Rose Reynolds was left staring at the two soft globes and the beautiful, delicately drooping neck of the swan where she saw them reflected in the hard tabletop.

"Did you find it?" her lover said again on the telephone that night.

—⁂—

The gun had entered her dreams now. She was searching for it even in her sleep. First it was immense and traveled on two long legs with insect feet. Then it was minuscule and she was searching for it on her hands and knees with a tweezers and a wet sponge as if it had been a bit of broken glass. One morning she woke up to find the barrel of it like a cannon bursting through one of her windowpanes. There had been a little nick on the barrel of the gun that she had lost, she remembered it. Now it appeared in dreams as cuts in the earth and on the sides of trees. She had seen now forty-two people killed by it while she slept. Why couldn't her sister-in-law just speak with her about it, if her sister-in-law had found it and taken it away? But then, Rose had approached it badly, Rose knew she had. Almost hourly, Jacky Alaska called to ask her whether she had located it.

—⁂—

On Saturday when the sister-in-law went out with her brother for their weekly game of golf, Rose Reynolds began to hunt—through all the sister-in-law's closets and shoes and hatboxes. She peered under the mattresses and in the backs of drawers; and, in the attic, she had even begun to open all the trunks. Under the eaves where it was impossible to stand, her brother had rigged up a little trolley out of a square board and four casters. Rose found that she could sit on it and nip in under the rafters like a child among all the stored curious things. In one corner her mother's old college yearbooks lay, and in the opposite: her brother's. And Georgia's first high school report card. On the other side of the room, she discovered one of her own scrapbooks open on the floor, the pressed corsage of her high school boy friend, Peter, dead in the war, molded into the page. Rose Reynolds was thinking now that anyone who carpeted the tops of furniture might hide a gun in any place.

Rose had just opened the wedding dress box belonging to her sister-in-law when she thought she heard the distant sound of tires in the driveway. She sat steadying the cart, barely breathing, as if bolted to the floor. And then, when there was nothing at the door downstairs, she lifted up the white net veils. There was a picture of her sister-in-law walking down the courthouse steps on the front page of the newspaper. LOCAL VETERAN'S DEATH RULED SUICIDE, it said. From below, a volley of voices shot up the stairs: her sister-in-law's rapid one, and then her brother's very low voice, at their early return. "What are you doing up there, sweet potato?" her brother Freddy was calling up to her. "We came back early. Ginny wasn't feeling all that well."

"Freddy!"

"What's of interest to you in the attic?" he called again. "Can I help?"

"No!" she called out, putting away the wedding veils, as the sister-in-law's younger face stared up at her from the printed page. "It's O.K.. I'm just looking for some of my old high school things. I think I left them with you in the other house. They must be here somewhere."

Then she heard the sister-in-law on the stairs where she must have come out of her room where a drawer, she knew with sinking certainty, had been left hanging open in a telltale way. "What are you doing up there?" the sister-in-law asked very brusquely. "What are you doing in my attic in the middle of the day?"

"I'm looking for something," she called shrilly but she didn't have time to explain.

"I'll bet you are," the sister-in-law called out angrily.

"What's the matter, Ginny?" Freddy said below.

"She's rummaging in my things," Rose heard her sister-in-law say, almost in a whisper, but too angrily.

"Oh, I can hardly believe that," Freddy said.

"I don't suppose you can," the sister-in-law said in a harsh voice. "Your sister can do no wrong, isn't that right?"

Rose Reynolds was freezing now from head to foot in the pounding heat of the attic under its thin non-insulated roof.

"Come along, Ginny," Rose Reynolds' brother said. "She has a right to look for her things. She's been with me a lot longer than you have. Come on, cheer up. She's a pack rat just like all her clan."

Rose Reynolds could hear the sound of footsteps surrounded by silence as they knocked down the stairs and onto the kitchen tiles.

—⁓—

As far as Rose Reynolds could ascertain, the gun was not in the house itself, but then she didn't know all the cubbyholes and nooks of the building. Perhaps she had overlooked it in the most obvious place. Perhaps it was outside in the garden or the tool shed, she thought, or in Vivien's car, or with Vivien's friend Mirth. Or perhaps Vivien had thrown it into the water; that would be something Vivien would do, secretly and dramatically. To protect her. Because she loved her. Or had. Rose Reynolds looked into the rafters of the old house and wished for serenity. All she had wanted was to be alone and paint; now she was involved in this. She would have to buy another gun and try to put a nick in it. But surely someone like Jacky would know the registration number to his own gun; he would know the feel of it even in his sleep. Or maybe the gun was not registered. An impression of a gun rose up from the knothole in the wooden floor at her feet. Her mother had been a crack shot with a rifle. Finally her mother had admitted it and started to instruct her, partially to get rid of Rose's Annie Oakley obsessions, as her mother called them. Rose had joined her mother regularly for a time in shooting down tin cans in the country and also clay pigeons at the firing range, with her brother looking on, after their father had left them. I've never believed in killing, Rose said to herself. I've never believed in it. I've never wanted a gun. Now here I am pursuing it. Mama never believed in it, Freddy never believed in it. Grandma and Grandpa didn't believe in it. I don't believe in it, she said to herself again.

The man in the gun store was most sympathetic. Yes, she was sure it was a .38 she wanted. Not a .22, or a .45 caliber.

"You'll have to sign the registry," he said. "And then it takes a week."

"A week!" she said. "But it's right here. This one right here." She tapped the top of the glass cabinet. There it was, right beneath her fingertips.

"In this state, you have to wait a week," he said bristling sternly. "That's the law and that's the way it's got to be."

"Couldn't you make this one exception?" she demanded of him. "I know it's unusual. I don't want to shoot anyone with it."

He looked at her oddly and set his wire-rimmed glasses up onto the front of his forehead. He looked out from under them. "And you were going to shoot horse flies with it, my dear? Or maybe you don't consider your 'flies' to be anyone in particular."

"I want it for protection," Rose said. "We've had a prowler coming around at the windows. I'm afraid at night."

"Then get yourself a boyfriend," the man said to her. And he turned his back on her. His voice came at her as if from out the back of his head. "It's stupid to live alone these days," he said.

"Are you sure I couldn't just come back in three or four days?" she asked. It was not natural for her to plead. Yet a plaintive note had entered into her voice. "Three days or four, please. He always comes around on weekends."

"I'm dead sure," he said, turning around and setting right his spectacles. "You can have it in one week, just as is according to state law. Do you want to sign the register or not? "

So Rose Reynolds had found herself leaning over to sketch her own name in her own hand in a book that she herself did not illustrate. The thought of it froze the pen above the page. "All right, all right," the man said. "You don't have to drool on it. If you're so scared why don't you call the police?"

She was to pick up the gun the following week.

—⁓—

Jacky took the boat down to the same beach with three or four other yachts. When they had joined the others, he told her that the old man, the one he called Uncle Vince, wanted to see them in his cabin. He took her gently by the hand—it was something touching that the man at school had hardly ever done with her, taking her by the hand; and they went into the teak-paneled room. Three armchairs were drawn up around the divan beneath a shelf of books. A chart of channels and currents was on the wall beside his small desk. The old man sat down and motioned her into the chair beside him. He stretched out his hand and took hers into his own. Above she could hear the man who had rowed them out starting the engine to the yacht and then again the churning as slowly they put out into the waves.

"Jacky's been telling me about you," he said. "I'm glad to get to know you. Tell me—what kind of person would you say you are? I'm always glad to know Jacky's friends. He's like a son to me."

"Why I don't know—" she said. The old man's kindly eyes looked upon her. "I guess I'm basically a creative person," she said. "And honest. I guess that's about all I am."

"That's good," Uncle Vince said. "That's very good. Honesty and creativity are very important. Without that, there's nothing among friends." He patted her hand again. "Here, do you like art magazines? Jacky and I have something to talk about. I like to buy paintings. I like them to be very good paintings. I don't like junk. I like things that last. Do you feel that way?"

"Yes," Rose said, suddenly sad. "I am tired of losing things. I seem to have lost a lot of things in the past few years. I prefer things that last."

"You sound too sad for your age," the old man said sympathetically, looking up at Jacky and motioning him aside. Jacky stepped back behind the bar again and began washing up glasses and drying them.

"I've lost many friends in my life, a son, and—even my youth," the Uncle said. "I used to be quite handsome in my youth. I could attract a lady without a glance. But, I can still get around, thank heaven for that. I haven't gone completely under. You can ask my wife Silvia about that."

"I can see that," Rose said. "You seem to have a new young family." She liked the sparkle in his dark eyes.

"I like things that last," he said. "I hear that you paint."

"Yes," she said. "I try to—"

"Do you paint fictions or do you paint from life?"

"A little of both," she said. "I start from a setting or figure I know, and then the painting turns into whatever it wants to be, but it never turns out to be fact. I wouldn't make a very good journalistic photographer. I'm not much interested in reporting."

"That's good," he said. "I don't much like stark reality myself. It's so often distorted—lies—. Sometimes it can be dangerous. I prefer imaginative things. The joyful life."

"Yes," she said. And then she added, "Often the imaginative seems more real than the actual anyway. It would be self-defeating to do it any other way—for me. I'm here to reinvent the orange, not take notice of it."

The old man laughed then, he tapped her on the forearm with his pencil, thinking about the orange, or so she thought.

"I understand you've lost some precious things in your short time." He reached across from his chair and patted her knee in a grandfatherly way. "Jacky was telling me about your mother."

"Yes," she said. She wanted to tell him about what had happened to her at school, about the boyfriend she'd had and the baby she'd miscarried before coming home to stay with her brother and his new wife. She didn't know why she wanted to tell him; she hadn't been able to even think about it herself, it had pained her so much. But then, suddenly, she was going in a different direction entirely. "I've lost a gun," she said. "I didn't think I had but I must have."

Across the cabin, Jacky cleared his throat.

"A gun?" the old man said, a little surprised. "That's a pretty bad thing to lose. You wouldn't want children coming across it, for instance. That could be quite grim."

"Jacky gave it to me. He told me to put it in my purse. It was at McDonald's. The next time I remembered it was at my brother's house. I woke up and looked for it and it wasn't there. I hadn't seen it since he put it in. I didn't move it."

Uncomfortably Jacky turned to study the wall chart. "We could rendezvous at the island if you like," he broke in.

"That's a good idea," the old man said. "A very good idea, Jacky."

Uncle Vince looked at her again. "What were you saying? Jacky had you take a gun into McDonald's. I could sincerely wish he hadn't put you in that position. I suppose that's true for you, too." Behind the counter, Jacky was wiping water spots off the stainless steel sink.

"Check," he said just audibly. The old man nodded just as Jacky looked up, just as if that part of the conversation were so serious that in a fraction of a second like the firing of a bullet it could be over and would never have to be addressed again.

"I don't know what happened to it. I've looked everywhere," she went on. Vince was stroking the back of her hand with his grey one, much as she had done for her own mother when she was in such pain. "It couldn't have fallen out, the bag is just too deep. It's heavy, the gun is heavy. How could it have fallen out without my noticing such a thing?"

It was a cut glass that Jacky handed her, intricately cut by hand in diamonds around the base. Jacky leaned over them with a bottle of brandy and poured some out for them. Her own hands seemed very pale around the glass, she was thinking. Her mother's veins had stood out a little like that, she was thinking. And of course there was the ring, her mother's ring transferred to her own hand. Here she was sitting with strangers talking about guns she didn't care about and drinking brandy with her mother's dead hands.

Stiffly Jacky Alaska sat down on the other side of her. There seemed to be no anger in him now, in this older man's presence, only awkwardness.

"It's a beautiful ring," the old man said, reading her thoughts.

"It was my mother's ring; it's not all that beautiful. She didn't have much," Rose said. "She's dead now."

"I'm very sorry," the old man said. "She can't have been very old."

"Just in her early forties," Rose Reynolds said, swallowing a little. She sipped up a little of the brandy, trying to steady herself. "Just three years have gone by."

Uncle Vince shook his head and looked down onto his own old hands. It seemed as if rivers of milk were flowing through the backs of them. And his eyelashes had gone very white as well; they couldn't have always been that color. "I was very fortunate," he said. "My own little mother lived to a very old age. Still—when she died, I cried like a tiny baby. I can still remember how she held me when I was a little child. She was the most important person in my life. I will always say that."

"Yes," she said softly.

"Yes," the old man said, "we are all little children when our mothers die." He pressed her knee again, firmly and innocently, to bolster her up. There was a brief silence in the room then and she realized that there was a large wooden clock in the cabin of the boat. She had almost forgotten she was on a boat. The clock was ticking reassuringly. "Would you like another little sip, before you go on?" he asked.

"No, no, it's O.K." she said. "I lost the gun somehow. I tried to buy another one but I didn't really know how. I can shoot one, but I've never had to buy one. I think I know what happened to it, what might have happened anyway. It's the only thing I can think of."

"What's that then?" he asked matter-of-factly, as if it had been a roller skate key she'd been seeking, and not a weapon.

"Well," she said. "I think maybe my sister-in-law found it and took it away. I've been trying to paint some portraits of my mother, and my sister-in-law doesn't understand that it's a good thing—all this thinking about my mother. It helps so much to paint. I'm not just painting how it was; I'm inventing a story that never occurred. It gives me peacefulness. But she won't leave me alone to do it. She thinks I'm too maudlin now."

"Maudlin, you say? She thought maybe you were going to kill yourself with that gun, Rose?"

"Yes maybe," she said.

"But no, that's incredible!" the old man said abruptly and rather loudly, sitting his chair onto its back legs. "A girl like you would never kill herself. It's not in your character. I can see it in your face. I know people. You rescue people, Rose; you can't stop from doing it. You don't kill yourself."

"Of course not," she said. "I tried to tell her. Still, she's a little jumpy. You see—her first husband shot himself. Because of the war, because of Vietnam, you see, he couldn't recover—"

"Did you ask her about the gun then?"

"No," she said. "She's very conventional in her thinking, and flamboyant. She might, well, do something too extreme for the situation."

"That is quite an unfortunate combination, as you point it out: conventional and flamboyant! An unfortunate combination." He laughed then from the belly and knit his fingers together in front of his sweater. She wanted to tell him about the paintings on the wall then, but they seemed quite irrelevant. She wanted to tell him everything.

"I don't really mind if she thinks I'm a lunatic—if that helps the situation, I mean. I just don't know what to do about getting the gun back without scaring her or causing her to do something irrational."

"Yes," he said. "She might try to lock you up for craziness if she thinks you're packing a gun."

Rose Reynolds looked at him with her big eyes terrified. "I never really thought about that," she said. "Never once did I—"

"Now," he said. "Don't worry. It's only the remotest possibility—only if you were to allow things to escalate. And you won't, you're a smart girl. I suggest that you simply forget about it. Your sister-in-law will have the satisfaction of thinking she rescued you from suicide. Just try to enjoy yourself while you're in her house. Forget about the gun. The more you think about it, the more absurd you'll seem. That can't possibly help you."

Jacky set his glass on the edge of the coffee table and stood up. She stood up, too, then, as the old man did.

"But I've lost Jacky's gun," she said.

Jacky looked at her with a hardened face.

"Well, I wouldn't worry about it. I suppose he can get himself another one, don't you think so, Jacky? I can guess which one it was."

Jacky's eyes softened then. "If it doesn't matter to you," he said.

"I don't suppose it does much harm for one lost gun to be floating around the girl's house, does it? It doesn't sound like the sister-in-law wants to make use of it herself, or to show it to anyone. I expect it's very neatly tucked away—for eternity perhaps. Probably in the river."

"Yes," Jacky said, smiling. "Yes, I see what you mean."

"Do you think so?" she said as she felt Jacky take her hand. "You don't think someone will get hurt because of all this?" she said.

"Oh no," the old man said softly. "Really don't worry about it. If anything, you've done me a favor. It's given me greater confidence in you. Now go on out with Silvia. Jacky will be along in a moment. And don't think another thing about it. Jacky is going to stop bothering you about it. Chin up. Behave like a normal young woman at home, as if this whole thing never happened. That's a good girl."

She went out then, for the boat had gone back to shore, along the port side, and stepped over the bow into the dinghy. There a man rowed her the short distance. She wanted to say, I can row this boat by myself, but somehow there was never a moment to even offer since never once would he look at her or respond to her queries. When the dinghy was on the sand, another man was waiting to row the little boat back for the old man and Jacky.

When they arrived on the beach, the squat old man approached her again. The sun was brilliant on them standing there on the sand in their deck shoes. "I brought the magazine I mentioned," he said. "Sometime, maybe all four of us can go to an auction in New York. For the good stuff," Uncle Vince said. "I prefer the French Impressionists whenever one turns up. I've been buying a few for Silvia to hang up in the house. Without art, life is so extraordinarily dull."

She thanked him then for the magazine. "Oh it's nothing," he said. "Consider it a token of what art can mean in the world."

"Yes," she said genuinely. "I will."

"And if you find that other little thing," he said, "you'll let me know?"

"Of course."

"That's a good girl," he said for the second time. "But I suspect you never will. Now run along and have a good time. I certainly don't think you're maudlin, but I think everyone deserves a respite."

She smiled at him sincerely then, for he had given her so much relief in such a short span.

—◊—

The sausages were grilled a golden brown and the pasta served in clear glass bowls. The sand was still hot beneath her as she lay on her back; the old man's children nestled in beside her like colored bobbins under both arms. She looked up with Silvia at the clouds meandering like sheep across the very blue sky. Every day, the middle-aged woman was saying, she had great contentment in her life. Every day she took care to embrace some new thought in depth. Since her marriage, she had never spent a day without reading for nearly as long as she wanted. She loved most of all to read philosophy and the works of great men and also women.

Sitting on the blanket alone for a time, Rose Reynolds was thinking how the sculptor had offered to help her find another place if and when he moved to another town, how he had planned to take their baby in his arms. Perhaps she had made a mistake in not going with him as he had asked, but then the baby had not lived. And the sculptor had never asked after it, had just assumed that she had betrayed him and had aborted it. She was thinking how his eyes had been so much harder than this Jacky's were; but the face had been softer in some way. How could she manage to speak to a man who had stopped asking after her and had not accompanied her to a hospital when she was bleeding? Well, after all it was not his fault if she had been too ashamed to tell him that it was going quite so badly. A wave of sadness was sweeping over her at the thought of all this when the quiet conversation of the old man, who sat quite far from her on the beach, speaking with Jacky and another man, crept into her experience.

Matter-of-factly, the old man was describing the attributes of a newer model of silencer. Neither of the young men looked at her, yet there was a certainty in the old man's manner. At one point the old man looked up to find her watching. After a moment he waved his small wrinkled hand. Now the picture of the anonymous man came back to her. She turned away as though she could not hear their voices carried to her on the wind. "Hit man," one of the men on the beach said self-referentially, as though he could not sink so low. At that point however someone shushed him, but already she was making quick chatter with Silvia about cookware.

"I live so much in reality," the old man smiled as she and Jacky departed. He took her hand. "If you get a spare canvas someday, just a little one," he said, "if you wouldn't mind so awfully, I mean, I've always wanted to leave my portrait, for my children—" Protectively he kissed her hand, his eyes gazing up from her fingertips.

—⁓—

That evening when she and Jacky were back on his own boat, Jacky took off his clothes to change and touched her again. He stood up then, pulled his jeans on over his long legs, and fastened them, without bothering to put on his shoes or shirt. "I want you to marry me," Jacky said. "I'm going to the end of the dock for a Coke. When I come back it would be nice to have your answer." So, she thought, Uncle Vince had given his O.K., or maybe the old man had even suggested it—that was one of the reasons they had talked so long that day. She could see that.

When his face appeared at the cabin door, all she could do was look at him with astonishment. "No, I don't know, I don't think so—" was all she could say. He pulled her onto his lap and held her curled like a child, kissing her eyelids, first one and then the other, not frivolously but firmly and seriously, holding her face like a robin's egg between his hands, fiddling with a curl of hair between her legs. "How can you drift like this in your life," he was saying, "when you have work to do? You know how to paint. What do you need school for when you already know how to do it? Of course you know how to do it; of course you do. Have some confidence."

"I don't know," she said. "I just don't know."

—m—

Jacky came home with her for the first time, insisting that he accompany her in the little car he had given her. "We've decided to get married," he told Freddy and Vivien in the front hall. Firmly he pressed her hand where it hung between them. "She's frightened of marriage, of course," he said. "But she'll adjust. She's just a little skittish. If it's all right with you, that is?"

Jacky Alaska shook hands with her brother who was staring into her ashen face. Beside him Vivien was all smiles. "Well, we'll see," said her brother. "She's plunged a lot of time into her university. Maybe Rose has to think about it awhile. Maybe she'd like to take her graduate degree. I thought she planned on art school."

"Yes," she said quickly. "I think I'd like to finish something in my life," she said. "I'd like to finish one thing first. Just to be able to say it."

"Oh, don't worry about it—" Jacky said. "We've a perfectly good university here. She can have her degree and anything else she likes. I can take over the school bills for her. They must seem extraordinary after awhile. I would never stand in the way of an artist. That would be suicide in her case."

"Well, we'll see," her brother said. "It's not something a young woman like Rose wants to rush right into, I expect."

"Oh don't be such a stodge, Freddy," Vivien pronounced. "This girl has finally found someone who loves her! This is absolutely what she needs now!"

"Ginny," Freddy was saying.

"Let her have her own life," Vivien said. "Why do you have to stand in people's way?"

"Just give her some time is all I'm saying," her brother said. "Don't you see that she looks very tired?"

"Yes, yes," Rose Reynolds laughed brutally. "I think I'll at least sleep overnight on it. Freddy is right. And if nobody minds, I'll just go to bed this minute. I thought the sun unusually bright today, didn't you, Jacky? If I don't take something, it's going into a bad headache. If I don't go now, it's sure to be a migraine—"

With that, Rose Reynolds pulled away from Jacky Alaska. She went up the stairs under the beak of the fractured bird that should have brought her peace, and perhaps was; here everything seemed to turn upside down around her. The bird seemed to dive down now out of the window to drive its bullet-like tongue into her head. "Yes," she chattered nervously as she disappeared into the upstairs bedroom. "It is going to be a migraine." Her sister-in-law below was asking Jacky Alaska if he'd like a drink, or perhaps to stay over. But almost in the same moment her brother was saying perhaps they should all wait to socialize—until another day, until Rose could be with them. Surely Rose would not appear from her bedroom until late tomorrow morning with such a headache.

Rose fell into an old dream then that she had often had as a child, a dream of guns and people falling off horses in dramatic poses. Don't ever betray me, they said, much as Jacky Alaska had said to her when she'd first met him. The stone angel waved his arms over his head in dismay at all the things she'd done to risk oblivion in a household he found all too familiar. When she woke, she woke with the horrifying realization that it was already the day when she was supposed to pick up the gun she had ordered in the gun shop. And she'd had to leave her address and phone number.

—⁂—

The house down the block was for sale, the sister-in-law said at a late breakfast after Freddy had gone to his office. It would be so cozy for all of them to live so close like a real family yet at the same time to separate; to consult one another constantly without stepping on one another's loafers. She herself, the sister-in-law, knew how important it was not to interfere. It was her first mother-in-law she still blamed in part for her other husband's suicidal death. Yes, there had been sadness in her life, too, the sister-in-law said, as in the life of young Rose Reynolds. It was something that deepened the character and drew together people like them. It had drawn together Rose's brother and herself— But that conversation was all too quickly truncated.

Rose was horrified to see that Jacky Alaska had arrived before them in her brother's garden, even before they had set down their teacups on the patio. "No, run along," Vivien said, insisting even more than Jacky Alaska. "You must go along, Rose. Don't worry about me. You've got so many plans to make for your wedding."

So the strong man had taken her by the arm and placed her in the little green automobile, which he had now had again since the previous evening. But when they entered his house, he sat in the white-tiled kitchen, answering the phone quietly and repeatedly, saying yes, then no, murmuring from time to time, about seemingly abstract times and places. And then he set the telephone in the cradle and looked into her eyes with intensity.

Rose thought at first he would say something touching or worrisome, about the gun perhaps. Perhaps he would ask her about it again and her natural temperament would cause her to shout at him and reveal the fact that she was afraid now that it had all been a lie, a test even. Perhaps Jacky and Uncle Vince had dreamed it up between them—a test to see whether she would betray them even in a subtle way.

"What's so startling?" he asked. "You look petrified."

"Oh, just something Vivien said—"

He joined her at the table then and looked tenderly at her, more genuinely it seemed than he had ever done. Then he said in a soft and sympathetic voice something entirely else. It seemed at first to Rose Reynolds that it was absurd that he had looked at her and asked her for something so ridiculously small, and inconsequential. He had asked her to make him a sandwich. A sandwich? she said to herself again. He was looking at her as if it was the greatest favor he might ask, and he'd asked it as if the bread and knife and sandwich spread had not lain between them. Deep inside she felt the waters of her indecision, of his unborn children who would certainly come to her after a time, cascading about in her womb, chilling into lumps of ice at the thought of his profession. It was her sister-in-law's advice that came back to her: You have to stop taking care of everyone else and have a life of your own.

On the tabletop, the bread lay like someone's body, white and impoverished in its bleached materials. "Look," she said. "I really have to go home. I shouldn't have come with you just now. I'm sorry." She pulled her purse onto her lap and stared again at the sandwich spread he liked; it was sitting right in front of his placemat.

"Oh sit tight," he said. "What's your rush? This is a special occasion."

"I forgot I was supposed to meet Freddy today for a walk. It's important to him. And it's important to me. Freddy is very important to me."

He went on as if she hadn't spoken, sipping at a cold drink he had pulled from the refrigerator. "Why do you think you have to go to a university to learn things like painting? You have to live in your own head in this world if you're going to do anything of interest."

"I like taking painting classes there," she explained. "There are things you can learn you can't learn anywhere else."

"Like what?" he challenged. "Why do you have to go back there when you can learn everything here? Look at Silvia. She studies constantly, and she lives here. She doesn't have to sit in a class of intellectuals to learn. Live this life. Live your life. Stop living in your head."

"There are things you can't learn here," she heard herself say again. "It isn't a very good university. There are lots of things." She reached into her bag to find her keys. There was a hard-etched surface in the bottom, like the butt of the gun. She felt her face go red.

"Give me one example."

She looked down into the bottom of the purse but it was a shell she had thrown in, a particularly pretty one, she had forgotten. She had meant to save it for the time when she went back to the city again, back to school, when she would surely be missing village life and the water.

"Well," she said, annoyed at herself, and again increasingly at the simplicity of their conversation. "If you wanted to be a doctor, of course you'd have to go to a good university—where they at least taught medicine. Wouldn't you?"

"Ha," he laughed. "Ha. That's what you think. Let me show you something now. Look," he said, taking her with him, rummaging in the closet in the far bedroom behind the blackened curtains where they slept.

"Look." He pulled the white canvas bag of tools from the back of the shelf. From that bag the long glittering handle with the delicately curved blade of the scalpel emerged. "I have done so many things in my life," he said. "Even you can't begin to imagine them. And I never had to go to school."

And then he told her how he had done everything Uncle Vince had told him, how he had even been an abortionist in the city.

But it was not the blade itself she was staring at, not the razor's edge. It was the darkened stain on it and the small dirty tuft of some woman's pubic hair that had been cut off with it, before or afterwards, perhaps a souvenir. She was remembering the pain she had felt as the doctor at the clinic scraped the remains of her own miscarried child and their own promised future away in the clinic so she would not have to pay money she did not have at the hospital.

"I have to go home now," she said staring coldly at the razor he held out before her. "I promised I'd go out with my brother today for a walk, I almost forgot about it. I don't know how I almost forgot it; I almost lost him once—in the war. You don't know how it's been for us with him going near crazy after the war and my mother dying—" Then she said it again as if it were the most important of all things. "I'd like to make you a sandwich now, but I can't. If I don't get there right now he might start reliving it, his time in the jungle."

With vehemence and horror she was staring at his cold face and the instrument between them, thinking what her father and her brother both had taught her. It was the simplest thing. No professional ever left a dirty tool behind and she had never done it herself, nor ever would; she had never killed anyone. Even Jacky could see the change in her. Before her, his face had fallen into despair. A line etched itself onto his brow as she retreated into the kitchen once again for her purse. He did not put the knife down as he followed her, nor did he seem to notice it.

It seemed to her as if for the last hour or so she had been tied to some trajectory between his bedroom and his kitchen—without hope of getting away from it. Everyone she had ever known, except this man, had abandoned her in some way, it seemed—by choice, or death, or fate. Now, as he followed her into the kitchen, the thought of the ham sandwich lay before them again and the thought of those women drawn up before him and the entry of the filthy blade between the tender pink labials. The life spilling out of them.

"I know exactly what you mean," she said, picking up the keys to his small green car. It was a senseless conversation now, for all she cared. "I've done so many things in my life I never thought I'd do. Like meeting you—which has been utterly amazing."

"I can do almost anything," he professed. "All you have to do is be yourself for me. You are what I am most interested in—in my whole life. You think I don't notice things. It isn't about sandwiches. That's for ordinary people. You're more than sandwiches to me. You know, I never thought it would happen to me. I've never loved anyone like I love you. You're so funny and cute," he said, "and you're so incredibly smart and talented, that's the main thing."

She looked into his face and could feel it with her fingertips even without touching it. A sudden weakness went over her, accompanied by nausea and dizziness; and she found herself sitting down, in order to maintain her balance in the window seat, paralyzed, again in the kitchen. She thought the most absurd things then, about how she seemed to be losing everything: her baby, her lovers to the war, her mother, part of her brother, and in a way now the confidence of her brother's new family.

A gentle rain was falling at the window, up and down the steaming streets of August, over all the slick automobiles that meant nothing at all to her, when all at once she rose up out of the window seat, beneath the bulletproof shuttered window coverings. "Oh no!" she cried, "This can't be right." She grabbed up the keys.

"Oh look at this," she cried falsely, rushing toward the front door with him close behind. "I forgot to remind you—to put the top up on your car!" She ran out of the house and into the rain toward the car that he had so generously lent to her, exclaiming falsely about his beautiful fast little car that was soon to be soaking wet with its top down. She rushed about, but he was right behind her wherever she turned.

She heard his voice gaining on her. At least he had left the scalpel in the house, she could see that much. "But this is the day you're supposed to pick up the gun."

"How did you know that?" she demanded, turning on him. His eyes were like two black pellets in his head. "How did you know about that?"

"Oh," he quickly said. "I saw it in your address book."

She stood stock still in front of him, glaring at him now. "I guess you must have been going through my purse," she said. "Putting things in and taking them out? Like handguns?"

"I was looking for the gun," he said. "A temptation came over me. I wanted to know what it was you did with yourself before you came to me."

"You were looking for the gun," she said. "Did you find it?" She stared hard at him then, unflinchingly.

"No," he said with equal resolution. "I'll take you over to get the new one," he said, "on your way home to meet your brother."

She looked into his hardening face in the middle of the street then. "You don't understand," she said. "I can't marry you. You don't understand me at all. I don't have any need for guns," she said. "I don't believe in them. And I don't have any need for your games with Uncle Vince."

His eyebrow went up then slightly in his hard dark face.

"I really don't believe in them. I've never believed in them. I could never marry a man who carried a gun—even if it was just for protection," she added quickly—"like you do."

"Oh don't be silly," he said. "Don't let silly things come between us." She was soaking wet now, and pools of water lay in the car on the black leather seat.

"Look, I'm not passing judgment on you," she said. "I stood in front of an army tank for the sake of doing away with guns in Vietnam. It was not a World War, I know it. But neither is what you're doing. Do you think I'm going to change now? It doesn't matter how I feel about you personally. I wouldn't be able to look away. I don't know anything about you. Let it go before any harm is done. Just let it slip away. I don't know anything." Hurriedly she was wiping down the seats with a towel from the beach. "Put the top up," she said. "Don't just stand there. Protect the things you love."

The rain came down in a cascade against the windowpanes. "I'll take you home," he said, as if she might have been merely a baby-sitter for his children.

In the car she was afraid he would do something to her; she had learned to recognize the bulge just over his belt that other people were not meant to see. But the ride was calm and slow and he didn't drive even as quickly as he usually did. Slowly, methodically, he delivered her to the front door of her brother's house. "I'll be going now." He looked at her across the vast expanse between them in the tiny car. "Good-bye."

"Good-bye," she said.

"I'll never once forget you in my life."

"Neither will I," she said stiffly. And then she was in the house again, leaning against the inside of the heavy door. She had thrown the lock behind her.

—·—

"Where is he?" Vivien said coming into the entryway with a towel on her arm. "Where's your man anyway?"

"I haven't got a man," she said with no emotion.

Vivien's face fell dramatically. "Why what happened, darling?"

"Ginny," Rose Reynolds said firmly. "We had serious, incontrovertible differences."

"Well," the sister-in-law said sympathetically. "I expect he was drawn to more exotic women. Still I can't help but think he made a mistake, leaving behind a smart girl."

"I wouldn't say it was exactly like that," Rose Reynolds said. "He isn't my type."

"Have you ever met your type?"

"Oh yes," Rose Reynolds said, trying to change the conversation. "I saw him on TV once," she invented wildly. "Oh yes. I saw him on TV."

"On TV! You're such a dreamer. How do you ever expect to settle down?"

"Oh it wasn't a dream," Rose Reynolds said, looking at her sister-in-law's finely chiseled features. "He was in a band."

"Not a rock star! When are you ever going to get some sense in your head? You know what men like that are."

"Ginny," Rose Reynolds said, seriously. "All men aren't the same—no matter what their category. You have to look at the individual man."

"If you ever do meet a man like that," the sister-in-law said, "watch out. You have to watch out with big guns like that. They're completely insincere."

"That's right," Rose Reynolds smiled. "I'd have done better with a quiet man like Jacky Alaska, someone from the neighborhood."

"That's right," the sister-in-law said. "Someone from the neighborhood. Someone predictable."

"You know something, Ginny?" Rose Reynolds said. "I've been wondering—have you ever shot a gun?"

"No," she said, "I never have. I always figured if a gun was meant to go off, someone else could do the triggering."

"Genevieve," Rose Reynolds said, staring at her new sister-in-law, "you have very dangerous ideas. You know, you emanate danger from your very bones. And you don't even know what you're doing."

"Do you think so?" the sister-in-law cried in exuberance. "Why that's the nicest thing anyone ever said to me. That's the very nicest thing."

"I didn't mean it as a compliment," Rose Reynolds said, but the sister-in-law laughed and poured herself a drink on her way through the living room. On the patio she shot another spurt of lemonade into the summer air. In her bright green jumpsuit she sat down on one of the marble benches, where the dappled light moved through the maple trees in a golden stream, first over the statue of the man behind her, and then onto her hair.

"You know," Vivien said, "I nearly convinced your brother to have you committed during the middle of this summer, you were acting so strange," she said. "But then you got so happy suddenly. Now when I look back on it, I think what a terrible mistake that would have been."

"Good grief," Rose Reynolds coughed, as if it would have been a joke, being locked away for the rest of her life like that on a mistaken whim. It had never truly occurred to her that the old man might have been right. Perhaps she should have been grateful for that. But a hard pebble had begun to settle inside of her, a disagreeable rage.

"How did you get so much power in your life?" coldly she asked her sister-in-law. "How does it work with people like you, Ginny?"

"It's hard to say," the sister-in-law laughed, pouring from a bottle of gin into her lemonade, and working the zipper up and down on the front of her top a little, as if she had been fiddling with a necklace or someone's ring.

"Sometimes I think I'm twisted inside out, but perfectly, ever so perfectly. I thank God I was born myself and not someone weak like Davie." And then she looked straight up into the angel's face. "My poor Davie," she keened and then she started to cry. Tears dribbled down her chin and onto the marble disk that encased the man. "You know they made him from a photograph. It looks just like him, it really does. My poor Davie. I'm so lucky your brother understands. He lost so many good friends."

But all Rose Reynolds could say was, "You were really going to throw my life entirely away. You were going to destroy it, just like that? Without even talking with me? You were really going to have me put away for not marrying that horrifying man?"

"No no, not just like that," the sister-in-law was crying. The tears ran down. "With a lot of anxiety. You can't believe the pain I've had in my life. The pain is so great sometimes I can't bear living it. I should have seen it coming to Davie. I should have stopped it. "

When Rose Reynolds stopped staring off over the wrought iron railing, after she had walked around the gardens and the pool to return, she found that the sister-in-law was crying still; she was sitting on the marble table top itself, her arms and legs enveloping the naked torso like a vine, her sobbing face pressed into the belly of the winged man.

"Me? Me? You were really going to lock me up in an asylum—for not appeasing you? " Rose Reynolds muttered at the woman's back. She stood aside then and walked into the house—away from her brother's wife shattering around the marble statue in her new backyard, while she herself, Rose Reynolds, was shaking inwardly from head to foot. And when to her great surprise the knock came at the front door, she opened it. It was unclear at first for whom these policemen were meant or why her sister-in-law had called them. Rose merely pointed toward the yard and, as they went, picked up her purse and walked toward the street, the sloping hills, and the bus that would, she hoped, carry her away in time enough.

CHAPTER IV

Behind them walked the only living thing that shared their
pilgrimage, the dog. And by degrees they reached the briny sea.
Then, with souls well disciplined they reached the northern region,
and beheld, with heaven aspiring hearts, the mighty Himavat .
. .Whereupon the lake was lapping, the lilacs were blowing, the
chenars were budding, the mountains were glistening, the waterfalls
were playing, the spring was green, the snow was white, the sky was
blue, the fruit blossoms were clouds: and he was still thirsty.

—Under the Volcano
Malcolm Lowry

THE HEAT, THE SUN. I think they have begun to crack open my eyelids, the Lover said, further and further away.

Long orange-lit summer hours seethe with scent: country grasses, clover, last of the lilacs, climbing fuchsia, roses. And in the morning the balloon races will go off just after sunrise at the pop of a gun. Fierce orange flare of the warmers and then the vast, silk, pastel parti-colored eggs luffing here, there, chatoyant in the clear-blue breeze. Rose's Alfie, only three and a half, lunges skyward after the baubles: "Please don't leave me behind!"

Rose scoops him up, her sister and William running at her side. Rose's Alfie must get down again, cry out in his little rooster voice, and leap, too, in the grain: "Mommy! Mommy! Let's run! In tall grasses! Tall grasses!

Let's run in tall grasses!" The four of them bounding after the hundred silken balloons, the dangling baskets at the uncut edges of the open field. Long grasses wild with dew at the sisters' legs, at their waists, at the little boys' gleaming faces. Rose is smiling so hard that Georgia reaches out to squeeze her hand: "Tall grasses! Tall grasses!" And then they are far away; the colored bulbs are scattered over the sky.

———

At night the summerhouse is quiet, but for the ocean's breeze sweeping the curtains out beside Rose's shoulder. Rose lounges in the scratchy stuffed chair, embroidering. Georgia, still in her sundress, sits cross-legged on the couch, drinking raspberry tea and eating hot baking-powder biscuits. Half-heartedly, she plucks crumbs from the flowered napkin. *No crumbs on the sofa!* Rose can almost hear her mother. By nightfall, the rug bends in a braided blue, coming apart in surges and swells, winding in on itself. They can hear that their little boys have subsided in their whisperings, are curled up with their favorite bears upstairs. Their damp hair has been slicked back with a comb from each pale forehead. There is sand in the shoes at the sides of their twin beds. On the windowsill lie two sea-green squid, painstakingly constructed out of *papier maché*. Out beyond the window sleeps the water that Alfie says Orion strides over. Others, too, have actually walked on water! Did they know that? So Alfie announced. So they have taught him in Sunday School.

"More than one?" Rose asked.

"Yes," Alfie said. "One walked over it, and then along came his mother looking for him. That's the true story."

Georgia cocked her eye at her sister; Rose the painter smiled so proudly at him. Now the sisters make time for private conversation:

"There's something peculiar about Hibbie, George. He never wants to leave home anymore."

"Sometimes I don't understand you, Rose. If you're miserable why don't you leave him?"

"I'm not exactly miserable; it wasn't that I didn't want to tell you. I was looking on the bright side, George. Grammy said to me—*Never, never tell stories on your own husband. That is the beginning of the end.* At least when we have company then Hibbie might eat something orange or green. I think there's something wrong with him, George. You know how people seek my advice; it's not as if I were full of bad advice. He doesn't listen anymore. I just can't understand."

"Orange and green? What are you talking about? Fruits and vegetables? You have a perfectly wonderful husband. Some people should be grateful for what they have."

Rose wants to tell her how she and Hibbie found themselves on the beach, another sign, she thinks, she in a dress and he in a suit. But now she cannot. All she can do is relive it and quietly make her stitches around the miniature scene play out on her embroidery screen. Her sister nonchalantly lifts her cup.

It was only two years ago, Rose Reynolds thinks. Yes, the Husband has taken off his shoes, yes, as she has. But he has left on his socks. And she has laughed at him flapping about helplessly in the waves in his wet grey feet. She is lucky, she tells him, that they don't live in England where as a lawyer he would have to wear a professional wig. Rose laughs out loud. At this, in a similar situation, her sister the lawyer would have laughed with her. Hibbie does not find this reference to his profession amusing, he says. Then he squeezes her hand until she is crying and her hand has gone white. Hibbie has never before done anything like this. She would have liked to tell her sister about it, but she has started out by saying it wrong and now

Georgia is not likely to listen.

"Would you like a biscuit?" Georgia says, "Before I eat them all up?"

—⁂—

In tennis, it is said—and she has watched the Lover in tournaments—it is hard to keep up with him because of his exhilarating odd rhythms; it is hard to know what he might do next.

—⁂—

Today Rose and her lover have driven to the top of the mountain. It will be her first time. Hold on to the kite, the Lover says, like this. Hold tight and when the plane takes off, move your feet like this. Don't let go until you're sure. Don't hang on when you're close to the ground. Skim over it, he laughs, apply the gesso with your feet, Annie Oakley.

Oh you. You wild man. Below her the land falls away and a terror rather like freedom grips her chest wall.

—⁂—

Into the desert this week, the Lover has taken with him a film crew, has international coverage, an ultralight plane, surveying equipment, dried food, much water, Arabian guides, and one pair of his wife's high heels for the wife who refused to stay at home and he swears he has had to bring along, so he has laughed over the telephone. And tents.

You're too visible, Rose, he said. Of course you can't go along with me. Besides, wouldn't you rather be on the sand beside the water? I can't imagine you in a waterless land.

—m—

When the sisters wish to swim, one holds the blanket around the other as she flings her blouse over the top and the skirt drops into the sand around her feet. Then Georgia perhaps will mention the deep nut brown of the cow's eye Rose Reynolds kept floating in a bottle of formaldehyde for half a year on the floor of their closet when they were girls. Rose will recall how she disposed of it finally in the very top of the bin—to frighten the garbage man who had once evilly kicked Rascal their dog. They will laugh at their long-ago dog's assisted triumph, at the recollection of the mean man running down the street to the sound of his joyous bark.

Then they will be in their bathing suits with their little boys, holding them aloft, dipping and splashing, pretending to be giant sea snakes and turtles, monsters from the deep of oceans yet far away.

—m—

Paint thick as clay. She lays it on the canvas with a knife. The blue floats off the wall like sky. Twenty feet long and six feet high. "It looks like hieroglyphs," Georgia says, her tennis shoes squeaking on the shiny floor as she rocks back and forth. "It's hieroglyphics to me."

"But what if the paint cracks, Georgie, and it all falls off? Oh—I should have used a commercial paint."

"Oh stop. You're always worrying," Georgia sighs. "This is the most beautiful piece you've ever painted," Georgia says. "It has everything in it— It's as ancient as— as—" She finally laughs, "It's as ancient as dirt."

"Thanks, George. Thanks a lot."

"I meant that as a compliment."

"I said *thanks*, didn't I?"

—⅏—

First the pale yellow car, then a glimpse of light catches the top of the Lover's elongated forehead, then his azure eyes, his straight teeth, the high crests of his cheeks. The squat door swings open over the antiquated running board and there are his shoulders in the colorful shirt, the khaki pants and loafers, his pink tongue. Behind him, the automobile: highly polished, pale yellow. Once it was just an average car, in the twenties, rather long ago, when such cars first came out.

—⅏—

Along the garden, alone and wading through high dry grass, a streak of white paint almost like a question mark, just above one eyebrow, she spies the myriad Japanese beetles among the asparagus, their thick green and copper-colored shields, lanterns pressed almost flat and shimmering, almost phosphorescent, behind the brief fence. There the black, then the white, in alternating stripes like oars cast down along the juncture of abdomen and back, as if to steady themselves in their mating dance. Exotic they glow among the wispy and towering asparagus with its firm green balls of seed.

The Lover is a copper light now on the inside of the window, his hand waving: a conveyor belt of greetings until he can pull himself away from the others. The Lover, at the window, already inside, is sun-brown as a biscuit, almost rust-colored; now he has lifted up the sash a crack. His light brown hair, his trim beard, grow sandy with sun in the uppermost right pane, and with him the ghostly reflection of a fern sprouting affectionately out the side of him.

He sends a sudden greeting as he sees her: he lifts up his hand, and then there are his apologies to the curator of the local naval museum. He extracts himself *ad nauticum*, as he says after wrenching himself from the naval curator's tour, overly emotional, of rows of nautical hooks, ropes, pulleys, portholes, and miniature demonstration models of bunks and bilge, fore and aft, not to mention all the various model decks from hold to poop.

A set of creases like two white flashes of the artist's brush spring up at the corners of her lover's eyelids. Broad open laughing frescoed mouth. Then his head tilts suddenly behind glass. His warning to Rose. Something of consequence behind her? Abruptly she pivots. Just in time to avoid the drunken dance instructor bandying himself toward her on pegged legs. "Ho!" he slurs, "Back from your escape? What do you say? See any ancient grief in the plains? Ho Ho!"

She strides away from him, beyond the garden now, the cotton dress floating and airy around her calves and thighs, sandals sticking very slightly to her feet—shush-shush, shush-shush—as she moves away from the party. She can hear him then, behind her in his linen suit and the soft tawny leather shoes, stepping closer among the sycamore trees with their giraffe trunks. The radiance of his heat moves rapidly toward her. Over field, thicket, or gorge.

Twigs snap behind her, beneath the Lover's shoes; and yes, she smiles at the sound of it. Now the two of them have it, that creak, how peculiar for two men to have it. There is a little creak that appeared a few weeks before, while Hibbie was crossing into the living room. Up over her reading glasses she glanced at him.

"Why! I've got a cricket in my shoe of all things," the Husband complained. "If there's something I can't stand it's a cricket in my shoe."

"Ah, Hibbie," she said, already reading again. But then he stepped off, noisily, into the other room while she went on, redesigning in her imagination the dimensions of the new space telescope about which she was reading. Reconstructing a missile that would carry the telescope up to have a look at a few other worlds: surely many were just as good.

Now the road wound slowly along ahead of her, ahead of the Lover, very rutted: a runway once for farm implements. All over the lane, grass cast itself skyward, in this hole and that, among the antiquated brittle cakes of cattle dottles and the occasional bared scattering of quartz and basalt. Ahead of her, among other trees: the smooth grey bark reaching up into a large leafy beech and beneath it an immense boulder flat like a table, big as a low-riding auto. Her lover's hand then, his fingertip gentle under her hair at the side of her neck. His voice a whisper. "How are the little fellow and Georgia?" His low murmuring. "William appreciative of his Aunt Rose? Alfred behaving himself? Glad to have his Mama home?"

These days he is looking for a small artifact in sand, he laughs; he looks for lost souls, and, if not that, for Aristotle's tomb. It might as well be so.

She turns around to nuzzle his chest, where—what miracle—his shirt has already been undone. Her face presses against the scent of him, in the wealth of golden-brown hair. If it were not for him she would be entirely chaste these days, for a year or two more. What ails Hibbie anyway?

"Your sister wasn't biting?" he whispers. "Not in one of her moods?" The long-time lover's voice is already husky at her ear. "At the station, everyone cried after the funeral when you went away?"

She breathes against the taut pink nipple in the thick coat of human fur, exhales, "Everyone, absolutely— strangers, yes everyone—cried when I left them—"

His warm hands encompass the sides of her face. She looks into his eyes. She crushes his lapel.

"Good," he says. "I'm glad they gave you the send off you deserve."

Her voice has disappeared now. She pulls at the bottom of his shirt.

His hands are at her waist, then his finger points toward the far side of the road. *Look! What's this?*

"I didn't know!" Rose cries out in surprise. The back of her skirt drops against her as he turns.

"Will you have a look at this," he says, going toward it.

The snakes, like two lime-green garden hoses, rise and fall, intertwined. They stand together watching.

"You didn't know what, Rosie?"

"That snakes had them."

"What?"

"Private peckers, parts, you know—"

Abruptly the Lover wielded a stick. "In snakes they're not private."

"Oh no!" she cried, grabbing at his arm. But already the creatures made ready to race away. Already they had ceased their dance. "How could you? How could you have done such a thing? You've stopped them in the act."

"They're snakes. I did it for you. Think how you hate them," he protested. "More little snakes all over the world. Think of it. Yes." He poked at them with his stick, and they went writhing off separately through the humus that underlay the woods. "Besides," he said, wagging his pointy beard. "They were the ones to break the sacred act. Not us."

Blankly she looks at him staring at her.

"Rose, they interrupted *us*—"

This is the one who is always there when she hurts or needs. This is my true husband, she thinks suddenly. Then her long cotton skirt is swaying between them again and the back of each bare calf flexing taut beneath the full hem. The palms of her hands are at her waist where the large belt nips in; pines and poplars sway overhead. His hand touches at the back of her neck again.

A slight coolness of evening moves up their bare legs. Gently her skirt flutters as if from out the sides of their slender, combining waist. A dragonfly shudders on a plateau of bare rock, watching as the flowered skirt hikes up, still fastened at the waist and she bows down. Her blouse is nestled elsewhere in the underbrush, on top of his pants. Her hat hangs in the foliage: still life in an offshoot of early elderberry. His socks make knots; very comical, on top of his shoes among the habitat of small animals and last year's resigned leaves. Low tones and a language without words, her cries burnish, like rough cloth, his whole hide. She turns her head nearly halfway around to meet his flushed face; tongue moving up, then down, lithe messenger, coursing in the vault of his mouth. How glorious are bodies.

Against her back, softly furred as a moth he is now—his belly and thighs, his chest buffing her. His sweet, mechanical voice in her ear, squeaking like a spring. Winged rocking chair. Ecstatic stuck torso, whirling dervish and thin butterfly. How long has this gone on? Iridian Pegasus. Far away the slight murmurings of abandoned festivities. His cries are restrained, match hers. And then the arching of their one true back sighs an agony.

But what was that? Something solid and hard like a tennis ball. Something fuzzy as a rabbit. It has thumped him squarely on the back between his shoulder blades. Under him still, she lifts her torso from the granite slab, and together they peer behind toward the earth. There—in the grasses—what is that round ball of fluff? No larger than a potato. *Weren't we alone?* Two completely round yellow eyes nictate wildly off to each side of the grey hooked beak. Infant owl fallen from the skies, completely stunned, at this couple's feet. An early spectator.

"Rosie?" he asks while she sits on his shoulders to put the little owl back into its tree. He holds her very gently in his arms then. "My Rosie," he says. She sits in his lap and he strokes her hair. "My dearest dear," he says. "My dearest darling one," he says. "If ever you're hurt," he says, "you let me know. That is my job in this life: I lick your wounds. I make it better."

—⁂—

Rose Reynolds stares out across yellow dunes that sweep in crowns of pink roses that in a few moments will turn to red rosehips. "Rosie!" Georgia exclaims, "You're going, of course! You wouldn't miss your lover's documentary?"

Rose sighs a small protest.

Georgia smiles, matter-of-factly. "My goodness," Georgia says, "he is pompous, isn't he? He out and out assumed you wouldn't go just because he said you weren't to. You haven't acquiesced?"

"Perhaps? Maybe?"

Georgia grumbles, then Georgia asks, "Do you think he's stable?"

"I guess."

"I mean the Husband, your husband, of course."

"I don't know now. What would you say?" Rosie asks.

"Completely stable."

"Yes, Alfie and I are the ones likely to go insane waiting for Hibbie to enjoy our wonderful life. But we do enjoy it, we enjoy it anyway, even if he won't do it."

—⁂—

She is fussing; she is pacing when she should be painting. She is pacing back and forth. What significance is there in paint? In a riddle, back and forth she strides before a wall of hidden meanings created by herself, none other. She lays the paint on a corner of one small piece. She knows it belongs there; she can't say how she knows it. But it does go there.

Swimsuits, picnic baskets, beach balls, sand shovels, presents for the children of friends. Alfie is skipping toward the car, laughing. He does what is called pony riding, not quite skipping, and not quite a run; in his high sweet voice, he is singing the spider song. Rosie whirls him into his car seat with his stuffed bear in tow, jumps into her own seat in front and sets the music to playing in the tape machine. They are so happy! For once the Husband is coming along! He looks in the rear view mirror, scans the car. "Hello," he says brightly. And then his face falls. Oh no, it is that ominous look again. "You know I can't see with all his stuff in the backseat."

"What do you mean?" Rose Reynolds asks. "There's nothing in your way; it's only his bear anyway, it's behind the back seat. Why don't you take off your jacket? It's hot out, we can relax."

An inexplicable anger rides onto his face. "You are not the one driving. How can you possibly know what's clear from the driver's seat?"

She looks into the back. There is nothing but a small basket beside Alfie, who looks up in alarm. Then the Husband has thrust open his car door and opened the back. He yanks the basket from behind the seat, then the swimming bag, and then, too, the stuffed bear from her little child's arms. He slams the door and thrusts bear and basket into the trunk.

Alfie is crying so hard that Rose is out of the car with her own set of keys, retrieving the frightened bear, comforting her horrified child. Then they are on their way—in a bedrock of silence.

"He won't allow us to go anywhere he hasn't already been. Grammy says—"

"A lot of what Grammy said was utter foolishness."

"It was not, George. It most certainly was not. Name one thing."

"Oh, all right. I can't. I was just feeling contradictory."

—⁓—

And so my wife has gone into the cave with us. I turn around and she is actually kicking at the remains, the Lover tells her. The femur of the skeleton tips, then lifts up and points directly at her face like in a horror story. I will be the first to admit that once Armand died, I was totally in over my head. But that's something everyone seemed to forget. We swore we would never ever ever go into that desert again, but of course as soon as we were out we were planning it again.

—⁓—

Rose pulls the towel around her shoulders and relates the conversation for her sister. Water runs down her sister's back and sides, streaming from Georgie's blue-black hair and buttercup suit.

Georgia says instead, "Remember when the Man with the Scar on His Chin rides up to the log cabin? Every time I see that movie I think when the door swings open that it will be Mother standing in the door, tying up her hair."

"Well, so—" Georgia says, burrowing her arched feet into the damp sand. "You know I don't mean to be dogmatic, Rose—but perhaps if you didn't have your lover all this time, your hubby would be more alive, so to speak?"

"It didn't happen in that order. It wasn't my idea, it was his."

At this, Georgia throws both hands up and shrieks. Just as quickly, she brings them back down again. "No! Your own husband did not insist you take a lover, Rose?"

"I cried like a fountain. That's the least of it."

"But it was *his* idea, Rose?"

"In the end it seemed almost a good thing, George—since there wasn't any deception in it. That's what it came down to, I guess. After a year or two, I stopped feeling guilty and forlorn. And now it's just—well, extended family, I guess."

Rosie puts down the thickening tapestry. She musters a feeble laugh. "I stayed in my marriage for the sake of loyalty—to Hibbie at first—and then I stayed in it for the sake of Alfie being with Hibbie, of course. And then for the sake of the Lover so he wouldn't freak. And then even a little bit for the sake of the Lover's wife and kids since they had gotten to be a part of it, and then for the idea of loyalty itself."

"I see," Georgia quips, her eyes gleaming as she tosses a grape at her from the blue and yellow bowl. "Nothing for yourself, of course."

"Aside from the fact that I love both men—of course. I didn't think of that."

"Anyone else and I wouldn't believe it. How many have there been?"

"What do you mean?"

"How is it you fall into such tantalizing desperate things? How many lovers have there been? "

"Since I've been married? Why there's only him. And I wasn't kidding, George. I did it for Hibbie in the beginning. He begged me to—to take the pressure off, and the guilt. He was never with me and when he was he always had his nose in his work."

"But, Rose! All this time married. And you've only slept with two men? In your whole life! And you're still with them both? That is absolutely incredible. I know you didn't sleep with Peter in high school—or that college kid who went down in the helicopter—not to bring up that whole sad subject again."

"I didn't say in my whole life, George. There was later on in college after all."

"Oh yes, there was college of course—one or two more."

"It's not something to be ashamed of, George, having a little virtue left."

—☊—

The world turned round and round. I began to see the possibilities in dehydration now. Dehydration, a tantalizing word.

—☊—

A glint of bone had begun to show beneath the children's sand pails and shovels on a Tuesday. By Thursday, Georgia and Rose were digging, too, rather silently for them. At first the sisters had worried that it was a small animal, maybe a dog, and for a while the two women scooped sand beside the children, fearful that they would find, with the children, a human set of bones intact and stretched out in a damp, beach repose. It was only after nearly a week of the children's frenzied excavation that the animal's metamorphosis from puppy to boy to horse and then to shark; and even beyond, came to an end. Finally the skeleton of the small—-could it be a whale?—with the help of some sturdy metal twine and screw eyes—swung intact from the central beam in her studio. All that night and the next day she examined it, drawing sketches on her pad.

"What is it?" her sister asked, watching the children for her. "What is it you're staring at when you see those bones? It gives me the creeps some times when you look like that. Sometimes I get afraid you'll look like Fred when first he came back."

"Entirely different thing."

"Oh, you artists are all the same."

—☊—

At the end of that same week, it began to rain, and after three days of taking the children into town for movies and library, they'd stayed home while the children played upstairs. Georgia lay back on the sofa reading briefs she had promised herself not to read while on vacation and Rose brought over from her studio some handwork for her thinking, something she could do in the front room. Rain sluiced across the panes and kept them cozy by comparison. Out to sea, foghorns were groaning, and the lighthouse cast about for lost adventurers with its single yellow eye. Sugar cookies were rolled out with the help of the little boys and cut into shapes, decorated with frostings colored with the blues and reds of berry juice. Batter, spoons, and bowls were licked at eagerly in the little kitchen while the cookies baked. As it slipped through dense fog up the sandy drive, the sleek, petal-yellow automobile parted the pale green of Queen Anne's lace.

Mid afternoon, Rose looked out the window and exclaimed to see the Lover sitting on their porch in the straight-backed rocking chair.

"Good heavens! How did you find me here?"

"Investigative reporter," he said and bowed.

—⁂—

Georgia is rubbing a corner of her dress between her forefinger and thumb. A nervous rash has gone up across her chest, just above the blue bodice of her dress. What an imp, Rose thinks fondly.

"A man is not merely some kind of vitamin, George," Rose Reynolds says. A crystalline light seems to have transfused the air, Rose thinks. See how the light is so bright around all the objects in this room, haloed around Georgia's furrowed face.

"Well then, I don't know what a man is after all, it seems," Georgia said and smiled.

Sometimes, I don't know why, when I'm around her, I feel like a sore about to form, Rose Reynolds thinks.

—◌—

That night Rose Reynolds and the Lover slept in her little room, the one with the pink and green rose wallpaper, facing the water—he stroking down her hair, down her sides, under her waist, taking the small pillows of her breasts again in his hands and burying his smiling face. And she, in turn, pressed the thick, stolid substance of him against and into her. She was dreamful and sighing of a world where two little boys could dream of squid and she could be with such friendship and reliable tenderness again.

"You didn't tell me about his smile," Georgie says.

"I did," Rose asserts. "You forget."

"You told me," Georgia says, "But you didn't really tell me. It's so brilliant. He has a stunning, radiant face—for a lover, I mean."

"It's bad luck to say such things."

"It isn't bad luck for me to say it. Only for you." Georgia grins and then she falls silent for a moment. "I understand the need for comic relief, Rose. It's nice he's come to see you now when things are so bad with Hib."

What is it, Rose thinks, what is it her sister always knows without ever telling her? "Georgia!" Rose Reynolds says. "Why ever would I need comic relief when I'm here with you?"

—◌—

In the kitchen then, just the three of them.

"Just looking on the bright side?" Rose asks her sister. "You never told me this." For one moment Georgia's face tips between sadness and flippant generosity. Then it sails: a yellow dishtowel across the sky-blue trimmed room. Rose has caught it before it comes near her face.

"All right, let's hear it, Georgie," the Lover says. "I want to know the end."

"Yes," Rose Reynolds says. "You've been keeping back the bad parts. How odd, George," she says. "I thought only I did that."

"It's a ludicrous story really," Georgia says. "Embarrassing."

"Ah, embarrassment—" the Lover says. "We can handle that." The Lover has leaned back on the white legs of his chair. His ankle rests on his other knee, his coffee mug in hand. "I—" he laughs. "I tell nothing."

Georgia grins her sunny smile: "That's not acceptable."

"That's right," Rose says. "That is not in the least an acceptable thing."

"You can't bow out this time, Sir," Georgia says to Rose's lover. "I want to hear about your wife."

Suddenly Rose's coffee cup has made a stain like a rotten apple on the tablecloth. "Georgie! That's not your business."

The Lover quickly answers: "Oh, it's O.K. My wife's a good kid. Everyone likes her— There—I'm done."

"Did you know Georgie had polio once?" Rose asks. "For three months. Tell him about that."

Georgia smiles brilliantly into Rose's nervous face and presses on. "Not so, not done with your story, Mr. Adventurer. Why do you stay with your wife anyway when you could have Rose? What does your wife do to earn her keep? Who is she anyway to you?"

"Georgia!" Rose reprimands. "I have Hibbie you know. I am not divorced nor leaving Hibbie ever, you know."

The Lover clears his throat. "My wife doesn't do anything, really—not like you two. She doesn't paint or write legalese or defend the abandoned and innocent. She doesn't represent anyone or anything. She's a sweet kid, that's all."

"I want to hear about the wife and then I want to hear about this desert thing," Georgia persists.

Georgie's face practically glows, Rose thinks, whenever the slightest interrogation begins. Now it glows in reflection.

The Lover takes an immense bite from his jellyroll, chews quietly, the movement of his jaw rippling up even on to his forehead. He looks back and forth between the two of them. His iridescent eyes shimmer in his tanned face. "All right, you've got it," he swallows, sips his coffee once. "All right. The desert thing. But we have to hear your story, Georgia—all about the polio, and then another one—the most upsetting experience you've had all year, George. And you, too, Rose—" He touches his hand to Rose's knee. "A story from you, too, sweetie, something I don't already know."

"I'll think of something innocuous enough," Rose says stirring up the cream in her coffee.

"Innocuous begets innocuous," he says. "Reap what you sow."

And so the game had come to a close, because Rose would not tell anything.

"And so it goes," Rose replied. "And so I prefer it to go."

—⁓—

Always I have been led by love, I said. Or something very like it anyway—I just don't know.

—⁓—

The Husband removes the clothing from her shoulders, rolling downward as if he were helping her to shed the thick skin of a snake: blouse, slip, bra, stockings and underpants roll down into a thick rubbery tire at her feet. She stands naked under his relentless gaze. There is just one thing: she is not to take her mouth from his mouth at any point, even in the most awkward of moments. He is not beyond reminding her of this. He holds her face tightly in his hands. He will not kiss her anywhere but on the lips. The Husband has never kissed her on the lids of her eyes for instance, as the Lover does. Nor rarely her brow, she realizes from time to time. Nor hardly ever her hair. Nor any other softer place. What can she think?

—w—

There, still it hangs: the crenated crepe-paper donkey, the red *papier maché* saddle-stitched in green. A yellow bridle of yarn, and inside—every kind of individually wrapped sweetness for Alfie on his birthday. The house is tidy now, the other presents extravagantly ribboned.

It is hard to believe that only a few years before, her nephew William had placed his moist round birthday fists like bundles of dough into her hands. Now her own Alfie nuzzles his face in the hammock of skirt slung between her legs. Here it was again:

Today, yes today! Bright moments! It was Alfie's birthday. It was such joyfulness, this summer together at the summerhouse even though Georgia and William had moved to their own cottage down the lane. "We never could stand to be in the same room, Rose, why did you think it would be so different now?" her sister said. Georgia was bringing William by in the afternoon for his celebration. Oh how Rose and Alfie had planned. There in her son's tiny face was also the face of her own nephew William and of her own sister as a child. Alfie was small for his fourth birthday, with a tiny winged impish-looking scar at the bridge of his nose from where he'd fallen off his tricycle just the month before, pretending to be a bird. A "weenie teenie one," he'd said. The goldfinch, as it turned out, was just learning by flapping its arms to fly, he explained, and had somehow lost control of the handlebars.

Alfie sat on the floor, new short trousers pressed to the linoleum, hands on his lap, watching the small cake in the oven beginning to rise. "It's a hap hap happy day," he sang. The little scar wrinkled up. "A loo, loo, loo, loo day—"

"That cake is just yours and William's size, Alfie," she said. "With enough for Aunt George and me, too, of course. And then we have your piñata. Won't William and Aunt George be surprised?"

Then the frosting was in the mixer ready to be stirred, Alfie peering over the side. "Watch your fingers," Rosie said.

"Mama, mama, mama," Alfie taunted, dipping his fingers toward the bowl, making fun of her. Rose smiled. "I just have to say it, Alfie; even if you already know. Watch your fingers. That's the kind of thing mamas say. They can't help themselves. Just be sure you do it!"

"Mama," Alfie laughed.

"Watch those fingers!" Rose cried out, her heart in her throat. The yellow bowl went around, almost whistling under the mixing machine. The sun made a white mist as it streamed through the flutter of white curtain over the sink on a sea breeze, and there was the phone.

"Mama, can I have a lick of frosting?"

"Of course you will, in a minute,"

It was Georgia's voice, rather cold coming from the little cottage she'd taken at the other side of the inlet. "Why what's the matter, George?"

"Do you mind if we don't come over today?"

It was as if someone had clamped a cold hand over her heart. Alfie looked up expectantly. Her child. She tried to take the phone in the other room, but Alfie is following along and it is such a small house. "But everything's fixed for Alfie's birthday. I'll come by, George, and pick you and William up, if there's something wrong with your car!"

"Something's come up, Rose. We are entirely behind around here."

"Honestly it would be all right, Georgie. I wouldn't mind at all fetching William. Alfie's been looking so much forward to it. Then you could do whatever it is on your own—"

"Can't you ever take no for an answer?" Georgia shouted quite suddenly and erratically.

"You asked if I minded, Georgie. I was only trying to tell you that all Alfie's little friends have gone away on holiday. We were planning on William— It's not me you're hurting, Georgie. It's Alfie. You're his entire party, his family. It's his birthday, Georgie. He won't understand." Alfie is looking at his newly four-year-old hands.

"Oh, Alfie," Rosie cries. "How could she?"

"Mama," Alfie softly says, fighting back his tears.

"And William will be so heartbroken, too, Alfie. I know he wanted to be here with you on your special day. Something must be wrong. Maybe Aunt George is feeling sick and didn't want to say it on your birthday. That might explain it to us."

—∞—

"My god," I say. "Ho! What vertigo!" Or has the horizon shifted again? Acres and acres of sand shift by in front of us.

—∞—

Rose Reynolds and Alfie have been sitting under the dangling colored donkey crying, the child's face heaving against her breasts, the mother's tears in the crown of his hair. "There there," Rose said, "we'll have your party together. We're together. I love you so." There were devastating breaches in their lives as sisters, moments that Rose would never be able to explain, and that her sister in her hardened reticence would never venture to help Rose with. But wasn't this true then of everyone she knew— this lack of perfect understanding. Wasn't everyone calling across the wide water of confusion and experience? Still it seemed unfair, cruel even. She had lived through the repeated insensitivities of those she knew, had come to think of herself as negligible in some way, of attracting silent viciousness. But to see it transferred to her little child.

"Mama," Alfie sobs. "No birthday?"

"Alfie, Alfie."

They are on a downward spiral now. And if she had abandoned all those who had acted thus, relatives and friends, she would have had no one at all. She and Alfie would have been as isolated as her own mother ironing relentlessly in the basement family room. The woman who never went out for her own reasons, for any purpose in her own life. Perhaps her mother had found a kind of solace in this severe loneliness; perhaps anything was less painful than this. Her sister had called it once a social suicide—-this withdrawal of their mother from everyone but her children. But now Rose thought of it as an act of stamina and bravery—to avoid moments such as this. But then, it had not occurred to either of them then that her mother had already been ill, dying even, for sometime.

—∞—

"Rose," the Lover laughed, "how can you work like this surrounded by dug-up bones?"

—ɯ—

Alfie looked up at her with his startling red eyes. "You have broke my heart, Mama," he said and then he sobbed.

Yes, she'd thought, I have broken your heart, my darling, by somehow holding out a natural hope to you, that on your birthday you might have a family, if a tiny one. It wasn't my fault but I have broken your heart, against all my will, on your own special day. What is it, she asked herself, that keeps my sister away? To say nothing of his own father who has no time to come out here.

—ɯ—

"My baby," Rose says to the little boy. "My one and only love. Come on, we'll take your little cake to the beach and make a party with someone there. Surely some wonderful little children would like to celebrate with us. Come on help me take these wonderful balloons. We will stop by and see if William can come along. And even if he can't, we will have our fun."

—ɯ—

On the way they had driven over there to find William crying on the front steps. She put him in the car with Alfie, rolled all the windows down, and then she came around the corner of Georgie's rented summerhouse and went inside, and there they were. She had never seen her sister with her legs apart. That was the first astonishing thing. She had seen her naked a hundred times, yes, in the shower and getting dressed, as an adult and as a child. She had seen her mother strip Georgie's damp flannel nightgown off when she'd wet the bed, but now it was the central part of her own sister thrown open directly before her. It was the small pink puckered part even.

It was almost as if she had walked in unsuspecting on a surgery, and without prior warning seen a corner of her sister's grey-pink lung flapping open in a bloody slit. There was that, the bulb of her sister's heart: fatty tissue, cords, and the purple vein that was pounding next to it. Rose's breath caught up inside her chest somewhere and she fell against the wall. It seemed disembodied, seen at such a great distance. She leaned up against the sharp casement of the door.

What was she thinking? And why did she not move out of the room to the little boys who were playing in the yard, so that she might breathe again? It made a perfect loop of red with all the attached skin sucked along behind it. The bulb came out and went into the loop; the eye seemed to be turned inside out then, sucked inside.

Georgia gasped and cried and gripped the Lover's back and even in her frenzied passion thought better of it. Her sister did not scratch the Lover. The red loop was out again. The bulb rested a moment in mid-air, and went in again. Surely this was the beginning of all paralyzed things.

—⁂—

The vertigo sets in, round and round as if we have fallen into a volcano and are falling still.

"I can't stop coughing."

"This vertigo means the dust storm is certainly coming."

"No," I said. It means something else. I have a fever."

"Always European or American has fever in the desert."

"No," I said, "something isn't right."

"No, or yes, what does it matter?" He lays his hand on the back of my neck. "Inch'Allah. Today we see very much sand."

—w—

The Sister was panting terribly, flinging her head back and forth on the pillow. Her long pitch-black hair was swept across the flowered sheets in sheaves and was harvested again. Her sister was making noises Rose did not want to hear; she called out Rose's lover's name. The only movement in the room was just before her, going back and forth. Alfie and William were happy now; she could hear their unintelligible happy chant and felt unending relief— Her sister's bed made strange noises she had never heard from her sister's bed before. They sounded oddly like the songs her own bed made, the little thump against the wall. His testicles swung back and forth as if in a children's game.

In what mirror was he not seeing Rose, looking so beautiful for Alfie in her enchanting Alfie's-Birthday dress? But so frail, suddenly, come to retrieve her sister on Alfie's birthday, the two little boys downstairs. She could see them through the window, digging in the sandbox there by the big fence. The Lover cried out hoarsely then, looking up perhaps. Did he see her fainting there against the side of the bureau, welded then to a wooden chair, watching his buttocks as if in a fun house excursion moving forward and backward from all angles in the mirrors around her sister's bed with his swollen self out in front of him? There, too, lingered in her thoughts the Husband too busy to come an hour out to the shore for his child's birthday. Very white and drawn there, nearly pre-Raphaelite in her long blue dress with her hair pulled back at the sides above her ears and the soft tresses collapsing down around her shoulders and to the center of her back. Yes Rose Reynolds could see that her small face was smaller now, her diminutive white hands twisting together, her small torso in the lovely light blue flowered dress reflected now, so minuscule in all the room. She is merely a tiny emblem painted at the lower right corners of all the mirrors her sister has added to her room. How long, she thought, has my mouth been open just like that in horror? Her bodice was wet across the top from what her eyes put forth; and her knuckles had gone white almost blue from gripping the back of the straight-backed chair just inside the door.

Right in front of her, they were looking into one another's eyes, with tenderness—was it tenderness? Then their eyes were shut. Already he was on the final upward tilt, already carrying himself into his final cry, that cry which she knew so intimately as if it were again in the side of her own hair, spiraling its comforting heat down into the paths of her own right ear, their shoulders locked together, his belly against her own, the mat of his chest against her breasts, the pike deep inside and barging against her deepest gut—

But she was outside of this experience. She would always be on the outside now. She could see the back of his shoulders, the way the muscles rippled up, as his weight traveled down his arms into the heels of his hands. She could see the tilt of his pelvis.

But he had seen nothing of her, had only moaned. The way she had cried with her little boy over his birthday only moments before came back to her. It was as if he, too, were crying for her in her ear. Already he had comforted William. Now the reason for her sister's absence became clear; strange that she had not foreseen it. But then she had never put the Lover, or anyone, before either of the children. Now the Lover had closed his eyes again; though he rocked back and forth on his arms still. She could see her sister's head nearly jolting against the head of the bed. Now the Lover was lifting Georgie up, Georgia had wrapped her heels around the Lover's back as if she were sitting like they used to sit, playing Indians, soon to be impaled by warriors. The Lover lifted her sister up and drove her down onto the front of him repeatedly. How strange that her sister made no protest.

Life had begun to twist now, and there was perhaps no stopping it. No they couldn't have seen her there, seen her inability to cry out or yell or scream or walk angrily or painfully from the room. If only she could reel it all back in. Then, starting over—if it could have been—she would never have introduced them. She would never have trusted her own sister. And she would have left the Husband long ago. She wouldn't have trusted any of the people she cared about most. It was pathetic, she thought. She might have laughed out loud. Or broken something.

But now in all the icy ponds the mirrors made, the Lover stopped for the very slightest moment. For a moment he caught sight of her own face, of Rose Reynolds in her blue dress painted into a corner of the doorway. It was the briefest look, a mere tic in the surge of ongoing energy.

Her sister's eyelids fell back into her head; and her own mouth clamped shut. She leaned forward trying to catch her breath, a cramp in her upper chest. Was that herself in a silent film now, grasping the sides of her own face?

The Lover could no more stop himself than an arrow can cease if one says cease at the near end of its run. It was as if Rose Reynolds had caught him in the very moment of strangling. His hips tilted forward. She saw the spasm, heard him groan, the little twitching movement centered in his tailbone and passed in a current that shuddered up his whole form. She could almost see the sperm go round the curve of his lower spine, as if they had come from his brain, along all those funny little knobs, up around the crease and under his buttocks, up under the double-hanging bulge. She could almost see the sperm shooting up, through her body, into her sister's heart.

Yes, something was missing, she was sure, and whatever it was now caused her to cry almost uncontrollably, silently, in the mirrors, and in the wavy front of the china cabinet, and in the sparkling sides of all the water glasses. She had never seen him look at her this way, in all of the years they had been together, married or not, every day together, she had never seen it. He had been the real husband to her, that's what he had said. He had seen her in every mood, had been her most reliable, amusing, beloved friend. And Hibbie had agreed. She had never seen herself destined to become another Emma Bovary; it was nothing like what she had dreamed. The way the two of them were looking at her! For this fraction of a fractional moment, perhaps a limb had fallen off of her somewhere. Rose Reynolds could close her eyes; but she could not move her own wrists or ankles.

His voice trembled, even furiously, worried and almost hysterical. "Rose!" The word seemed to fall back down inside of him as he pressed Georgia, falling, back into the bed. The sisters looked up at one another.

Even as she saw the still length of him, the Lover collapsed into the cradle of her sister's legs, his wide shoulders, the vertebrae as though fused, his white buttocks pinched together, his long stony white legs. "I'm sorry, Rose!" his pinched voice came. Georgia, too, had bent away from her. Was her spinal cord severed now at the other side of this column that held her throat? What had she been thinking when first she had entered this room?

Then the Lover turned, pulled his face out of her sister's hair. His face an emblem stamped now on her sister's bed. He spoke again. "For God's sake, go away, for a moment, Rosie. I didn't mean for you to see."

And then her sister Georgia looked and said nothing, just stared at her, as if Rose Reynolds had done something inappropriate. It was as if Rose Reynolds had been exchanged for something as shocking as the ghostly image of their mother—floating there in full view, in outraged and grieved multiplicity.

"Well, after all, you have a husband, Rose! That's more than I have."

"I'm taking William and Alfie to the beach," she said. "Don't you realize

William's been crying in the garden all alone? You've made both our little boys cry! And on Alfie's birthday! Pick him up tomorrow or next week. But don't come in my house. Don't you ever!"

And in the end, Alfie said it had been an absolutely delightful day, even if they had known none of the other children at the beach until then. And wasn't it wonderful to have William staying overnight again?

And yes, Rose said, maybe he could stay overnight more often. She had been missing him. She always loved so much to have William visit them. He was such fun.

—◦◦◦—

I'd blow my brains out if I didn't already know what would happen.

Mama, the girls cried out, mortified. What would happen?

Why, girls— Her Scarlett O'Hara voice. *Of course I'd sneeze—at the crucial moment—and blow the very end right off my very own exquisite nose. And then, just as surely as the two of you are standing there, I'd be a freak the rest of my born days.*

No, Mama, no, don't you do it.

Now, girls don't be ridiculous. Do you see a gun here? Of course not! Don't think another thing about it. Everybody knows suicide is the only unforgivable sin in the whole wide universe.

Why is that, Mama?

That's the one thing you can't ask forgiveness for, now isn't it true? How are you going to be asking forgiveness of God for something when you're already stone cold dead? They've had that straight in most religions since the beginning of time anyway. Except for a few. Except for a few, where it is actually a patriotic custom, but then—I can't say I understand them. I do not.

—⁂—

No she would not be blowing her brains out over any of them.

The donkey turned quietly on the breeze of her dream. They were announcing something in the airport, but no—it was not yet her sister's plane. They would be another hour at least. She tilted her head against the sweater she'd rolled up, and drifted again. And William would be staying with them for the rest of the summer. That, in itself, had been a great thing.

"I remember when we were small and you were always terrified," Rose was saying. "I would come to find you, Georgie, when you were hiding in that little park between the highway and our street."

"In the lilac bushes?" came back her sister's crisp voice. "In that triangular park? That was nothing but a median strip."

"That's the way I remember it, too. It seemed so desolate to me the moment the bushes went out of bloom."

"And all this time I thought you came to find me because you understood."

"I did. I couldn't stand you to be in pain when I wasn't feeling anything bad myself. Anyway we were only five. At five, it's hard to understand."

"I was four."

Against the back of Rose Reynolds's bare heels, she felt the coarseness of the animal's hide as she rode along. Alfie, enraptured in front of her, held in an uncharacteristic silence to the donkey's rope. The trail wound up the mountain. On the right, a stream slipped down its side into a cavernous pool far below.

"It's been one of the sadnesses of my life—thinking a little child could be so unhappy so young," Rose Reynolds said to the donkey. "And you my own sister, too. What was it? Tell me finally what made you feel so bad. There seemed to be nothing to do for you."

"Why, I haven't any idea," the donkey exclaimed. "What a strange thing to have tormented you all these years—something on my behalf, something I can't even recall. Sometimes you seem so ridiculous to me."

"Well," Rose tried, fighting back her tears. "I thought I was caring for you, Georgie. I love you so much."

"I got in the habit of feeling sad," the donkey, which now looked quite like her lovely sister, said out loud.

Rose gave the donkey beneath her a nudge, but the creature merely snorted and then refused to speak.

They went along the cliff trail for some time in utter human silence. Even Alfie had stopped his humming in front of her. Only the clatter of hooves on pebbles and the creaking of the saddle penetrated their overlapping worlds. "I wanted to have everything that belonged to my mother," the donkey said.

"Nothing was *your* mother's," Rose snapped at the beast. "It was *our* mother's, George! We *were* born of the same parents. On the very same day. But for a few minutes and a year."

"Oh, Rose," the donkey said. "You imagine such things."

"George! Three or four minutes was all, at most. The same day! Hold on tightly, Alfie."

"Leave Alfie alone," Georgia said. The clicking of hooves seemed like castanets flung down and living like animated snapdragons on the road. "I decided to be just like her, like Mama. Even then, that early. I decided to wear her sadness. And her loneliness, Rose."

"But you never seem sad, or lonely now."

"Neither did Mama. I wear it inside out, just like Mama did."

"But you had Mama, and Mama had you. You were like twins."

"It was devotion," the donkey child said proudly, looking back into a long ago past. "It was devotion, it was not sympathy—like yours, rushing into the bushes to ask what was the matter with me. Sympathy is easy, Rose."

"Well have a look at this," Rose cried in nearly the same tone of voice.

"Sympathy is nothing at all," the donkey said quite clearly.

Rose Reynolds twisted her head this way and that like a bird. "Why, Georgia!" she said quite artificially. She herself heard it come out that way, as if she had been made of quite some lesser stuff. "Did you see that little seaside town we just passed? It was the loveliest little town—just like I imagined you and Mama and Freddy, too, loving, so quaint with pastel houses and all the starkly colored shutters flung across. That's exactly what I imagined the three of you would have loved. I miss Mama so much."

The donkey's long, nappy ears perked up for a moment and then fell flat in anger against its straw head. "That's it, that's the very last word, Rose. That is quite enough for me! *Imagined!* If you'd just looked around you, Rose, just once in your life—at me and at Mama, at Grandma, too, you wouldn't be imagining everything right now! You would know."

"I know completely well," Rose said. "I knew them both better than surface or reality, or any other such confining thing. They told me things they never told anyone else. And that goes for you too, George! Don't you dare say such stupid, myopic things." And before she knew it, Rose had kicked the donkey with the sharp heels of her boots.

Very quickly it happened to them then. Just while going around the bend, her sister the donkey drew to an enraged halt. As if Rose and Alfie had been only two tiny pebbles resting between the shoulder blades of the beast, they flew off its back. Out over one crevasse and down the dry hillside, they tumbled, and then they fell: directly into a turbulent stream. For one moment, in the heat of the day, their ill fate seemed nearly to be a cool relief. Well, so much for dreams.

—⁓—

Five summers ago, looking out through the telescope into the stars, she had watched the small streak of light like a fuse burning across the sky. What was the offering, the gift in these times? That morning she had lain on the table. What were her symptoms? A tingling feeling in her lower abdomen, almost an itch. Cell division, she was sure of it, a growth, something effervescent inside of her, fizzing as it spun out of control, wild with determination. She had not mentioned it to anyone, not lover, nor husband, not Angie, nor to Georgia or even Maya Lane. No, it was not a good idea to worry them, especially not Georgia—to make her sister conjure their mother's death again. Since she'd noticed it, she'd thought daily, almost obsessively, of calling the round forthright judge, a stranger really, who had not so long ago laid the wet paper towel on her brow in the train. Maya Lane would have consoled her, yes, nearly always consoled her as Rose did in return; but she was in Copenhagen this week and then two weeks more—invited to speak at a large conference on drugs.

Rose Reynolds lay like a state of being on the table in a pervasive sweat. The paper gown they had given her to cover her nakedness clung to her skin. She stared at the light overhead in its small square frosted glass box. A rash of goose bumps overtook her arms; why did they always keep the temperature in such places so torturously low—no matter the season?

The doctor wore a mid-calf white skirt under her lab coat, and there in the doctor's glasses was Rose's face in a contortion of anguish Rose Reynolds recognized as one side at least of herself. Yes, yes, Rose said to herself, be still; but there was the worry like a wild animal reflected in the doctor's dark eyes. Dr. Straus lay her hand on Rose's chilled arm, and it was as if she had been injected with a comfortably warm oil. Out it came from Rose's own mouth in a jumble, hurried and high pitched: all the illnesses she was certain she had.

"Whoa now," Dr. Straus said. "Just tell me the symptoms; *I'll* give you the news—if I find anything."

Yes, there had been those moments of dizziness, perhaps a brain tumor that had metastasized to the uterus or the reverse.

"Whoa, whoa, whoa," Dr. Straus said firmly, smiling slightly—with restraint, in case the tumors came to be a truth— Rose observed everything. "Whoa now."

Dizziness and the growth buzzed away in her abdomen. "Now let's not think of that," Dr. Straus said. "Let's have a look."

It was always a strange experience, not sexual, not much of anything. It was the circular warmth of the light only that seemed embarrassing. "Ah," Dr. Straus said firmly looking between her legs. With no commitment or implication in her voice. "Get dressed, we'll talk."

It was the matter-of-fact fraction of moments that marked turning points. She turned her face into the pillow and, to her own astonishment, cried. She could think of nothing but *The Idiot* now. Dostoevsky's *The Idiot*. Over and over it came back to her, this book. The light was gone; she was lying on her side, the doctor's hand on her back. "It's not what you think," Dr. Straus said. "Not any of those things." Rose Reynolds looked up, surprised to find the woman still standing in the room. Other women had had similar symptoms, had in fact died.

"Get dressed and we'll talk."

Sitting in the office, before the large desk that squatted between the doctor and herself, Rose stared at the family photographs like clay pigeons on the mahogany. And there, too, the leather rimmed blotter with the calendar paper in the center of it, the neat stacks of scratch paper from pharmaceutical companies off to one side, the light pouring in as if out of the fingertip of God.

The doctor was speaking now.

"There is a moment when you look up and the first little pin-pricks of the stars break through and the sky is still very blue. It is as if you are looking at the bottom of a blue china bowl," the doctor said all too seriously. "Your cervix is blue."

Even as the doctor hesitated, Rose held her breath. "That blue uterus inside of you—the way it's tipped up now—" The doctor was comforting perhaps. Blue china bowls? Rose asked herself. The world is about now to change.

"You're very swollen. Were you and your husband planning to have any children now?"

Rose Reynolds looked at the doctor blankly for a moment, and her spirits sank into a pit somewhere. "I'm to have a hysterectomy. I understand," she said. "Will I—be all right? I mean—will I be likely to live, a long time, I mean—"

"No. Not at all," the doctor gruffly said. "Pay attention. You're going to have a baby, if you want one that is."

And so Alfie had begun.

—⁂—

What a sigh of relief as the toast popped, yes there were the crumbs of a late night snack all over the counter. How these minor trespasses pleased her still. Rose unplugged the toaster and fished around inside it with the butter knife. The twin halves of the muffin would not come out. A raisin had caught itself on the vertical grid, offering up a thread of smoke. She pried it off.

"There it is: some things never change, including the private language even of the intimate." He patted her on the shoulder. "Here, here," Hibbie directed, in a fatherly tone of concern. "Close your mouth for just one second, take a deep breath. I'll put some cream in your cup as well. That is—if you think you could drink a little coffee. Wouldn't want to force feed. No nothing like that. I could always call the resuscitation people to see you through."

"What were you saying?" Rose asked, staring still into the vacant yard.

"I haven't the slightest idea," the Husband said.

A car started up with the rattles and knocks of a badly needed tune-up and then slid backwards out of the churchyard drive across the street.

—⁓—

When she opened her eyes, a mossy substance was collecting almost like flesh along the back of the stone next to her; and then it began to curve like a scythe. One line grew into an edge and then in several places a similar transformation occurred. Wiggling and shimmering, the slender filaments expanded toward the light that fell toward this her son and herself.

Far overhead, above the two of them, wavered an elongated matted face and the gigantic ears of her sister. "It was the way of our mother " the donkey called out, as if it were underwater itself rather than somewhere above them on the treacherous watery cliff, "It was the way of our mother to be honest and honorable even if it meant being mean."

"Alfie?" Rose asked in disbelief. "Did you see that beast?"

But the little stone child had seen nothing extraordinary at all, it seemed. "I had a gold fish once—" the little one said. Before her, he had begun to grow on his grey speckled surface, small grey wedge-like fins. On the back of him a tail now wriggled, testing itself on the bottom of the stream. And then far above, on the bluff, the creature that was her sister called down loudly, and all too clearly, something truly irritating.

185

Just the same Rose called back, "I didn't hear you."

"Get a horse," the donkey called, braying hysterically.

"I can't quite hear you?"

"I said get a horse, you parasitic thing."

"I'll never be able to hear you, I'm afraid," Rose called back. "You might as well go on without us—now that you've bumped us down this well."

"It's not a well," the beastly sibling shouted nastily.

"And you're not a horse," Rose screamed, "so go off and have your jaunt when everyone's down and out like you always do. Go off and be your stubborn internally raging confined and wretched self." The clicking of the hooves was recognizable in retreat. Whether the sound accompanying it was laughter or sobbing could not be said. No, Rose Reynolds thought, it could not be sobs. The Sister never sobs. And if you were to look beneath the fur just beneath her chin, on neck and chest, you would find that donkey blazing rashy red, Rose said to herself. A sunburned hysterical wretched and unhappy red.

While I am not altogether cool, Rose Reynolds thought, as always I find myself rather in a predicament.

A cool ripple of water swept out behind her, and she could not tell whether she herself was riding or making the small wake. An odd feeling came over her then; it was as if she had just pulled off a pair of tight riding pants after a very long day. "Suddenly I think very fondly, Alfie, of your two pet fish."

"Me, too," Alfie squeaked. Along they sped then, a mother and her son, calling from time to time to each other about the nature of the elements.

In among the yellow-green haze of the seaweed, a speckling of black and white shadows appeared, then the sycamores, black and fully leafed, and a rubbing sound like the violin strokes of crickets as the road opened out into the night. Stone walls leapt against the headlights; and the Husband, driving beside her, gently touched the top of her head and said: "I didn't know you were awake."

—◆—

CHAPTER V

There are always two deaths, the real one
and the one people know about.

—Wide Sargasso Sea
Jean Rhys

HERE WITHOUT THE ONE AND NOT THE OTHER I am the compass
without the needle.
Or I am the needle spinning aimlessly.

—⟋⟍—

At Alfie's birth, the mirror was like a full moon hung up in the night.
The midwife's arm went up inside her—to rotate, she said, the small
unseen shoulder within her body so that the baby's arm would appear first.
"Here," the woman said and pulled Alfie's wrist. "Hold your baby's hand."
In the mirror she saw the tiny fingers coming out first, all wet— And they
moved. She felt them, too, in her palm; then they wrapped around her
forefinger, squeezed it tight. Somewhere in the room her Husband had
cried out in delight at the sight of them already holding hands like that
before his face appeared. The mirror held it, too, as in a photograph, as
out it came: miniature lavender hand gripping and squeezing, the arm and
shoulder, now the dark back of Alfie's head suspended for a moment just

outside of her, the doctor's hand turning it gently now. Finally her little child's purple wrinkled face, squinting and smiling up at her. Mayan figure: two heads, top and bottom, Alfie poking out of her. Then, folded up small: the other arm, and suddenly the scrawny bent legs, slipping frog-like into a world, eyes agog, Mr. Peepers! Blinking very briefly, for the moment, silent with awe.

—◊◊◊—

Snow had fallen against the windowpanes! How unusual! On this summer day, and frosting the evergreens—

The willow trees swung down, their glistening green ropes festooned with white. The midwife worked under the sheet slung over her deadened legs, and then the Husband held him up. It was the dark blue, infant eyes. On and on mother and infant stared, mesmerized.

"Alfie is his name," the Husband said, somewhere in the room. "Just as we planned." The snow swirled behind him against the lightly frosted pane.

"Yes," she said. "Our magic elf. He has arrived."

—◊◊◊—

On early summer mornings, Alfie plays with his little friends; afternoons Rosie picks him up and they are off to the park or the zoo, to the museum, or to play ball in the deserted stadium. Saturdays, it's Alfie's team of preschoolers. The Midgets play the Mosquitoes, Beetles, Hedgehogs, and Gnats. "Oh, Alfie," she found herself saying. "Hedgehogs? It's such a clever name."

"Hedgehogs!" Alfie cried out, his hands stuck to his hips much as his father used to do, when once or twice he came to games. Alfie, mortally offended, stamps one blue tennis shoe. "Hedgehogs! What kind of name is that for a baseball team?"

—※—

Let September come riding in. Glorious heat and a clear light, no breeze. But for the last two weeks of rain, the end of summer has been as summer always has. She relates it for her sister in a letter, the invigorating changes of light and pigment, air moving against her bare arms as she paints. In another week, her sister will return to get William. At home, sweat slips down her sides as lovely as tea; in her studio she cuddles under air-conditioning in a long woolen sweater. On the canvas something moves. Life comes into contrast and juxtaposition; meaning forms. She throws the letter away. How can she speak to her again?

The Husband will barely speak to anyone now. At the office he seems to be nearly fine, or so it seems. No one has said otherwise. A certain resentment is welling up, so she has said repeatedly, her anger is barely assuaged now by the contentment she usually finds in her work.

The Husband has entered into his own work with a mania that looks remarkably staid. It has taken so long for her to notice what has been there from the start, or at least the seeds; she has always been so taken with him. Ten years he has worked in the attic, he can be found there anytime he is not at his office during regular hours. Just a minute, he says and there is the scrape of his chair, the desk drawer shutting, the opening of the door. Hibbie. It is so unbelievable to her. On weekends and vacations when he can get away with it, the Husband now fails to wash! She is always asleep by the time the Husband comes to bed. She cannot stand to be touched by an unwashed man. Between them there is this small interceding, growing, almost imperceptible thing on his skin. She cannot bear to tell anyone; she will not tell her lover, or her sister, or Maya Lane.

All evenings and weekends, she and now Alfie, too, are alone with him lurking elsewhere in the house, slipping away whenever they approach. She would rather sleep with Alfie on his narrow bed anyway, with bears and stuffed animals, or on the sofa, rather than sleep in the acrid air that surrounds the Husband now. She has moved into the guest room down the hall and tosses and turns at night before crisp, white curtains between the neat, clean sheets that her weekly housekeeper Jane Anderson helps her put on the bed.

—⁂—

This winter, to make up for Alfie's despondency at his father's strange behavior, Rose-Eleanor and her Alfie talk about buying a real animal—merely ideas now, these pets with no real names, only things like Hopefulness and Faith, to go with their cat Hodge. *We are trying everything now. Let it never be said, my Rosie, that you gave up without a fight.* Certain glass and metal items she has found on her Husband's desk only this week. She would rather not think of it, does not understand, refuses, too. Soon they are as forgotten, in the shock of it, as if she had never seen them there. Each day still he rushes off to his office, presents his cases, comes home in his pressed suit. Perhaps it is a dream she tells herself. She has had a strange dream or two.

One cat they already have, soon a Labrador, two parrots and a pair of finches, two turtles and a funny, red-spotted puff-up fish, and then a lap dog to go with the big one, maybe a Bengal tiger or a kangaroo . . . . Alfie, sequestered in a towering bathtub froth, studies his paired set of brilliantly detailed plastic animals and the bright blue boat with Noah and a woman they have called Zoë at the helm. What a surprise! Alfie has suddenly proclaimed that their own grey and orange striped cat Hodge, given a choice, would walk alone onto the ark. Also the purple plastic cat prefers to sleep alone, so Alfie says, not with Hodge who sleeps with Mommy anyway. Likewise, the purple cat lives its entire life by the soap dish at the sink, by choice. Noah did not know everything, Alfie says. Rose grows confused.

Hodge needs no mate, Alfie clarifies, sitting on her knee, because Hodge has Mommy to tend for him, he says. Everyone needs a mommy, Alfie says. Even Hodge. It is true: Hodge would accompany Rose anywhere— sleeps at night now, in fact, curled beneath Rose's fluffy hair in the pocket between her shoulder and jaw, partway wrapped around her neck, an orange striped cat, a kind of feather boa, long and flat. It is all a matter of perspective, Rose-Eleanor and the cat. They look a kind of Rousseau perhaps, with all these stripes, if seen from the door head-on; certainly this is nothing from John Ford, no matter the door, even if he had shot her just as her cat has tied himself around her neck and begun to purr. No this a moment of Rousseau, she thinks, going slightly mad, if studied from deep within the conscious body, within her neck and head itself where she listens to the deep reverberating hum of the living fur wrapped half way around her head. She can almost see the horse cart going by, the puffed up sleeves of Rousseau's passengers. Striped cat sneak-chews at her own two-dimensional hair whenever it catches her off guard—as she so often is. Merely herself: *Painter, Asleep with Cat and Child.* Dreaming unforgettable dreams. She tries to lay the hieroglyphs onto the canvas, and now onto a project commissioned by the city in the subway. Alfie comes along and paints, too. No, Hodge must stay at home. Hodge would not like it in the subway with all the people milling around and the trains shooting through and throwing off plumes of fumes. Alfie has never been happier, his brush dipping and slathering. Imagine his surprise, when someone threw a quarter in his upturned baseball cap. *Mommy!* he said, his little fists stuck to his hips. *Those people gave their money to the wrong little boy, make them take it back! Then take it to some other little boy. This money isn't ours. What would Gandhi do?*

—⁂—

I rest my elbow against my pistol to reassure myself that it hasn't fallen to the ground and gone unnoticed somewhere. The vertigo has begun again. I rest my head on her chest. I cry like a baby. I clutch at her as if she can stop the world going round. Every spiraling channel in me is drying, flaking and curling inward, going down in the undertow. Inside I can hear the completely tattered, flapping, tattered sails.

"What is it?" my wife says. "What's the matter?" I am holding to one corner of the earth. I am puking into a million pivoting grains of sand. Again and again Isabella puts her hand at the back of my neck. Up it comes, further evidence. The acrid smell turns around in me. And I see it again: the jeep moves, driving in circles, in search of the water someone I trusted holds. Their eyelids have curled back like dead leaves and dried to their skulls, their eyeballs mere burned out flashbulbs popping out of their heads. Around and around they go, bursting, as one of them points.

"Buck up, Birdy," Izzy says.

She knows it is my fault we have come here. I can't stop retching now. Whatever happens will be my fault. It already is.

—⁂—

For two days the Husband has refused to go into the office, has refused to call in sick. She has called for him, to save face for him. Over the past month she has had him see two neurologists and suggested another one. *Hibbie, you've lost your sense of humor now. You don't look yourself.* Now, here, suddenly, he appears across town, looking wretched in her studio. Alfie is playing at Jane Anderson's with her little boys for an hour or two every other day. She puts her palette away when she sees Hibbie at the door. The Husband's face is gray; he's lost so much weight. He looks even worse today. "All right, Rose, you're going to come along with me today."

"I thought you were going to the doctor today. The doctor wants to see me, too?"

"I'm the doctor now," he says, taking her out from her studio and down two flights of stairs by the wrist and pushing her toward the car.

"What is it, Hibbie?"

"Don't call me that."

"I've always called you that, Hibbie. You liked it you said."

"Well, I don't like it now. I have to show you something. Just shut up—until we get there, Rose."

The Husband stares into the road. For four hours he drives in silence leaning into the steering column as if it were some kind of psychic projection from his chest. He flicks the radio off, if she turns it on. She can evoke nothing from him. She becomes more terrified as he drives barely looking left or right. She takes comfort from the knowledge that Alfie is with Jane Anderson, is happy and taken care of no matter how late they are getting back. Jane Anderson will always know what to do if someone is late, she tells herself. When they reach the familiar thoroughfare, they drive deep into the upper west side, going up and up, even past their old apartment building from their student days, until she has leaned her elbow quietly onto the door lock and felt it go down. Then he has stopped the car and come around to her side. He taps on the window until she opens the door. He reaches in and takes her again by the wrist as if she has been some recalcitrant child. "For Heaven's sake, Hibbie, where are we going? This is a very rough area! What are you going to do?"

—∿—

Piers and Ramon lift me up onto the saddle of their arms. Piers puts a drop of water on my tongue.

"Every time I go on one of these so-called geographical explorations," Piers says, "some batch of these touring explorer types—stick out your tongue, I said—goes paralyzed. In rain forest last year, only six months and they all go crazy with arthritis, screaming I can't walk, I can't walk. You'd think they'd been beaten with a pipe. Here, the vertigo. Why can't you remember to drink what I told you? Open up his beak. He'll never get it in with all this shivering and twitching. I told you you'd have to drink more than you ever thought you'd consume. Now, 'Birdy,' —isn't that what she calls him? 'Birdy?'—Now, 'Birdy,' open up and be a good Capitan. Fearless leader, we're going to have to force some fluids in. Pour." She is laying paint onto canvas again. It's white and swirls. It has a hidden dimension. The Lover is away again, looking for a king or what remains of him, looking for a universe lost in storms. The canvas seems to undulate before her eyes; she is feeling feverish. At the center already the painting can be said to have integrity. This one will be exceptional, not a throwaway, but there is an impinging red at the edge.

—∿—

"I want to show you something," he says.

"Hibbie, what is it? Can't you see I'm coming along, just don't yank me around."

"This is for you," he says. " I've been meaning to give it to you for a long time."

"What is it?" she asks.

"You've always got paint on your nose—you're so naïve, Rose."

"Hibbie, what's wrong?" she asks him. "You're not acting like yourself—for weeks, months. Maybe a psychiatrist could turn you around. No one would have to know."

"Here," he says. "Look at this."

There is no knowing what kind of animal or person is on the other side of the crumbling concrete wall, high and thick, with the hole blasted out just big enough for a man's or a woman's hand perhaps and arm to go through. "So?"

He looks at her expectantly.

"There's a hole in the wall. What is it, Hibbie? Let's get out of here. Look at this rubble, there must be rats. I want to go."

He takes her hand almost tenderly, to leave, she thinks. Whatever it is, it is over. It is a political statement about one of his cases, about something he can tell no one, that he has learned in his work. That must be it. But then, he scrapes her hand, pushing it into the concrete hole.

"Stop it," she says. "Hibbie! Are you crazy? You're hurting me!" His weight secures her to the barrier.

Now he has actually turned to one side, to vomit on himself. He turns back again to wrestle her arm in again, further in.

"See how it feels to be me for once."

He has his weight against her whole body and her arm is scraped and stinging up both sides. The smell of his clothing is overwhelming as it rubs against her. She can barely understand that this is the same man she has been living with, who goes to work most days dressed in a soft grey suit. He has been in the attorney's office for the last twelve years. That should mean something, you would think. Though lately she has been noticing him sitting in the dining room on weekends; he is wearing a grey sweat suit that he has not allowed her to throw in the laundry basket for weeks. She has had to sneak it away from him to throw it in the machine. Perhaps it is like a child's blanket, she thinks. Maybe he likes its familiar smell. Still, he doesn't seem to notice when she puts it clean in his dresser drawer. He works on such difficult cases, she knows; sometimes, there is the danger that they will suck you in. This is all about one of them. He has gone mad now; now she will have to put him away—for a little while anyway, maybe a few months—if he keeps up like this and if he will not let her or anyone help. Her arm is burning where it has been scratched by concrete, and glass, and broken vines. This is nothing Alfie should ever have to see.

"See? See? Your arm is in that hole," he stipulates. "What would happen if someone came around from the other side?" he asks. "With someone twisting on your wrist? Anything could happen to you, couldn't it? Rape, Rosie. Lust. Love, misery, torture, dismemberment."

He is giving her a metaphor, she thinks, some weird instructive metaphor he must have been conjuring up for months. Something terrible must have happened in this place. It isn't that she hasn't tried to get him to tell her about all of it. In the first years he used to tell her about his work, he used to tell her so many things. She wishes now for someone to come rescue her. Perhaps the Lover would arrive; she wishes for the Lover's ordinary sanity. And strength. She wishes for someone, a stranger even, to pull this mad man off her so that she might run away like an insect about to be trapped.

—m—

The wall of sand seemed nine thousand feet tall, and perhaps it was, swirling above the dunes, in steely blue dust. A wall fully of sand. "It's completely Biblical, " Piers said, without one grain of humor in his voice.

—⚊—

She has always had a fear of being touched by strangers. Once recently a man reached toward her on the bus, picking up a paper she'd dropped, and actually touched her breast with his fingertips. She could not stop thinking about the horror of it at night. She could still feel him, see his startled, happy face.

"One person holds from one side, Rose, the others might do whatever they want. "

"Why are you doing this?" His weight against her is pressing her arm further in; her face is wedged, cut now between the chest of his sports coat and the craggy wall. "Get away, Hibbie, you smell so bad. Let me go. I want Alfie," she whines in the darkness he has imposed on her merely by blocking all of her view. Rose is suddenly very afraid of him, more afraid of him than she is of her own circumstance with her arm and wrist shoved into the unknown. It's true that conceivably wild animals might tear at it, she thinks. Like rats. No, she will not think of that. Or, she might be trapped this way and killed or raped with this mad man here in this strange vacant, bombed out lot. Maybe never found again—or, perhaps some children playing in these waist-high weeds . . .

"You still don't, do you, Rose?"

"I understand," she cries. "I understand. You want it to go back to the way it was."

"No," he says. "You don't know, do you, even now? Even here?"

"You wanted me to have him, and now I would be glad to give him up for you, but I can't."

"Why not?" he asks. "As though I give a damn. As though that had any relevance."

"He's with Georgie."

—⁓—

Hibbie coughs out a laugh as though an electrical shock had caught him in the throat. "With Georgie? He's with your little sister now?"

So finally, he is moved by the thought of fidelity, she thinks, when before it meant nothing to him. So we go back to what so very briefly was ours. He has no reason for all of this, even if it is what he started and even wanted. His madness now will dissipate. We will go home and wash ourselves and tuck Alfie into bed, continue on, with or without sex, certainly with our old familiar ways. Our old friendly life will return to us. But he says nothing, and she cannot see his hazel eyes, or any more than that edge of his implacable jaw. She is suffocating, so she thinks.

Her wrist is torn. It feels as though it has begun to swell—and her arm and elbow, too, her cheek, swelling, her fingertips, part of her stuck out that way into a cool and open air. She curls her fingers in for protection from whatever is over there, on the other side of this ghetto barricade. His chest is against her head. He has never seemed so tall. But his demeanor is not one of relief; he does not seem to have relaxed the way she thought he would.

She is all too silent now for her own good, listening to the familiar voice ranting, saying unfamiliar things, the familiar friend and mate looking unfamiliar, smelling strange. She is listening with every cell. The syllables sound oddly elated in their tones, leaping up and around in alien scales.

Her arm throbs and stings. Spiders and rats may be on the other side. Terrible people, unexpected things. Once, her father told her, there were rats in their own home that her mother had contended with—with three little children under her care. Her father evaporated into a better earthly world; her mother evaporated.

"We used to do this before exams, between classes, Rosie. Think of it, Rosie. Us. Many of us. Your friendly barristers, as you prefer to tease, oh comedian."

It must be a college game, do or dare, something like that. The point is yet to come. He will be divorcing her. She and Alfie will be on their own, and just when the Lover has gone off to Northern Africa with his wife, has enrolled as one in her sister's private cache of noncommittal male devotees. She does not know how she will support herself; she has relied on Hibbie so. Her work brings mostly respect; cash in intermittent tiny spurts. "I understand, Hibbie," she says. "You can have a divorce if that's what you want."

At first she thinks he is crying, the way his chest shakes against her skull, scratching her face and eyelid against jagged foundation and broken brick, but he is laughing again. She has closed her eyes against the sight and sound and smell of him, all but for the wet wool odor, which she cannot avoid. "There was a line, Rose, right here where you are. Poor kids, wealthy kids, Vietnam vets, poor fucking bastards from both sides, every color, Rose, business, medicine, film, and law, even Brooks Brothers, students in fatigues, our ratty jeans. We dipped our arms in, Rose, one at a time. We volunteered. You understand that, Rose? You volunteer at the hospital, you work with the sick and dying to give them one last laugh, don't you, Rose? You bring them flowers out of your own pocket money, and books. You can understand what it is to volunteer a part of yourself, Rose, I know you can. One arm each, stripped of the sleeve, an arm in here. Feel it, Rosie.

You can see how it feels. Exhilarating, isn't it? The suddenly known has such profound eloquence. Now you can't help but understand!"

She does not understand. She tries to push him off, but he bullies back. Even before she hears it, she can feel the tapping on the other side in her fingertips. Who is over there? Perhaps he or it is close, perhaps quite far away but growing near. She goes slightly stiff, her muscles taking on a chill that goes all the way through the nape of her neck and into the crown of her hair.

"And in it goes! your wrist after your hand, Rose! and then the shaft! Arm, skin, bones, essential twilight veins, Rosebud, do you begin to see? Into the unknown? Where were you, Rose? While so much was going on? You have to put a lot of dollars, Rose, balled up like a tiny cannon ball, even a spit wad perhaps, in your fist. *Voila! Rose-Eleanor! Voila!* Far fucking out! Zoom in, Rose-Eleanor. It's like being born!" Slowly it begins to dawn on her. "To receive it, Rosie! The needle and the god in it, the plunge into the squiggling pulpy vein itself! Conveyor belt of inner glory. The metallic pain! Try it, Rose! You can try it now!"

Her knees have given way but he presses against her so hard she cannot fall. His voice bashes on, ecstatic, swarming in her ear.

"Who knows how many times. Hundreds maybe more! Ask a doctor how many times a needle can be used before it won't go in again. Doctor Glow, as we called him, might have pissed on it first for good luck. How did we know? *Très chic. Far out.* "

Rose Reynolds' hand is waving around frantically somewhere very much alone in the cold air, opening and closing like an infant's, signaling for independent help, for deliverance. An extraordinary sweat has gone up on her brow. The wall might go up three thousand feet for the way she feels. "I want Alfie," she begins to cry. "I want Alfie. I want to go home. Please, Hibbie, let me go home. You can have anything you want. Please let's go home now."

"You might get high, Rose, if the right guys come along back there. You might receive the blessed release," he laughs. "Find out how I feel for once, Rose. How I've been feeling for years."

An insect lights on her hand, crawling on the back of it. She shakes it off. Her voice is hot and hysterical. *Get off of me. Get off. Let me out.* He is a tall man, she is thinking. I have married the tallest man in the world; what was I thinking then when I did that? If she could only turn partway, she might know how to fight him off. The side of her face scrapes concrete if she moves. She has kicked backwards toward his leg now. She has brought her heel down on his foot only to hear his glib response. She can feel the gun between them that he has begun to wear while prosecuting criminals—'for safety's sake, Rose.' Surely he has gone completely mad, her Hibbie, around the bend; maybe none of them are coming back, not even herself.

"There is no need for further sex, Rose," this his most tainted voice. "After you've had the needle, a little bit of fluid is all, water really, with a bit of horse, and in it goes. No need at all. For any other penetration after that. Who needs to penetrate when you can penetrate yourself?" He brays at his joke. He is an impersonation of himself, with sliding lips, mammoth teeth, and fantastic ears.

Surely soon he will let her go. "No need for further sex?" she says, choosing to follow along with him, perhaps to cool him down. She questions him. It's true they have not had sex in years—not since their marriage really, after which he'd oddly stopped. And then the little times before Alfie was born. Once last year, but it was good. She thinks she would not have given in to the Lover otherwise. She speaks now only to herself, because it is clear by Hibbie's eccentric breathing that he is not listening to her. She would have been the Lover's friend, of course. But she would never have gone over to this life, not without Hibbie's insistence. She would not have condemned it in the lives of others, but it would not have been her choice. She chides herself. She might have gone into a convent of the mind, accepted her lot, after all the life he gave her and the one she had given herself had so many good things to it. Surely that is what she should have done, at twenty-one. But now, she thinks, her husband has come here not to tell her anything as he has said, but surely to kill her in this place.

A putrid smell has gotten into her own hair now, runs down like egg yolk onto the side of her face. "Now you know what a crack lawyer, your husband is. Only my secretary knows!" he cackles. "Your prize! How long could I have fooled you, Rose? And you living in the very same house!"

She can feel his hard skeletal frame undulating, the weft and warp of his cotton shirt, the silk tie sliding still clean against her forehead. She wonders if the sun has gone behind a cloud or whether it has already gone dark out there beyond the oblivion of his coat. She would not want to be caught alone, even with him, out here at night. He rambles on and she thinks to comfort him; she cannot help herself. "Come on, Hibbie. You've had so many terrible things to think about, that horrible Robards case. Let's go home and I will make you some soup. You can have the little oyster crackers in it." She is aware that her voice has elevated in pitch, that she speaks to him like she would to any hurt child—but maybe it will work. The weeds have begun to scratch against her legs, too; one weed seems to have a broken thorn on it and it is at her leg, has torn her slacks right up her thigh. But suddenly she knows it now, something she would never in her life have expected. She could have imagined even her own murder, but not what he tells her now.

"It takes courage to give a stranger your vein, Rose. If you give all your bravado to him, oh and a few bucks, he might plunge it into you, Rose. You, too, could know what the icy shaft can mean. It's the sex of all sex,

Rose! It's the vein, and you have to give nothing out!

"No anxiety, Rose, about the globule of your terrifying god-damned life. You will be killed completely dead, no more fear of dying, Rose, no more fear of that stupid telephone frying you in the tub, no more terror of mosquito bites and flu and war and wasting disease, and best of all—get a load of this, Rose—you'll have raging self-confidence."

Hysterically she laughs now. It is an hallucination in itself. But she is also sobbing hard. "Who shot you up in college? Who was it? Hibbie? Let me go— Why are you making all this up?"

"You don't actually grasp this concept, do you, Rose? So much innocence, Rose." His feverish breath scores his little love symbols onto the side of her temple. With this motion, the distant afternoon crowds across the vacant parking lot come into view, over there past the busy avenue under a stack of high-rise concrete blocks and steel girders. A supposedly ordered civilization stands abruptly up to the edge of the ghetto there and slams shut its eyes. An insect walks on the inside of her wrist, half-crawling, half-slithering, she feels, carrying disease. Who knows in what filth, on whom, the animal feeds? It pauses to put the needle in. Frantically she shakes the burning off, again and again. She makes believe that she can hear it buzzing, but it is only her husband humming in something like a schizophrenic break, she tells herself. She has never seen a schizophrenic break, but this must be close. There is nothing but madness here, and loneliness, devastation, and loss of the unified self. The rest is all make believe. How can he have come up with such a rabid story, located this his alter ego's appointed under-realm?

"There's a spider on my hand, Hibbie!" she cries. "It might be a spider on me! Hibbie! Or an infected mosquito! Please get it off." He pulls his head back so he can meet her with his enameled eyes.

"Point at any one at all. Close your eyes, Rosie. That's who shot me up, that's a good enough guess. Are you listening, Rosie? I can't make it much clearer to you."

"Shot you up? Stop it, Hibbie. Get off of me. Please, Hibbie, I'm afraid. I want to go home to Alfie. Get me out. Not DuPruis, not any of the rest of them. They wouldn't do that. You and Hamilton and Williamson? With complete strangers? No. Why are you making all of this up? I've never done anything to you that you didn't want."

"No, not DuPruis. Of course not! Are you completely stupid, Rose?"

And then as if this declaration were all he had been aiming for, suddenly she is released. "Oh, Rose, don't be so bourgeois," the Husband says. He slumps down beside the wall in a pile of refuse then, his head in his hands, and laughs until he pukes again, a yellow-green bile all over his oyster-colored tie. "I've been trying to tell you for a year!" His laughter dribbles out of him as she leans panting with her back to the wall and her raw arm stuck out in front of her again, scraped and bleeding, like a sausage but retrieved. Mercifully it is still afternoon. "You are ever trusting, Rose, ever the old champion of my cause," he calls after her as she stumbles across the lot toward their car. He is close behind her, getting out the keys. But she is already in the driver's seat.

The vertigo sets into her. It is not a game; she sees this all too clearly now. It is an external misfortune greeting her. A cataclysmic shock coming her way. Round and round they spin, as if they have fallen down a typhoon, are still plummeting even now.

—⚭—

The salve she has rubbed on it has bled through the gauze in yellow lakes. There is a scrape like a grimace inside her palm, and up the rest of her arm it is as if she has been scoured with a metal brush from the shoulder down. Just there in the hallway lies Georgia's scarf, in the middle of the floor where, as Rose knows, it was not lying this morning when she came in. She knows because she lay there herself sobbing on that floor after the children were safely away from seeing her in anything like a worried state.

Lately she has been having horrible dreams. Last night, after Hibbie brought her back to the Cape and lurched off in the night, Rose dreamed that her sister was drinking with the mad man, the one they call the Rapist. "Old worn-out tennis shoes. No socks. Grey—the tennis shoes, the kind with no padding in them and the white elastic under-threads that come reeling out like worms—you know the kind, " Maya said. Basketball shoes. They come up on the ankle and lace to the top. "It's that guy," she says, "who sits on the ground in front of the trinket shop by the last dock. You know the one; he's always there. Collecting change. They call him the Rapist. As a joke." The policemen are taking notes; they sit in the armchairs while Maya and Rose sit right next to one another on the sofa.

"Did your sister have a reason to run away?" the policeman asks.

"No," Rose says. "Not that ugly one by the trinket shop."

"Your sister went off with him," Maya says.

"Did your sister have any reasons to run away?" The policeman asks again. "Did she have any reason to—hurt herself?"

Maya and Rose Reynolds look at one another. "Yes," Rose says. "She had reason. Yes," she says. "She had a very difficult week. She lost her lover and she had a shock."

"A shock?" the policeman says.

"Yes?" the other one says, writing carefully on his pad.

"Her health is in question," Rose Reynolds says.

Maya looks at her.

"She thinks she may have AIDS."

Maya's face goes white and she tugs Rose's arm.

"But I saw her with that man," Maya says.

"And," Rose Reynolds says, "my sister has a little child. She might go mad, but she wouldn't harm herself, I don't think. I don't think she would harm herself—for William's sake."

Rose Reynolds, alone now, goes upstairs to look for her sister in her own bedroom. The door is ajar. Rose Reynolds knows her sister has been and is in this house. Always she has been able to find her sister when her sister is lost. Perhaps she is crouched somewhere under a lilac bush with the man called the Rapist. "Well, if it isn't the Rapist right here in front of me," the owner of the bar said just the night before in front of Maya as she was leaving his pub. Rose pushes her bedroom door open with her fingertips, too afraid to call out. "You have every right to hate me now, Rose," Georgie had said. "But you'll never hate me as much as I right now hate myself."

"I doubt that," Rose said. "I doubt you can understand how much I hate you right now. You've never been much good at imagining anyone."

When the door is open, Rose sighs to see the made bed under the overhead light. The house is completely silent, but for the waves rushing at the shore at the end of their patchy lawn and the usual creaking of the riggings on the boats. They are to leave the seaside in merely a week, the end of the Labor Day weekend is already in sight. The air already has a cutting edge to it. A loose halyard strikes a metal mast, the sound of it a small bell high and distinct. It is a still and immensely starry night. Perhaps a night for northern lights. Rose's summerhouse is too far from the other houses for noise to drift to anyone else. Rose feels her sister is here anyway. She goes from room to room as if following her just a little late, on her heels almost, seeking a lost child.

Nor is Georgie in the boys' room. Not even on the floor between their beds. She feels it, her sister's presence. She doesn't know how. When Rose comes downstairs, the Lover is in the living room examining the backs of his hands, sitting on the couch: the Lover is reading a letter that Rose found that morning on the table. The sight of him is most terrible. Rose sits down abruptly on the stairs. Go back to your arid places and your camels, she thinks. His face screws up with concern as he reads; the letter trembles a bit in his hand. Just between his eyebrows the pigment in his skin goes bright red then white again, the white spreads out over his forehead and then down into his cheeks and jaw. He looks a little green and she is afraid he will be sick, that he will ask her to hold his head. She sees him clench his teeth. She already knows what it says.

I know you are having troubles—the letter says. It is badly typed, addressed to Georgia. It is worse than mad.

I know it is a bad time for you and I will visit you tomorrow.

That would have been yesterday, before Maya saw Georgie at the bar, Rose says.

I do not recognize the Bopa, the letter says. *I am neither Roman Catholic nor Protestant. But I have ways with evil thoughts and evil deeds. I can do them in, if you need. You do not need to find me. I will find you when you need.*

Almost against her will, Rose begins to explain to the Lover about her sister's disappearance. My sister is not a mad woman, Rose thinks. Rigid, impenetrable. She has always been that. Absent for most of my life. She is not one to drink with hardened men who write insane letters like that. But, Rose explains, Maya saw Georgia with the man in his battle fatigues, falling off her chair onto the filthy floor of the bar. It was as if a doll had fallen past a window from another floor, on the inside, Maya said. It had truly startled her, especially when she realized it was Georgie. All her straight, blue-black hair floating up into the window as she fell.

Rose stops in the middle of her worried explanation to stare at him. This is perhaps the worst dream she has ever had to endure, she thinks, but she always thinks that in a bad dream. She conjures ways to get out, even while the dream goes on. She has to leave the room to get a drink of water, to crouch down beside the kitchen cabinet and cry awhile, blocking the door. She will not let the Lover come in, or touch her arm or face, or hair, even though he taps at the door, even scratches at it with a pin. She will not let him step past the threshold. "So," she says with her voice contracted in her throat, "I thought you were not coming back from your desert for another month—"

"Rose—" he says through the door.

"When did you get back?" she says. "Or maybe you never left? Maybe you've been here with Georgia a long while. All along maybe."

"We had to come back early. Things were not exactly great. It was horrible really."

"So you thought you'd just spread it around. Is that it?"

—⁂—

"I found it. I've found it!" someone yells.

"How can you not look at it, Monsieur Bird?"

"I have to tell you something," he says, "about your sister. There are some things we have to face."

"Face them yourself," she says. "You have no idea what you face." She has not told him in the dream or in life, yet, about the illness. As far as she can determine, every one of them might live with it: Hibbie, herself, the Lover and his wife, her sister now, and even—Alfie. But William walks on water, even in her mother's grave. That is some remote relief.

—⁓—

The Lover wedges himself into the room and pulls her up toward him. He hunches his shoulders slightly, as he leans down to her, purses his lips. He is in the living room again rubbing his cheek where she has slapped him; and she is on the sofa in the opposite corner. He is fingering the letter. He looks at the scarf strung out on the floor. "We had another little thing, even before, when you were away with Maya. I'm sorry. It didn't mean anything. I'm sorry to upset you. For us to see you standing there, well . . . . you can imagine Georgie's shock. I came back to straighten it out. I was worried about both of you."

Rose looks at him without visible emotion. She knows this for a certainty. Unfortunately she can see herself in the mirror in the entryway. What is real and what is not? Her face is so white it is almost yellow—beyond ectoplasm, beyond the unreality of other lairs. If it were only streaked, she thinks, we might be able to roll out pastries on it. "My *sister's* shock?" she repeats. "Not mine?"

"I care about you, Rose."

"I heard you."

"Georgie called me at work. I tried to tell her it was you I loved. It's always been you, all along. She didn't sound herself at all. I didn't think she would get so emotional; she's always been so practical. She knows I've always been with you. I'm so sorry. It's my fault."

The Lover is holding the letter in one hand, face up on his knee. He is looking straight at her with those eyes she once thought beautiful. Now she sees they are like a Siberian Husky's. Wild, fixed as if with gunshot at the centers, coldly insane. She has not spoken to him since Hibbie showed her the hole in the wall. He knows nothing about it. Have you cost me my sister? she wants to say. Have you cost my nephew his mother? Have I cost you your life? And what about my child?

"I don't know why," Rose Reynolds says. "I don't know why you told my sister you love me when after all this I can't give a damn about you."

He looks struck down. "Oh Rose," he says. "How can you say that after all? It was an impulse, Rose. That's all it was. Try to see it."

Every word seems to be chiseled in the air. "She is my very own sister. Doesn't that mean anything to you?"

He looks at his hands, perplexed by what she's said. He tries to embrace her, but she will not. It is like a first hug from a teenager. She stares past his shoulder, fiercely, doggedly, fumbling away from him as though running on ice. She grapples her way to the other end of the couch again and slumps down.

She hears the Lover's footsteps going up the stairs and through the rooms of the cottage. She hears him opening the closets—something Rose was too afraid to do after seeing the so-called Rapist's letter. Georgie must have sounded that bad to him on the telephone, for him suddenly to come down here. A thought haunts Rose now: she didn't even know he was back. But Georgie knew. He is lying. That much is clear. Then she hears him coming down the steps.

"I know she's in this house," she says. Rose points at the dreamy scarf lying on the floor, long and twisted as an eel.

"Gone," he says, sitting down, lighting a cigarette. Now he's not looking at her again. "Maybe she's gone again. Maybe she's gone back to the flatlands. Maybe I've driven her out. It looks that way."

"Without her child?" They both look at the letter on the coffee table, the heavy script on it as if it had been written with a crayon.

"Ah," he says. "She will not have left William."

Rose Reynolds is looking at the scarf; the turquoise strip twists on the slate grey painted floor, with the rose-colored pattern. It looks like something that should be scaled.

"Caroline has the boys; she said the boys came over looking for George. It's not like her. The children were all alone and I didn't even know it. Georgia never leaves the boys alone. She would never ever do it, unless— something bad had happened to her." Rose is looking at his knee. She tries not to imagine it bent in front of her on the bed, but she can see the pants fall away in her imagination, the fine hairs on his knee beside her sister. She is wearing a long sleeved-shirt over her scraped arm. Still, he is studying her palm. "Are you hurt?" he asks. She will not tell him about Hibbie yet; she cannot.

She stands up and goes to the broom closet and very quickly opens it, but there is no one inside.

The riggings clank along the distant docks, she thinks, where often that man they call the Rapist sits with his hand stretched out, the man she dreamed about. Others sit there as well, but they do not have nicknames like that man does. Rose stands in the kitchen with her back to the Lover, her face hot and weeping in a veil of sweat, all over her forehead and neck. He has no idea how bad it is. She is too angry to tell him. She wants to go get Alfie, but she is afraid for him to see her like this. He is safe with Maya Lane. She can feel the Lover creeping up behind her, then his hands, unwelcome on her shoulder blades.

"I'm so sorry, Rosie," he says. His voice is like a hopeless bassoon in a long glass room, echoing. "You and I've been together for so long. You've been another wife to me. Please don't let my selfishness ruin it."

"Don't call me that," she says.

"So what shall I call you?"

"Nothing," she says. "Don't ever use my name again."

The Lover has no idea what she's been through this week at the hands of her once beloved husband. She doesn't know how to tell him what the doctor said may happen to nearly all of them. To hear it is not to imagine it. To see. There's a lot he doesn't know. That she will have to tell. He doesn't know her arm has been thrust through a cleft into outer space. Doesn't know that's what's sent her sister nuts, drinking, going to doctors, calculating left over and projected time, the possible collapse of their entire world. He thinks the whole thing revolves around him, his presence or even worse, he thinks, his absence. The way a lover thinks.

There is only so much Rose Reynolds can take. Rose will tell the Lover about this threat of disease when her sister is safe—if she is. Right now it would seem like revenge—to tell him now. Later Maya will say, You should have told him that you think revenge is sweet—when so very deservedly spent, on a scoundrel like him.

I'm no less the scoundrel, Rose thinks, though I never would have been, I never would.

Rose turns toward the chimney just in time to see something like a ping pong ball drop out of it. Out of the chimney it drops as if out of the hand of God. It makes a peculiar high, hollow sound as it hits. The Lover sees it, too. It is a long moment before either of them can move. And then quickly, as only a sister or a parent can, she rushes to the chimney and sticks her head into the abyss. On the way, as if she has been in slow motion, she has imagined it, her younger sister hanging there in the chimney by the neck from some outcropping, a ping pong ball clutched in her hand and finally released.

She looks up into the shaft, afraid to see her sister hanging naked above her with her bare feet, legs, the bottom of her rump and blue cut, only the raw tips of the breasts dripping from the form above. The face she can imagine, thrown back as if with ecstasy, as if Georgia would scream right in front of her with delight and sexual release. But the eyes stare straight ahead. They say: Don't say a word. The fear in Rose's gut is immense. In spite of everything, it is her little sister to whom she always turns even though her sister often is hard, or does not reply. She is afraid to see her sister's waxy feet. But instead she sees no feet, no throat or wrists. She sees instead a light off to one side in the dark column of the chimney and out of it her sister blithely calling. Incredibly, there is a large square of light, and in it there is the entrance to a room there, perhaps from the colonial days or later, it is fairly common here, a place for hiding runaway slaves. She has heard of this. In this part of the country, secret rooms and passages have been built early on for hiding children, whole families from the British, from the French, from warring tribes. Oddly she cocks her head. Without saying anything, she stands up into it and pulls herself up the jutting stones into the small brick room in the chimney.

"Whatever are you doing?" she hears the Lover shouting somewhere beneath her now, perhaps lounging in the far-off living room. And then she can see her, Georgia in this completely unknown place. Her sister sitting alive and well on a red pillow, surrounded by lilies and wine bottles, laughing as though completely mad. "Rosie! Look what I found!" Georgia screeches waving her hands around her head. "Here we are: safe in our very own house!" Georgia sobs again as Rose puts out her arms. "I read about rooms like this, but I didn't believe." She brays again with that hoarse sound only alcohol can make.

Far below they hear his voice, calling their names. "Rosie, Rosie, whatever is going on?" It is Rosie's name he calls this time; she can't keep from noticing. She holds her sister's hand.

"It's O.K.," she says. "There there, Georgie. In some way it's got to be

O.K."

"Snow is water running in place," the Lover will later say.

—⁓—

In the theatre, Georgia leans so closely in. "Do you think he's given it to you?" Georgia whispers too loudly and with such urgency, as the curtains draw away from the screen. Such a foolish extravagance, Rose is thinking, a curtain over a screen for a documentary. As if it were live theatre, as if this were Broadway.

"But Rosie, Rosie," her sister whispers. "The disease, do you think? He shoots up with dirty needles and everything— Do you think he has it, do you think?"

Rose blinks her eyes several times as if the movie had already begun, as if the camels were rising out of the distant hillocks, their nappy hides bleached by sun. She stares at the vacant ever-so-slightly textured screen. The auditorium is packed from front to back and into the balconies. She can't believe she has let her sister talk her into coming here.

"I'm sorry, Rosie," her sister whispers. "I'm always careful. Or almost anyway. I was careful with him. I can't be sick, can I? But Rose, but you. Why would you be careful? Hibbie's your husband. We can't even trust our own husbands now."

Rose does not turn to her sister, will never turn to her sister when Georgia speaks of such things. It would be too much for her sister to bear if Rose were actually listening, and then her sister would attack or abandon her just when Rose shows she cares. No, she would not turn to her sister now, though Rose herself would find it reassuring if she did.

Rose can feel that her eyes are floodwaters in her head as the lights begin to dim, and her voice is broken into little bits of glass. Who said that passing diseases was a solitary if amorous tragedy? "Listen! Now Hibbie says that it was only after Alfie was born that he started those things, not in law school after all. But who can believe him now? He said at first he did it because he knew he would be drafted, he thought he was going to die anyway. But now he's changed his whole story—"

"He's changed his story?" Her sister clutches her arm too tightly. Her voice is in agony as she thinks of it, for the first time. "Not Alfie?" she whimpers.

Rose is totally disemboweled by the worry of it. Perhaps she has become her sister the lawyer now, she is that stiff. "Shhh," Rosie whispers rather calmly, staring into the vacant screen. "Shhh now, shhh now. Alfie will probably be all right. Oh, don't you think?"

"Of course Alfie is all right," Georgia says a little frantically to Rose under her breath. Still they have not begun the show in which their lover will appear with his wife on an expedition about which both of them have heard relentlessly. Rose calmly watches Georgia's Adam's apple jug up and down in her neck as the lights go dim. "I would look after Alfie, Rose, you know I would, if anything happened. I could support them both— William and Alfie, too. You could come home, Rosie, if you got sick—"

"There, there now," Rosie says in their mother's gentle tone.

The Lover's tired face appears on the massive screen, and the sisters go white with fear at the sight of him. Now the camel under him is barely interesting.

—⁊⁊—

Her husband is a spot of green-black ink on the white tablecloth, running into mouldy threads with his illness.

This is Rose and the Husband's house. This is everything she owns: curtains, windows flooded with light. The floors shining in spots where they do not need refinishing, floors reflected in the polish on the tabletop, red dust everywhere like spider mites.

—∞—

The first thing Isabella did was hit her head on the dashboard when the jeep took a lurch. "That was stupid, Iz." I said.

"You hit yourself, too," she said. "You're just as stupid."

—∞—

Because Rose like Jane Anderson does not truly care about dust, cares instead about texture and color and books, and even more—it is dignity she cares about. No, no, not her own dignity. She did not care a thing about that in comparison. All the little children flowering seen and unseen and wretched somewhere, she and Jane Anderson grieve about that. She laughs sometimes at herself. Her Alfie. Perhaps her Husband has not lied to her this one time about such a precious thing. Tonight she will be home again; she will ask him again and again until she is certain. He cannot keep avoiding her.

She has gone to the place with him, where it began, to the crumbling concrete wall three stories high with the hole in it like a vacated dinosaur's egg. Put your arm through, the Husband said. He first knew of it when he was a student, he says. His embroidery of the story can only have begun in the last few years, that recently.

We are what we believe, she thinks. For a brief time anyway.

—∞—

Isabella walks off alone. I see her body disappear behind the earth from the waist up, and then, too, her head bobs down behind Dune 86.

—⁂—

How uncharacteristic, Rose is thinking in the balcony, for her sister to gush like this. The hall is long and narrow with the movie screen a blanket of light at the front. From the far right, the Lover enters. The Lover's Wife moves against the white background, suddenly a wash of red hair and sunburned complexion. She is very thin, stately, her hair in a French roll at the back of her head. Slender, not short at all, as was first conceived.

All Rose says to her beloved and traitorous sister, in a hoarse whisper, is this: "You would do anything, Georgie, to get me to come back to the flatlands. You would even offer to feed me with a spoon to get me to come back."

"Shush!" Someone says, "It's starting."

"I don't ever want to come back to that place."

"Oh, Rosie. That rotten husband of yours has surely killed us all dead."

At which, both sisters have broken into tears just as the house lights have gone down completely and a sound of trumpets has begun.

"But not William," Georgia begs.

"Not William surely!" Rosie says. "Maybe not Alfie."

"Not any of us! Maybe!"

And now Georgia has stood up, her blue-black hair flying, and thrown her rolled up program directly at the man sitting behind her seat. "Shush yourself! You patriarchal hog!" She hisses like a snake and sits down in a blaze of red rashes and embarrassment.

Together they sputter at the sound of it, laughing through their tears.

They cannot help themselves. There is the trumpet again announcing the start of the Lover's film, or the film about the Lover. It is a documentary, after all. In real life, perhaps everything will turn out all right.

That was always their mother's theory of comedy and tragedy: Anything worth anything should begin and end with trumpets, no matter how stark, no matter how funny. The trumpet jokes have pervaded their youth.

"It just figures," Rose sobs into Georgia's ear. "It just figures he would do that. Isn't it just my luck? Did you tell him about that—the trumpets?"

"No," Georgie says.

"Oh, I did—"

"Shush!" Someone says, "Would you please shut up."

"There are people dying in here!" Rose screams ever so quietly to herself. "Shush up? You say shush up?!" Georgia has hunkered down into her seat beside her. And there are the opening credits, all too suddenly.

The Lover has made a rather vulnerable looking appearance on the screen, and there, too, is the jeep; the camel beside it is chewing vigorously. A nasty looking beast surrounded by dunes, a blinding white undulating sand absolutely everywhere. Heat shimmers in waves of waterless air behind his stricken form. Rose, looking at him, can barely see a thing—there is so much moisture on her face.

—〰—

CHAPTER VI

THAT WAS THE WAY ROSE FOUND HIM, the Husband then, several weeks later very suddenly and unexpectedly, with Alfie at home and awake downstairs, in fact coming up the stairs after her, calling, "Mommy, Mommy, there's a scary part on TV. It's too scary for you, I think, Mommy, so I came up. Mommy, where are you? Mommy, why did you close the door so fast to Daddy's study? It's the scary part, come quick, the scary part to my movie."

Rose sits on the floor, her back shaking against the door of Hibbie's study, trembling from head to foot, barring the opening of the door so her child cannot come in. But there the Husband is: lying on the floor unnaturally that way; her husband next to the spike, as he called it, he was truly very dead. So many moments have occurred but these are the ones she will remember. She holds her own hands. All sound seems to have been blocked out and then it comes in undulating waves.

"Are you okay, Mommy?" Alfie whispers, through the door. "I thought I heard you crying. Are you feeling scared about the Blustery Day? Mommy, what about the Blustery Day? It's the scary part but it'll be over soon."

"Go downstairs, Alfie. I'll be right down." She is shaking with cold. Hibbie is lying on the floor. The floor runs under the door. The same floor she is sitting on, and the Husband is dead on it. Never to be spoken to or consulted or held or laughed with again. So much has happened that it begins to seem hilarious. She throws back her head and begins to laugh. She laughs again and again.

"Are you having fun in there with Daddy, Mommy?" Alfie asks.

"Shhh," she says. "Don't wake Daddy up, Alfie." There's a certain uncontrolled shaking in the arms and hands. It's best to sit on our hands at such times. "I've got to call Aunt George right now. Please wait downstairs for me."

"But it's the scary part, please come quick."

"I'm coming, honey, please go down now and put it on hold. Please go down. For Mommy, go down and I'll be right there. I need a moment now, Alfie." She is surprised that he can even understand what she is saying, she is shaking so.

"But, Mommy. I can't go down, Mommy. It's the scary part."

"Please, Alfie. Please, please. Wait downstairs for me." She is in tears now. She can tell that much about herself.

"Mommy! I'm going to be frightened without you there!"

"Please, Alfie, do what I say! I'm frightened, too."

"I want Daddy," Alfie cries out. "I want Daddy if you're going to be that way. Daddy! Mommy won't come down for the scary part and I have already started to cry."

"Alfie, please!" she whines, or is it harsh? She can't register her own tone now. She means not to scare her little boy. "Go downstairs and I'll be right there. Daddy can't come out, Sweetie. Please, Alfie, please, for Mommy. Listen to Mommy just this once. Please." Yes, it is a whine, a plea.

"But I want Daddy to come out." It is going to be a tantrum on the other side of the door. Occasionally it is, and then there is no stopping it. This is the turning point; she has seen it before. She cannot bear a tantrum now. She cannot stand to hear the wailing now. She would wail herself. There will be no stopping the floodwaters then.

"Alfie, stop," she says. Her normal voice is back. She is an authority now on child rearing, on telling children that their Daddies are dead, though perhaps right now is not a good time. Her voice is perfectly clear.

"I'm coming down with you. I didn't mean to leave you out here during the scary part. You know I'd never hurt your feelings on purpose, my Sweetie. We'll go downstairs and call Auntie George." But Aunt George is out—perhaps with the Lover. How would Rose know by now? The Lover would seem to be able to appear nearly anywhere in the world. The telephone machine reports it rather curtly, Rose thinks, considering the circumstance that her sister is out. "*If you like talking to a machine, leave your message please.*"

She quietly shuts the door to the study and goes downstairs with her child. For moments, hours perhaps, she lives in a wash of pastels, falling into the images on the television screen, holding her warm sturdy boy on her lap, rocking him, trying to conceal her silent tears in the crown of his silky hair. The curtains float out above the room, lift the room sky high; and then a second time; they live their own lives. Alfie pools into a warmth on her lap, cries out from time to time to watch the floodwaters whirling around the small almost human pig-like creature who cries because an owl is shooting a stream of intellectual nonsense at him while he the tiniest most innocent Piglet is sure to die by drowning almost immediately if owl does not help him on a very blustery and scary day.

You must call the police, it occurs to her, *you must call the police right this minute.*

"It must be hard," she says silently, "to drown in words and water at the same time. . . . But then I wouldn't know," she thinks, "I have been drowning not in words but in Hibbie's silence for so long. . . ."

For compassionate words, she thinks, right now, I would give my life.

She nestles around her only child: perched there so happily on her lap, watching his movie, chewing on the back of his fist as the tiny pig swirls about in the whirlpool. The harbinger owl whirls overhead in an outpouring of irrelevant conversation. Through the soft shirt on his back, she breathes her baby's soothing scent.

And if he did not inherit the disease, do the times he used his father's toothbrush count against him? She has read of that possibility.

"I'm hungry, Mommy," Alfie says, suddenly, so suddenly that she doesn't know whether she has gone to sleep or not. "Could we have dinner, Mommy?"

"Why, of course!" she says, and jumps up. An image of something sticking out from under Hibbie's desk fills up her head and disappears. "I'm sorry, honey, it's just so late, I forgot what I was about." Together they have a healthy dinner in front of the nighttime television set. She cannot go upstairs now, can no longer consider it more than a bad dream or a cartoon. Hibbie is a dead body upstairs in his study. It is the first time she has neglected her husband, she thinks. What a juggling act. "I like this movie," she says, for they are watching it again, perhaps for the third time. "I like it very much."

"It's a Blustery Day," Alfie says, snuggling his head up to her neck. His hair stands on end a moment, caught in static electricity, tickling the very tip of her nose.

"A Blustery Day. . . ." she says vaguely, holding him as tightly as she can without hurting him. "That it is, my little elf." She is almost in tears again. "We'll remember this day a very long while, my poor sweet elf."

There they sat. She watched it again with him, the great flood, and then they watched it again until it was time for bed, and then again until it was midnight. "I think it's time for bed, Mommy," Alfie said.

No one mentioned Daddy; even the little boy knew not to mention him somehow.

When her child was asleep, she stood next to the desk where she had so often stood running her hands over the Husband's arms and shoulders while he worked. She was a failure certainly, she thought, certainly she did not know what to say to her child. And now that her baby was asleep downstairs where he wanted to be on this one night, on the sofa, now she did not know what to say to his father lying there upstairs half under the desk.

Then, without dialing it seemed, Rose had called the hospital. "My Husband is asleep," she said, "I can't wake him up." They would send someone right away. She couldn't be sure she had given the right address. In time the ambulance would wail, she decided, if she had given the right address. She could not bring herself to sit down in the chair, nor to leave the room. Why did you do this? she cried just as she supposed any wife would have done. Why did you do this to my little boy? He needs a daddy, he needs you. You have hurt my little boy more than anyone can ever know. While she waited, she kicked the Husband repeatedly in the side of his best soft suit. She kicked him until later on they would say he appeared to have been bruised posthumously, they said. She would have laughed, if she had not been crying so.

—w—

"I kicked him with the toe of my shoe," she said rather quietly. Policemen shuffled back and forth. The ambulance men came into the room. How surprising, she thought, that there is light coming into this room.

"Why did you do that, Mrs.?" they asked.

"Where is my little boy? What will I tell my little boy?" she cried. "He doesn't know."

"Why did you do that, Mrs.?" they said.

"Now I <u>start</u> to understand," she whimpered. "All those years I thought it was my fault. He tried to tell me a few months ago. I understand now, I can understand it all now. It was this."

"What did you understand, Mrs.?"

Then she looked him straight in his coroner eyes. Small trains ravaged the Coroner's pupils then, carrying the body away. "Have you?" she said to him, the Coroner. "Have you ever been much for lies?"

"He has bruises all up and down one side," came one of the other voices.

"I didn't kill him," she said very quietly. "I wish I had now. You must understand: now I wish I had killed him, now and a long time ago. But that would have been a lie, wouldn't it? To take someone else's life away, someone you actually loved—that would have led to further lies. I didn't kill him, I wasn't smart enough. I never understood in time that he needed it. I just kicked him in the side. I could never kill anything. I wish I could have killed him now. But you see I never believed in it, in leaving anyone, or making them go away for good."

Who were these people anyway in Hibbie's room?

"There there, poor lady," the Coroner said. "There's nothing wrong with kicking someone who's already dead. I expect he needed a good one in his life by the looks of this."

"That's not why I'm crying!" she shouted almost angrily. "Shhh—don't wake up my little boy."

"Your housekeeper is here with your little boy. Mrs. Anderson came in just as we arrived. She said you thought to call her; it's easy to forget how well you're doing when these things occur. She is looking after your little boy downstairs just as you asked her to."

"Mrs. Anderson?" Rose said in alarm. "I don't know any Mrs. Anderson. Oh yes," she said. "Thank you very much. Jane Anderson has Alfie now.

Yes, Jane Anderson is my saint. She is a saint you know. Alfie doesn't know, does he? He doesn't know about his Dad, does he?"

"I don't think so, Mrs. It doesn't seem so anyway. It's hard to know what children know."

"That's good," Rose said, sitting down abruptly on the floor again, her back sliding down the wall like a doll that is made to play dead by a greater force. "I don't think Alfie should ever know his dad is dead." She is rattling a bit, she thinks, when she talks now. She can't seem to help that part of it. Now she is talking much too fast, or perhaps not very fast at all. "Alfie had some idea of course last night. Just as I did when I saw him there. I knew he wasn't breathing anymore. At least I saw it. Already when I found him, he was cold. I had a chance of believing Hibbie was dead. Alfie didn't even know on the very day. I knew it but I couldn't believe, if you see what I mean. I couldn't imagine that he would do such a thing—to all of us. He was a very good kind man, you see. At times he was truly gentle and elegant. And—his fingers when I touched them just like that; they were just like popsicles. I started to cry, I couldn't stop until Alfie made me watch the scary movie so he wouldn't be afraid. I had to stop for Alfie's sake. I didn't want him to be afraid."

The detective picked the syringe up off the floor with his blazing handkerchief—just as she and Hibbie had watched someone very like him do in the detective shows they liked so much. But this time it was a stranger taking her hand. It was not Hibbie at all. Hibbie was looking toward the baseboard underneath all the furniture on the opposite wall. "How could I have been so dumb? How could I have been so dumb?"

"There there," the Coroner said. "Poor lady."

"You must have so much misery in your life," she said to the Coroner suddenly, looking into the landscape of his eyes, the tiny railway running there in each eye, round and round. There was the small wedding party at the station now, and the going away valise. "So much misery you see every day. Poor lost man."

"No," the Coroner said. He patted her shoulder, then her arm.

"An obsession with death, my own wife said to me. 'You are so obsessed with death,' my wife said just last week again. 'Why can't you be a normal doctor, tend to some guys who still breathe?' But it's not like that at all, Mrs. I'm not seized that way, Mrs., like they say I am." He cleared his throat. "I'm hooked, if I'm obsessed with anything—I'm hooked on getting over grief." The stranger held her hand, a coroner.

A terrible feeling went down her spine; her stomach fell in on itself. A familiar voice, the Lover's, seemed to catapult itself across the room then. She looked up at her Lover as investigative reporter, sometimes explorer, coming hurriedly through the door, in his bright white shirt, and the new Armani coat. She stared at him quite blankly, and put her head against the Coroner.

The Lover, the Traitor as she now called him in her mind, addressed the crowd of reporters in the room. She had no idea how all these people had been invited into Hibbie's study, into her home. " Can't you keep the jack out of here—until the Wife gets straightened out! Show a little respect, Macs. Yeah, I heard it downtown on the way to the club."

"It's the Deputy Attorney General dead in there for shriek's sake," the reporter said. "Don't tell me you're gonna pass this story up while I give it a blank. And you, not back in the country two weeks."

The Lover's shoes approached soundlessly across the carpeted room. Why, she thought, it's nearly the biggest room in the house. It is nearly bigger than the living room. The Lover crouched down next to her. On her other shoulder, she felt his all too familiar hand. She could not look at him. "Hibbie," she cried into the Coroner's chest. "My own dear Hibbie is dead."

"Go on now, leave her alone," the Coroner said. "She's in good hands."

"Hibbie is dead," she said again. And so it must have been, for there he lay in his tweed jacket and beige corduroy pants, one arm pulled out of the coat and the sleeve rolled up and all his beautiful arm exposed.

The Lover stood there a very long moment, looking broken-hearted for her. But she could not open her eyes without seeing her sister spread out wide and graceless for him. At the touch of his hand on the crown of her head, her stomach nearly rose up into her throat.

In real life it was always so, as her grandmother had told her. One disaster leads rapidly into another; it seems none of them will stop when the disasters begin. At least in my life, she was thinking. She couldn't account for other lives right then. The way it went on and on made her know it now: it really was happening. It was too horribly real to have been a fantasy. The Lover lingered beside her, hovering.

"Please go out!" she rasped. "Get out! You horrid newsboy leech!"

And then he, too, miraculously was gone.

"It's not your fault you kicked him, Mrs.," the Coroner said.

"Hibbie," she cried. "My Hibbie is dead." And it must have been true for there he lay in his tweed jacket, one arm pulled out of the coat.

"It's not your fault you kicked him," the Coroner said. "It's not your fault."

—∭—

There is no doubt that the oak floors of Hibbie's study need polishing. A little dust is on everything. The Lover is away with his wife in the desert again, gone for nearly three months now—since Hibbie's death. This week Jane Anderson has come to help clean, and in the middle of the sorting and throwing out, or perhaps it is the start, Rose Reynolds has sat herself right down beside Jane Anderson and has rested her head on the bottom step of the stairs. There is no need for tears; they are everywhere. And that nice Indian man who lives with Angie now on the third floor that Rose has had to rent out, he has come down to try to get the hopeless vacuum cleaner bags into the vacuum cleaner where she and Jane Anderson have crouched. All three of them are engaged so seriously around a task both futile and ridiculous. Every one of them knows it, all three of them, even before they start: it is all the wrong fit.

Even Jane Anderson who took care of houses did not care a speck for dust. She cared for the people within these modest homes; she arranged their things until their cells took on a similar crystalline structure, an orderly one.

They will reclaim the house to pay her husband's debts, now that her husband is dead. It creeps up on Rose; she sets it aside. No he was not truly dead, only in her soul; perhaps that was a way to look at it. A spot of black ink seeping in and through. And that nice Indian man who lives on the third floor paying her enough money so that they may eat, has shrugged: What does a few days' notice mean to me? He says, If you have to come to me this night because the house is sold, that will be time enough, in the way time is. Do not trouble yourself. I will find some place to live. He sits down and plays his sitar for her.

And he was not dead, the husband, her friend, who had married her. He was gone. Well, she had admitted that much anyway. And the other one, the Lover, was in the desert looking for buttons, or what not. What not, she said. We are all reduced to what not eventually, and what more was there to be said? After all this time married to Hibbie, now a month has gone by and she has never been back to his grave. On walks, Alfie says tearfully, *That house. Daddy must live in a house like that now. He lives in a dead people's house. Mommy, do you think Daddy's happy there?*

And the truly peaceful gentleman from India cooks eggs for her out of kindness, because he wants to, because in some way he has come to love her very much. Their eyes meet, though they themselves will never touch. He brings her eggs with hot spices in them while she sits in her living room, flooded with light that streams in through the window, through the crimson lids that refuse to move from her eyes, filling her whole red cranium. "With red pepper," he says.

"A little." She smiles inwardly. She cannot tell how much of her emotion has reached her skin. Even the cleaning lady, her friend, has stroked her head. There all three of them gather around this device. She will take the curtains with her, too, when she has sold the house, even if she has to take a hammer and knock down the valance boxes herself.

—⚹—

Unlike the rest of us, Ramon doesn't slip in sand. When he takes off a shoe, Isabella gazes at his arch and then the long slender brown second toe rising up over the first. The sand pours from out the interstices. Iz glances sideways at me and then at him. I am looking at my wife staring into the pupils of a man soon to be dead. Or so I imagine it.

—⚹—

"How can I not worry, Georgie," Rose Reynolds cries, "when I suspect someone's not telling me the truth? Isn't that cause for worry, even in someone as mesmerized by life as you?"

"I didn't know, Rose, that he cared so much about you. I swear. I thought you knew."

—⁂—

So far, Rose Reynolds and the child have escaped any signs of the disease. Though she begins to worry about the child, his listlessness, and his loss of weight. Today Rose is awash. *Get some rest, Rose; it will be good for him.*

Rose has no idea how she will make it through the night without his little body pressed up to hers if he needs her, or without the certainty of his existence in the next room. She relies on having to have that strength he must draw from her. With Alfie around, no! She cannot afford for one moment to sink into despair! It is a triumph that Alfie has wanted to do anything after the loss of his father; he took it so hard.

—⁂—

Isabelle goes over to the other tents to talk to the men. Her red pixie hair is ablaze against the sand, her white clothes. She has befriended Pierre's lanky girlfriend, Anne. They sit around laughing while I am drawing charts. We have covered this much ground, but the ground is shifting always and the bottom is a layer of shale. When the dunes part it is like a sidewalk of brimstone has opened in front of Richardson.

—⁂—

CHAPTER VII

FTER THE HUSBAND'S DEATH AND THE INCIDENT WITH GEORGIA, Rose has stopped responding to the Lover's frantic calls. She has sent back his letters and even his flowers. Remanded to: *From Whence It Came.* Finally the Lover says that it is time to stop, as if Rose has not now said it repeatedly after his great offense. It is as though nothing has ever gone wrong in the dunes for him, the way he speaks. He calls by way of radio. The air scratches between them in nearly perceptible lines. She pictures endless, whirling, arid dunes that sweep down into a gaseous sea something like the dunes she knows so well on the Cape. Amid the stone roses of northern Africa, the dunes he frequents bear no vegetation of the kind she had been allowed to appreciate. It is not that she has not wanted to go there with him. Still, she could not, would not, leave her child as the Lover and his wife have done with theirs, a boy and a girl. Heartless, Rose thinks. She pictures him there, where last she heard in writing from him. She would ride across the dunes if she could; it pains her to the marrow. *To the marrow!* As her mother used to say. Now he actually speaks:

"It's just that you're too visible now, Rose," he says. "The relationship is too viable—now that your husband is dead."

She wants to laugh at the irrelevance of what he says; she has been putting him off for so long now, trying to inform him of the end. "Too viable? Too visible?" She pictures him in his tent at night working his way through the alphabet, stuck now in the V's, trying words to end it with her while wild animals are outside strolling in sweeping gestures through white sand. Where is his wife during this conversation? In the next cot, or in bed with him? Rousseau's paintings come to mind: Lion and Man—the latter off balance in elegant robe. What will he say next when he comes to the hideous W's? Whimper whimper, I withdraw, with all due respect, I have had a small and wondrous moment with your sister, I must therefore welch out on you. I am not a man for words.

Her mind threatens to wander off, but the distant effect of a radiophone is scratching in her ear. Oddly he does not mention her sister. Perhaps her sister meant nothing to him. An added offense. She cannot bring herself to tell him what she fears. Without further evidence, why speak? "How did you ever stand such ambivalence all these years, Rose?" he asks. "I never got it before. Now I've finally understood you. For the first time I am actually torn. But, we were both married then."

"Fine," she says, "what a fine thing to say now, after Hibbie is gone." She puts down the telephone without telling him. Who can say such things to someone who is not listening? My little son is sick. You've been with me for longer than anyone, except for my sister. Please come home. She asks the questions she has for him, of herself. Do you feel better now? To have hurt everyone so thoroughly? No, I will not take you back again, no matter how many times you vacillate and beg.

And her paintings have never been better received though there seems to be little enough money in it. Museum work. For all the acclaim, one would have thought there might have been at least enough to support herself and one small child in something other than abject poverty. Soon they would move into a place she did not want to think about. She feels tired, as though something immense and immovable were strapped to her back.

—⁓—

233

Alongside the road: a long black semi-truck. She will buy Alfie another stuffed animal, to ease his mourning for his father, to ease his frequent sore throats, headaches and tummy aches, so frequent now. It is a small way to ease his many pains, the sadness and confusion in his small, trusting face. The bookshelves of his tiny new room are stuffed with animals she can ill afford. She buys them anyway for the moment of delight in her child. His little body presses into hers for just one moment of happiness before he begins to cry again. I miss Daddy. I miss Daddy. She dreams the child is running after the man in her sleep, when the child isn't waking her up with his screams. So this is the bottom, Rose tells herself. This is the vortex and apex of everything.

—⁂—

"Those drop-off boys, stoned again in the clouds—drifting and drinking tea, listening to the Police," Annie says sardonically. Now that the usual airdrop has failed we take measures. In the morning they head out with the jeep to the only known oasis in the sector: Gerard and Richardson. They saw it in the rearview mirror, they said, and reversed all the way back into camp. "What's the matter? You're the ones on the way to the H2O," I tried to laugh. "Don't tremble at the oasis, crouched over your own reflections, boys. Nothing too narcissistic out there . . . .Bare shoulders in a wet black pool. Don't forget to bring some back." Even after all my good-natured prattling, they were still speechless with fear, staring at me.

"Stop staring at me," I said. "Have you gone insane? I said I'd rather go. You refused. Do you want me to go then? I volunteer. You can stay here."

"This is insane," Ramon stepped in. "They must take the water to get the water."

"We must *keep* the water," I said. "The two of them must *fetch* the water." I sit down on the canister. Their eyes pivot like they're linked to Ramon's by remote control. "What's the matter? You've never seen a man sitting on a water barrel in this your private desert? Here I am. There you are. You'll be back in three hours. Without you we're dead. It's not like you don't have your canteens with you, and the cigarettes, and the chewing gum to generate spit. And two or three liters of your contraband you think I don't know you have. There's two of you, then there's all the rest of us. That's us. Better get going quick."

"We split it," Ramon cries out. "Of course. That is what you meant to say. We merely misunderstood."

"We do not," I say. "We do not send more water than that out to a watering hole." I hunker down on the tin and put the gun on my knee. "It's very simple, Ramon," I say. "Now that our tiny footprints might as well be the tracks of your favorite little sand grouse on Cape Cod. Even Piers sees the logic of it." Even Piers stands directly behind me now and nods. "Ramon? Richardson? Gerard?"

"But we have enough. To us it would make no difference. To them, if they need it, it makes everything."

But I refuse to budge. "What if they don't come back?" I must ask unpleasantly. "We won't have enough to go out again in search of them or anything. We would have enough to get through if the plane comes." As soon as they leave, a moderate wind begins, and then the drifting masses of dust. By mid-morning they have not come back.

Before noon a layer of sand hovers over the ground as far as we can see. Below our knees everything disappears. And then we see the dust storm coming at us like I'd dreamed it would: the great wall of China moves toward us. With horrifying speed, we drop tents, gather up, and take refuge in the vehicles. Inside, everything has never ceased by day to bake. Ramon sways back and forth in agony calling out the names of his friends and relatives. Iz will not say a thing. Somewhere very close are the other vehicles. Someone gigantic is throwing buckets of sand at us. We wrap shirts around our heads

"I'd rather it had been a peace pin—" Piers says, "if it had to be recent history, I mean. I'm so sorry I've been such an ass."

—⁓—

On the road to the Cape, teddy bears with artillery belts are propped against the dusty side of the semi-truck facing the road. Orange cats with suction cups to glue their paws and bellies to the interior windows of vehicles. The toy cats look to have been disemboweled then stuffed again. What kinds of truckers carry such things? But there is a beautiful one, full and loving and brown, big enough for a child to sit on top of, almost big enough for the bear himself to seemingly wrap his arms around a little child who has his own easel and loves to paint, a little child who says now that he is just too tired. The car is pulling over now.

She is getting out to find the roadman's face. He stares at her most peculiarly. For a moment she thinks she has paint on her face. It wouldn't be the first time. Or frosting. Or tears. She wipes at her cheeks. Perhaps she is crying.

Why is his thick hand on her arm? No one has touched her now for months. No one's arm has moved around her shoulders. Has she gazed at the roadman much too long? He is gazing at her strangely. No adult has scrubbed her back or touched her hair or shaken her hand or given her a cup of coffee or held out the toothpaste. Or handed her the toast. Not even a sister, or a friend. Maya has been gone now to Copenhagen for six months, not to return now for nearly another year. Her sister has gone home, having done not very much comforting anyway—talking endlessly about the gloomy possibilities and bringing up the Lover again. Troubles have always brought out the rigidity, even the viciousness in her Georgia as though she had been too suddenly roused from sleep—she wakes up swinging, when she does wake. Always Rose has managed to forget that fact until repeatedly it takes her by surprise, especially now when she has needed least to be surprised. "I'll just take this large brown bear, it is so completely sweet. It almost seems alive."

"Usually, in solitude," her grandfather recalled, "the prisoner commences screaming after a few weeks. I myself cannot recall my own screams. It is other prisoners' voices we recall."

Now then, enough of that, her grandmother seems to say. Let's not think up unhappiness unless it's to a purpose—a purpose right here and now.

"Take the big bear. You have a child, I suppose. I'll give it to you. For your child. It's not for you, is it?"

"Oh no," she stammers, noticing him fully for the first time. She looks away. He is most incredibly terrifying to her as he stands there beside the red stripe on the long black vehicle. Rows of corrugated tires spin in place beside him, and all the black mud flaps hang down under the muddy belly of the truck. His face is stationary beside her as she looks up into it. It is like a badger's in its shape somehow, almost imperceptibly pockmarked from neck to chin, over the healthy cheeks and nose, inflicted with some former agony perhaps akin to her own. Perhaps only an artist would have noticed it, would have looked so close. He is peering at her with great seriousness.

"But the toy isn't for me!" Rose Reynolds exclaims, intensely embarrassed in the act of observing him.

"It would be all right—" He clears his throat. His eyes are soft anyway and persuasive, "if it *was* for you. You'd be surprised how many grownups want their own. As you can see, I have a few." He laughs then a little self-consciously. "You look troubled. Take the bear, for your boy or girl. A pretty little girl like you. It's okay. Like I said I've got a few." He laughs again, a sparkle in his honeyed eyes under the brown and gentle furry brows. Hibbie used to sparkle like that, she thinks, whenever Hibbie was about to tell a joke.

"I can't sleep with all of these bears," he proffers, "but I like to curl up with a few."

She looks up at him, into the amber eyes, past the skin that perhaps no one but a painter would have noticed anyway. There is a real softness there in the way he's healed himself. His hands are broadly veined, too. He's tucked his thumbs under the overall bib of the bear she thinks Alfie would want. He cradles it in front of his own flat blue shirt. She smiles now, just a little, seeing him shifting his feet in the gravel and smiling down at her. He must be at least a foot taller than she is. Behind them, cars whip by, round the curve. A speck of dust has found its way into her eye. And quickly after the grain of sand has come a tear without emotion; and then innocently enough emotion follows too easily on top of that: the thought of her Alfie maybe being sick rushes forth, perhaps terribly sick, irreparably sick, horridly sick, ... The thought of Alfie's rounded little body snuggled onto her lap and into the corner of her elbow, his face buried in under her chin, his own arm held out and shaking as they took his blood just this week, the sweet scent of his hair, the thought of his little adamant laugh and his funny funny songs, his little funny funny ways and then of his tiny fingers being buried forever in the earth has overwhelmed her in a wave.

"I'm sorry I don't have a chair," he says. He helps her to sit down. Each day she walks as if completely submerged, her throat quivering as she thinks of her sick child. No one needs to tell her it might be true, although now she waits for official denial of the worst, hoping with her last hope that someone official will tell her it is nonsense, that she is nonsense itself to think of it. It is as if she herself is drugged with the wait.

Prove it a dream! She thinks: Make this life more real than what we soon may be.

Tonight Alfie will not be with her. Only visiting, only visiting a friend, she tells herself. Like any normal happy little boy might be. "Of course he should stay. Rest," the mother of Alfie's friend had said to her that morning. "What a hard time you've had. Go home. Recover yourself."

But I can't rest when he's away from me, she wanted to say. Please invite me, too. Please.

She could hardly bear to leave him at the door the way he clung to her and yet wanted so to stay overnight, be independent with the other boys on his friend's birthday night. In the end he had decided to stay. Now there is nothing to do but wait for his call or his return. She will go to get him the instant he calls, if he does. Perhaps she could go to bed and sleep heavily for once, undisturbed by his cries. She could sleep with the phone under her pillow in case he called. *Recover yourself.*

The Stranger has a deep voice. "I haven't had my dinner yet." He points. He drives a dark green army jeep. There it is, parked oddly beside the truck, which will remain here, he says, tied to its road at night.

"Oh, you drive a jeep," Rose says lightly and most uncharacteristically as if her voice were cast into her by a ventriloquist, as if she might wave her arms around with someone else's hand up under her skirt, or a set of strings attached to her knuckles and hips. Perhaps none of this is true. She has never been one to notice automobiles. She stands beside the huge cylinder of white and black fur she has been sitting on, aware for the first time of the giant head staring down at her with the one huge black eye bigger than a tire for the mammoth truck.

The Stranger with the kindly eyes has taken out a tissue now from the glove compartment of his jeep. He has dabbed at her cheeks with it and pressed her into his wide shoulder. He is a tall man, broad shouldered, big through the chest, too narrow at the waist and legs, almost as if two men had been stuck together. And stuffed, she thinks, amusing herself, coughing a few sobs down. Stork legs. It is almost inconceivable that he can walk so smoothly in that broad, light blue shirt and those pencil jeans. Then almost inexplicably she has followed him. All it took was his hand around hers. The scent of orchids surrounds them both. "Rosie?" he says. "You said your name was Rose? Would you like to go out with me just to get a bite to eat? A cup of coffee and a sandwich? A bowl of soup? I know an okay place. "

Somehow the jeep makes it all better, jauntier somehow. More unreal in this *pentimento*. It makes her try to forget what she never will. Perhaps because it looks like something out of a war movie. She tries to cheer herself: life as movie as comic relief.

—⚏—

She nods at the ground, trembling with horror that she has given her name to a stranger. That she has her face pressed into the Stranger's blue cotton shirt again, that she can smell the scent of sage in the soap and shaving lotion the Stranger must have used that morning when he shaved.

"Whatever it is, Rosie," he says. "Don't cry anymore now. You're in good hands now. There there, that's better now. I'll fix you something to eat now." He says it again and again: *now*. As if now is already here. Then already they are there; the wind has already whipped past the open windows of the vehicle; and the stiff carriage has jolted her up and down until she has actually bumped her head once on the roll bar, until he has made her fasten the belt across her lap. She had thought they were going to a restaurant. Isn't that what he said? Before long, she has entered the slightly acrid air of his apartment. *There must be a leak of natural gas somewhere, a gas cooking stove perhaps.* And then she sees it, yes, the stove with four tiny black burners like the dead eyes of twins staring out at her from the flat white plain, and then, too, the central pilot light. Now the Stranger actually makes her laugh a little by throwing a speckled egg into the fragile air above the eroded black and white linoleum. He catches the egg behind his back. Then, not unlike the Indian man, he has fed her scrambled eggs, putting them onto his own fork and gently pressing them into her mouth. Unlike the Indian man he has held the wineglass to her lips. But even as she drinks she is thinking other thoughts. I am alone, she thinks. I am alone and betrayed. By a living man and a dead one. By my sister as well. *And if I'd not had the Lover, she thinks, it would have been the same for Alfie, and me,* she thinks. *It was my husband gave it to us, not a lover. And if I'd not had the Husband,* she thinks, *I'd never have known my Alfie. And now she will have to speak to the Lover again. Locate him in the desert. To tell him the terrible future, the substance of disease. Because she was too much of a coward to tell him, even in her dreams.* She swallows hard. For the first time in years she thinks about her father, off somewhere with the new young wife, unattainable. For her child's sake she has tried. *Can you help me Daddy? I really need you now.* Yet, she can find no reason why her nephew will not survive without his mother, cousin, uncle, and aunt. His aunt's lover who once held him high over his head. His aunt's lover's wife, and one or two of their children. A picture of a vast open countryside interrupted by graves opens up in front of her. She can see her nephew dancing on water in a yellow coat.

The Stranger waits patiently, it seems. It is as if he is in the doorway of another room, seen at an angle, while she thinks these thoughts. She will not think, refuses to do so, about her own little boy's frail hands, the changes in his once robust face and chest, the appearance of the blue vein like a river at her baby's temple. Inside her head she listens instead to her little boy singing. *Fwoggy went a courtin' and he did go, a huh, a huh.* These are desperate measures she tells herself. Next week they will know the results of his tests. And hers. She is sitting in the Stranger's bathroom, her head in her hands, listening to the liquid running out of her body. It runs, too, out of her eyes. "Don't come in!" she exclaims as the door starts to open. Softly but audibly.

But he has come in anyway. The Stranger squats down in front of her.

—w—

These then are the flora of the desert: where the Lover lives: algae and lichens, drought evading plants, desert perennials. The former drying into the merest skins, waiting for the reappearance of a life giving water. The second living its entire life only in the presence of a short-lived moisture. The third, the succulents, with a sap that will not rise into its outermost branches.

—w—

The two of them are pressed much too close in this small embarrassing space. Her face is red, startled; she can feel it flush. He unbuttons and pushes his sleeves upward on his heavily veined arms. Some of his brown hairs stand for a moment and then bow down again like foreign priests. He has hunkered down, his face right before her, placing his naked wrists on her bare knees and gently taking hold of her hands. "But I'm not— Finished—"

"So?" the Stranger says. "You can talk, can't you? Here," he says. The Stranger pulls a handful of toilet paper off the reel. His face is directly in front of hers as he perches there on the backs of his own legs, his denim knees sandwiched around her own bare ones. She turns her head away from him, blazing in the face, her elbows wooden against her sides, the paper dangling from her fingertips. But when she looks at him again she finds that the Stranger has fixed his gaze so securely upon her eyes that now a sense of privacy actually floods into her, even as he places his hands on her kneecaps. Quickly she puts the folded paper between her legs and stands up. But he does not rise, as his eyes had indicated to her. She feels his eyes on her lower parts as she drifts in front of him. Hastily she pulls up her underpants and drops the hem of her skirt. When she has flushed, he stands up and takes hold of her wrist again, just as he did beside the road.

"No," she says, "I can't. I might be sick. You don't understand, I only came because I was afraid to be alone."

With his other hand now, he is fiddling with the dials in the tub. "Here," he says. "We'll have some hot water now."

These then are the breeding birds of the Sahara Desert: the sooty falcon; the sand partridge; the houbara bustard; the cream-coloured courser; the crowned sand grouse, and all the larks: hoopoe, bar-tailed desert, ordinary desert, Dunn's, Temmink's horned, black-crowned finch, and thick-billed lark; the brown-necked raven; the house bunting and trumpeter finch, the pale crag martin and desert sparrow, scrub and desert warblers, the fulvous babbler, and the various wheatears: desert, white-crowned black, morning and hooded. . . .

—m—

There is a tan on the back of the Stranger's neck just above his light blue t-shirt where a summer sun has warmed him more than once. She thinks perhaps that he has been harvesting grain on some idyllic farm. And so thinking she is swept back into her family again, a family gathering among grandparents and cousins and mad uncles reading Joyce.

No one can hear it but her voice has become an inner incantation, praying. Even though no one hears it, it is the only real voice in the room, this voice inside her head. The rest would seem to be happening far away, inconsequentially. Don't let Alfie die, she trembles to herself. "Why don't you take that off?" the Stranger suddenly says. She almost jumps at the sound of it. His fingers are moving emphatically down the buttons of her blouse. One at a time they come out of their buttonholes and air slips in, in shocking zones of cold. There are tiny nearly imperceptible purple spots at the backs of his eyes, she thinks, beneath the Stranger's kind eyes. She stands with her back to the wall and watches her bare arms out in front of her, waving around—in weakest protest, she thinks. Perhaps not enough to be noticeable, she thinks, to anybody else. It is as though she were watching a home movie from the back of a photography gallery. His fragrant shirt is up against her again, pressing against her as he feels her back in the intense heat of his apartment bathroom. And then under his broad hands and nimble fingers, her bra has opened for him, at its little fastener in the front and both her breasts have fallen loose into his grasp. Then without pause her skirt is unbuttoned, too, behind her at the waist. His arms come around again. He cups her buttocks as the colored skirt falls to the floor around her ankles. It is as if she has risen from the center of a flower. He steps back and looks down at her without smiling. His lips are pursed with determination. One of his sleeves slips down his forearm again as he takes hold of her nearly bare hip. As he kneels she can feel his breath moving down the front of her, zigzagging from place to place, the toilet bowl at the back of her legs. He slips her underpants down her thighs now and picks up her feet, one by one, positions her legs and then hangs the panties and the skirt behind him on the doorknob.

—⁓—

These then are the winds and air masses of the desert. These then are the many snakes and reptiles of the desert. These then are the baking temperatures of the daytime, the searing white disk of sun in the unending sky above you. These are the freezing shakes of the nighttime. These are the sentiments gone mad in the desert. These are the burgeoning loves of the desert. This is the love for the small unexpected life found burrowing beneath layers of rock and sand, escaping the climate.

—⁓—

Naked and frail, Rose Reynolds stands before the fully dressed Stranger, walking underwater now. It is as if she must swim naked toward the big black drain obscured at the bottom of the swimming pool. There on the drain she must find the tiny black object she has lost, the small black case that contains her life and her child's, down there on the drain. She must force her head even further down and swim, holding her breath, exploding in the chest and ribs and throat, her face going purple from the want of life in her. She might swim that far if she had any strength, but her strength is gone off somewhere, swept underground and out to sea. She looks up at the Stranger, speechless. The pain of her life has so subdued her. *Don't let Alfie die. Please. Please.* At the tenderness in that obscured face. Really, no one else would notice. His shoulders nearly fill the room. His blue shirt has pulled up out of one side of his belt to expose his flesh, a tatter of light brown hair. He makes no move to undress himself.

—⁓—

This then is the sunshine of the desert.

—⁓—

"Close your eyes," he says. His hands encompass her ears. The sounds of the world fade away, even the traffic beyond his window, even the stereo he turned on earlier to play innocuous tunes, even the sound of his breathing.

She must be looking at him oddly, she standing there in his shower where he has placed her, his hands clasped as before to the sides of her head. He looks into her eyes so long she has stopped trying to avoid it. She so thin and naked with water and soap running off her ribs in currents. *Once she was beautiful, she thought. Once Rose was beautiful and someone was to be trusted in her life.* The Stranger's voice is deep and beautiful in itself, resonant and reassuring now. "Close your eyes, my new Rosie. I'm washing your hair. You're miserable in there."

"I don't care about my hair," she says. "This is not a good idea." Her hair is clean. She has always been meticulous.

"So how slim are the chances, Rosie, that you are sick? Don't torment yourself like that. You're so miserable in your skin, Rosie," the Stranger says. It lurches, circling back on her again and again. Moments flash back to her, words, and scenes: how Hibbie had stopped washing himself. She forgets so much here, washing about in the nightmare her life has become. Surely she is not ill. Surely next week she will find out that they are all all right.

—⁓—

It is important not to let a paranoia take over what small forces of life that are left to us.

—m—

This morning, so early that even Alfie was still asleep in the tiny room, she pulled all the Husband's things down on her until she was covered with his cleanest scent, the one she knew so well for nearly fifteen years, the warmth of his clothes heavy as his arm around her, her own heat so loyal to him it hadn't needed sexuality under all that wool reassuring him, radiant as the heat two bodies make. It was hardly ever bad between them. For years he had been her closest friend. No, it was hardly ever bad, not until the end. No, not until then. So she is thinking.

"Rose, Rose," Jane Anderson is saying to her. "Come out, you'll suffocate in there." Tomorrow, she knew, Jane Anderson would help her pack Hibbie's things away. To think that this lovely scented man of hers had gone so wrong, until he had actually begun staying home, sitting in the same sweat shirt and knit trousers from day to day, refusing to give them up for washing, sour, his hair more and more oily, his breath gone far beyond stale. She had thrown the sweatshirt and trousers away, long ago it seemed, even before he died, hoping to activate him in some way. "Come now," Jane Anderson said. "Take yourself a hot bath."

She had a shower that morning; yet it seemed this man was doing something to her; he had removed all her clothes.

Yes, the Stranger is washing her entire body, carefully. It is not unlike what the Dead must experience on their first time out of their corporeal homes, she thinks. Not unlike what an undertaker might have done to her husband at the funeral home.

—⟋⟍—

Today I take the plane up. To look. For anything, I say, anything that is helpful. Searching for them, among other things. The headache recedes little by little and is gone on an expanse of clouds.

"To go home would be helpful," someone says. I can hear it even up here.

I have taken the ultra-light up. I am free of sand. I float on currents as if I am in a little boat. Shimmering waves of heated air stretch all around me. Far below, I can see an endless, waterless beach where tiny people dig an oblong pit. You don't have to tell me what they are doing. They are burying one of our drivers. You too are down there, Isabella, in the heat, with your shovel.

It goes unspoken. Water swarms around me. When I land no one speaks. This is your fault, they seem to say, for your ignorance, your selfish timing. Why couldn't you have saved all of us?

Go to your God then, I say.

"Ramon is dead," my wife says. She drives the umbrella into the ground like a stake. There are tears on her cheeks.

"May he go with God," I say. "May Ramon live with his God forever." A mirage of a freight train splits the temples of my clarity. The dunes spin around me, do not recede.

My wife slaps my cheek. Before I can stop myself, I have knocked her down. I stand over her, stunned at my performance. I have never before done such a thing. She lies, one leg twisted under her, staring at me in disbelief.

"I don't suppose the two of you could do that again," Piers says. The eye of his camera points directly at us. "I missed the part where the wife fell on the grave of her lover," he says.

—𝔪—

The Stranger washes her in the shower, using a sprayer, directing a warming flood into her long hair, between her legs, on her cheeks and chin; scrubbing around the flanges of her nose, her brows. No soap seeps in, he is that careful. Around her breasts, up and down her sides, rinsing her, leaning over to kiss her very briefly in the deep well between her ghostly breasts. And again. His hair is thick and brown and straight, alive, she sees, in her hands. She clutches at it. Crumples it. His hands have gone away now.

She looks up. He holds the sprayer again. Eyes open into the water coming down in needles all over her head. He has pinned her hands over her head. With its spray he rivets her body like a piece of aluminum foil against the metal restraint of the shower stall. He has let go of her. Her eyes open to see that he has taken the small square of metallic paper and peeled back the lid to reveal a lubricated rubber ring and folded penile tube.

She would have kicked him again. She would have kicked Hibbie again and again in the side of his suit until he came back to life. She should have kicked him so much earlier. She does not know that her error has been in being far too kind.

The man is fully naked now in front of her. He is strong and nicely shaped. He is touching her. His head comes down. The Stranger is kissing the tips of her breasts, her collarbones. His broad hands slip up and down her breasts, pinching her very gently. His body heat sears up and down, front then back. He kisses her shoulder blades and neck, sliding against her in a cascade of foam. She can feel the smallest slivers of herself slipping to either side between her legs with the motion of his fingertips. Each tendril of hair, top and bottom, is held stiff with soap. She could not speak if she wanted to as, all at once, she feels the upsurge of his plunge into her. A sharp pain shoots up from her cervix into the back of her navel as she cries out. He does not pull back. He merely looks into her eyes as if waiting for something from her. And if she could, what would she say?

In spite of her saddened state, while she is waiting for him to move, she is aware that burning coals have fired themselves somewhere between the frontal bones of her body, in her skull and ribs and pelvis, between her eyes at the base of her nose, and in the flesh in her face, between her legs. He is large inside of her, but he does not move. Her breathing is shallow and fast and fills the bathroom with too much steam and noise as she waits for him to begin. She would rather the Stranger put some music on so she would not have to listen to herself. He is kneading her chest now as if looking for wounds. But it is the sound of her own breathing that starts her up. Still he does not move. He holds her head forcibly under the spray, broad tongue lapping at her mouth. She laps back in fear that if she does not she might drown. She twists her head back and forth but there is no moving under the Stranger's hands. She can feel a slow almost imperceptible trembling coming out of him. "Too much water," she wants to say. "Too much water." But she is breathing too heavily now, waiting. It is running down her throat. The Stranger's groin is up tightly against her own, suddenly out then rubbing seductively on her belly and thighs, then into her, and she is slipping up and down now, against the cold metal wall, her thighs arched like a rubber band around his upper legs, and then around his waist as he is moving; she can't tell whether she is crying or not, her back is slamming against the wall so hard, his mouth sealed around her own.

It is as if he makes contact with himself somewhere inside of her, makes an electrical loop of himself by thrusting at the self-same moment with the same pulse, down her throat and up into her. The water pours down on them, freezing cold, but still he keeps up this throbbing motion, top and bottom. It makes no difference if she is crying she is gasping so much. She has never felt anything quite like this. Her backbone slaps against the wall, stops, and she hears, just as suddenly as he first came into her, in the dead silence, very deeply from the bottom of his chest, his groan. And then, too, in chorus, there is a sudden hammering in the pipes as if something trapped in there has been sending messages and wishes to stop; and then that, too, ceases. He reaches around her and turns off the showerhead. His arms tighten around her torso for one moment, and in the same motion he jerks out of her. Her organs fall in on themselves, and then the floor touches her feet again. Without once looking into her face, the Stranger winds a long, rough, white towel tightly around her and hands her her clothes. His back turns toward her then, long and flawless, even elegant, as he slides the rubber device from the front of himself, flushes it, pees, jiggles himself, and steps out of the bathroom. The white towel wraps around his waist again ahead of her.

Rose reaches to shut the door behind him but unexpectedly he has turned. He is looking at her oddly, tilting her head against the doorjamb to meet him in unspoken conversation again. He takes hold of her arm rather painfully and now she is cold and perplexed in the hall. The towel is draped around her feet. "Don't you have anything to say?" the Stranger asks.

—⁂—

These then are the dunes in the sea of sand: ridge dune, star dune, and crescent dune. Ridge dunes run parallel and are called transverse. They stand at right angles to a singularly directional wind. The star-shaped dune can be most magnificent in the Sahara, some reaching 260 feet. The star dune is the result of multi-directional wind. At the edges of the desert, where there is little sand, the barchan crescent-shaped dune is formed.

There the wind blows mostly from one direction, coming over the outer curves of the crescents toward the pointed ends. While the star-shaped dune is relatively stable, the barchan may shift location as much as five and a half feet a month.

I am thinking that to be lost in the sea of sand could be a fatal mistake.

Alone I have wandered out, in search of something or someone, I forget which. Thrice I have come upon the Place of the Button as Piers now calls it laughingly. Thrice I have come upon the terrifying knowledge of my circular self.

—⁓—

Rose stares over the Stranger's shoulder to avoid him, stares at her own arm, looks up again ever so briefly. But still he gazes at her face. In his eyes she sees the tiny reflection of her own flushed face, her high cheeks, the depressions under them, the straight nose almost long, the little v over her teeth, the cascade of his dark wet tooth marks across her collar bone. "I forgot something," Rose says. "I think I'll be going home now."

Her one arm is bent over her head, caught, wrist in his hand, balancing the second towel on her head. Soon it will come tumbling down she knows, and with it her wet hair all over his chest. He is kissing her now and they are beyond the bathroom, in the hallway between here and now and then and there. He is still a stranger now, she is thinking. A certain panic comes over her once again. Always she has been afraid of strangers, yet it has been the betrayal her own intimates, family and closest friends, have given her that has slain something deep inside of her. Possibly it has even killed her child. What is the difference between Stranger and Family now? Where will any of it lead? Should she, she wonders as his hands move into her, should she be able to foresee anything more than the usual cycles of color and light? Of blood and not blood? She has never been any good at foreseeing anything.

—◊—

For the fourth time I have come upon it. And the fifth.

—◊—

In just one moment perhaps, the Stranger will pull back the towel he has placed around her, and his bedroom, which Rose has never seen, will open up. He will surprise her by touching her again and again, probing her, perhaps in a more kindly fashion, when she had thought that they were already through. Only slightly will he be scratching her with the corner of his thumbnail now while Rose emits merely a sudden cry, mostly an intake of air. She will find herself, this time, in the midst of a pile of inventory papers where he will place her, cold and awkward, on the floor.

Forcefully, and too pointedly, the Stranger takes the towel that he himself has wrapped her in, away from her. She spins, involuntarily, as in a nearly learned dance, out of control and up against him again, along with the clothes she holds to her breasts and belly. Rose looks up to see a myriad of orange artificial animals splayed and stuffed with suction cups on their tender feet, caught in a fishnet on the ceiling of his room.

And now in his bedroom, among the inventory papers, all the while his powerful shoulders are advancing and retreating, his groin trembling and plunging within and out of her, the Stranger is overcoming her with his life, his sex and how it feels to be the kind of person he is. He tells her how it is to be with her, how it feels to be inside her, surging like this, with her warmth pressing in on him, all around like a huge hot rubber glove. She isn't asking but he tells her how it is to be with other women, larger and smaller women, younger and older women, women with children, some more than one child, and virgins, too. He speaks to her of his philosophies on the topics of virgins, on the seriousness of governments, and on the nuances of his work including the grave importance of choosing stuffed toys with suction cups that stick extremely well to the windows of his car. He goes on about learning to shoot a shotgun as a child, about the first animals he killed as a boy, how it felt to see the blood running out of the small bodies as they lay vibrating in the dirt, and how it felt to hear the animals cry. Then come his questions, which she will not answer. But then, Rose will not be saying anything during this encounter. His lips, each time he asks her a question, cover her own. He pulls back a moment as if to permit her to speak and then goes on. She sits up, rolls to one side to extricate herself. But he places the heel of his hand on her chest completely staying her.

On the wall and ceiling, plastic eyes stare out from stuffed orange animals in a net. She watches this now while this man does things to her. He grows orchids, he says. The net of animals pours from one corner to another, along its adjacent wall, and across the ceiling. Everywhere are their eyes: the black, striped, ovoid irises with their pupils poked into them—as if drilled out by ants with ice picks or guns. The Stranger has put something cold into her, perhaps the petal of a flower, or his hand. Some fleshy part of it she feels deep inside. "Since you're here," he says. She cannot sit up.

There are orchids everywhere in the yellow stuffed room. She had not noticed it before. There is a penetrating funerary heat, so overwhelming in the moisture of flowers and artificial animals. A terrible mustiness establishes itself in spores throughout the contents of the overheated room. A pile of papers has been shoved aside; a pale green sheaf sticks to her bottom. These are the papers for the assignation of stuffed animals. He bends her over her own knees, unreels the paper from the back of her. She is not much more now than a stuffed animal herself.

—⚭—

They told me that the temperatures in the desert would vary greatly between night and day. Even gigantic dunes, as I understand it, were first formed when a fixed or stationary object, for instance a plant, halted drifting sand.

—⚭—

For one moment, he places her hand around the rubber sheath he has placed over himself, and squeezes it. She feels a tiny pulse deep in the center of the sticky, flesh-filled plastic bag; the pulse races back and forth squealing like a rodent across her palm, crying out.

Hatred is such a new emotion to Rose. She must consider these things, she thinks, very carefully. Rose turns her head to look at him now, this Stranger, naked, too, and smiling gently as he hurts her repeatedly. The Stranger who handles her so cruelly is not smart, but he is strong and perhaps even patient with her. Without him, perhaps even in this moment she might not have been able to have gone on. Surely Rose would not have harmed herself when her little child needed her so, but what might she have done? Slumped down beside the road perhaps? Wept beside the road, an easy target for any passer-by? At least she is alone now in this home. She is inside walls and not cast off to the elements and its unknown strangers. The Stranger is oddly familiar now. Somewhere she fears that she is bleeding. Or that she will collapse.

———

There is a certain terror when one finds that one is lost and cannot find the camp or any remembered object in relation to it.

———

"And anyway she was a blonde," the Stranger says. She can hear her own voice, low and rasping again in unintelligible syllables. A pain shoots up the back of her neck from trying to hold her head up again.

"But you're not a blonde, Rose. Probably you have never thought to consider something like that," the Stranger says. "There is a world of difference in how a man responds to a blonde, Rose, rather than a brunette. The blonde in my last girlfriend brought out the very worst in me. Blonde right down to her itty bitty wick."

It seems as if they are spinning now. His fleshy mouth could encompass her whole face, she believes. He has taken in her chin between his lips as well. And then the brown wilderness of his thick, sweaty hair presses hard against her cheek and neck, comforts her like the face of a big damp dog, as he jerks and groans. When he has pulled out, the inside of her falls into emptiness. He flips her over, too quickly, and she feels her stomach ride the air as it used to do when she was a child in the back seat of her father's car when they went too fast over unexpected hills.

"Please stop," she says very hoarsely. This is a voice in her own throat Rose cannot recognize. The Stranger pulls the pillows up against her waist and presses her face into them. He turns her head slightly so as not to suffocate her. And the pendulum of his testicles swings ever so gently again against the backs of her thighs. It takes a special woman to succumb, the Stranger says, to a total passion, so he says. The man who holds her addresses her then, saying that he would never hurt her seriously, except perhaps like this when he is so rough and penetrating. Does she mind? She doesn't really mind it this way, does she? Or perhaps only a little bit, when he does it this way, as he did with his last girlfriend when she had to call the police—sometimes these things happen when there is intensity, he says.

But it can't be true, Rose thinks, that the Stranger will really hurt her. It is not in him to cut her with utensils or actually murder her, though perhaps she can feel her insides falling in and out of her. She doesn't know anymore. He bends her over his knees and runs his hand into her backside. He slides a cool cream into her and then more and more of his hand. Please stop, she is saying. But no one has been listening for a very long time. Consequences must be thought out ahead of time, her mother is saying. And there is her grandmother saying, There there. A pain pierces along the underside of her spinal cord and then she is shocked and numb at her bowels tugging and ejecting him repeatedly. Her whole body seems to have congealed around the impulse to be rid of him and has begun to pulse. He bends over her again.

Rose watches it seeping out: her beliefs in what every moment has been. This Stranger, this seller of soft stuffed animals, would hurt her; but the Stranger would never sneak up on her, distort her life, her way of thinking. The Stranger would not confuse her and warp her child. Nor, it was true, would the Stranger ever say anything truly interesting. He would never understand her jokes or her descriptions of things. Yet for now, even this gold-eyed horror of a man would try to bring her fresh images of life, of his life, born of a culture she neither dreamed nor understood. No, this man could never drag her into his own depletion. He was completely other to her. There were rusted automobiles in his front yard, melting into a combination of red American dirt and air. And yet, she hears him saying,

It's good, isn't it? Is it good for you, Missy? Is it good?

Later on she will remember the feeling of his broad chest slipping up and down her vertebrae in a wash of matted hair and sweat, and how he was even then telling her how just last week his sidekick had been arrested for shoplifting. "My other partner and I had to calm him down. The kid's having a hard time growing up." She begins to notice her surroundings now.

"Why?" she finally gasps. "Why— rape— me? "

"Rape?" Suddenly there is no movement in the room. They are a frieze perhaps on the side of some painted and recently fragmented vase. "Rape?" he asks in horror. "You came with me, aren't you willing now?"

"Please stop now. Please not this way. Please stop now. I'm hurting so badly now. Please don't go on."

"We're only finishing now," he says. "We're only finishing what we started. We'll just finish it now. You know I think that's what I like about you, you're so frail. Crying like that and crying now. I know you don't like it that much, but you'll learn. Soon you'll be asking me for it. I know you will. Come in, please, my daddy, you'll say just the way you used to do. All right," he says. "We'll go the other way, if that's what you want. We'll go home like usual." He is out of her then for a moment but then he is inside her again, up against her womb, against the place which she has held to be part of her own spirit, the first home of her child, her family. "No, please stop." He is against it now, and it is her fault. She would never deny it. But then Rose has a tendency her grandmother would say to blame everything on herself. And then he is back and forth, in and out in a frenzy of finishing. It's her fault that she has ended here, though she will try to beat on him to stop him for a time and then stop again trying, overcome by a radiant fragrant heat that she has never fully understood before. She begins to cry for him now, too, desperately lost inside of her, unable to finish anything.

On and on, he would go until she would merely be a see-through coverlet for part of him, until her entire body would be worn thin as a formless nylon stocking, her body stuck to him in a paste. She has said something now. Her voice is hot and raspy, coming as it does from underneath her badly bruised body out through a pile of papers and stuffed animals, beneath his body hunched over her once again this way, a terrible crushing weight over the top of her back and lungs, her ribs nearly breaking over his arm as he pounds. The plastic sucker of some animal has attached itself like a third nipple to her side. Rose can feel the comfort of its faux limbs and tail flapping and motioning to her against her stomach and thigh. Perhaps she would delude the Stranger by speaking to him. She can think of nothing that would stop him now but speech.

"What did you say?" Momentarily he is frozen in his endless act. He says it again: "What did you say? Why do I like this job?" he repeats it after her. He is incredulous. "'Why do I sell stuffed animals?' That's what you asked?"

His hands release her for a moment and flail about in the air. He turns her like a roast on a spit, his hands leap like white frogs overhead. She is losing consciousness, she thinks. Everything has begun to float now. Pain is gone, and bewilderment. A feeling of warmth moves through her, like an ebbing of hot mud washing into and over her. How strange, she thinks that she hadn't noticed so many things about his room. This location for her greatest change. She has changed into something else now. She doesn't know what. She is lost now, or located. There is a little light at the end of the room where a stick of incense burns in the corner under the dimmed lamp. He has not burned her with it. That is something good, isn't it? It isn't just the perfume in his hair that would account for the florid scent surrounding her, she thinks. She can see in one of the black plastic animal eyes near her face that she would seem now to still be crying, even though her face does not in itself seem to be contorted. She hears no odd noises coming from herself. Only feels the dampness running down onto her hands. If Rose could think, she would chastise herself. How wrong-headed it all was, the very life of her little boy was now in question, and his happiness—everything so tenuous, so aching with disbelief. And just that day she has had to wrestle him crying, *Mommy, Mommy, make them stop,* on her lap his arm out straight while they plunged the terrible needle in and took away his blood. So far, she had never had a more terrible experience than that.

A watercourse is sent from the place where her body sees. Rivulets meet somewhere near her breastbones, somewhere under him. He has broken all his promises. He has risen up on his arms and lightly haired knees to speak to her. He leans forward, licks her cheeks.

"To earn my way, of course," he says, almost angrily, "to get the money for my restaurant." Perhaps he has been telling her about this all along. His fingers are moving in and out of her. "It's not so bad, Rosie," he says to her, "selling goods off the back of a semi-truck. You wouldn't think so, but it's possible. I can make some days two hundred dollars in one day. People aren't buying much right now—" he admits tentatively. She holds her hands against his chest and then his waist, to stop him, but he is going in and out of her again as he speaks. It wouldn't matter really what he said he did, whether he was a doctor, accountant, or nurse. The indifference toward her would be the same. Perhaps her wrists will break, she thinks and her hands fly loose about the room like the white hands and face of a mime in the dark. "The recession has hurt even the sale of black market stuffed animals," he says. He pushes her hands away from his chest, looks down almost wearily where she has tried to scratch him away. On his lower chest, almost his belly, there is now her bright red tattoo, like the footprints of a quail and all its young; it bleeds out through his sparser hair as if through tall grass.

"He gets them cheap, these animals," he says, "because they don't meet standard regulations. Buttons and things." For the first time, she can begin to feel what is happening to her. He turns her over yet again. Sweat runs down the side of her neck where it winds like the threads of a rope around and into his bigger neck, where he breathes into her ear, moaning then speaking, then somewhere in between he is continuing in a voice increasingly straining. "Merely my weekend job . . .This is only just a little something . . . . Painting houses . . . is . . . another . . . job." Decent occupations, all of them. The Stranger will tilt her now and then, shift his approach and for a moment he will stop speaking. He slaps her chest. He puts his fingers in one part of her. Through her tissues he feels his penis in the other part. He jerks himself up and down and now she is screaming. For him, he thinks. Surely it is a ludicrous dream. She has begun crying hysterically now, laughing and crying, wailing really, and breathing very rapidly. She sounds like a kind of machine with an alarm in it. Her voice is keening in a way she has never known herself capable of. She laughs and cries and wails.

"You wouldn't believe," the Stranger breathes, lunging ever forward like some sort of high-powered metallic device. "I painted over a wallpaper today. I was so tired I painted right over it, rather than strip it down. I might have gotten away with it," he confides in her. "But then the blasted bubbling began, the peeling off and all the running down the walls. It looked like oatmeal coming up inside of it. Not," he pants, looking down at her parts, "not unlike yourself, I might add." Her laughter is not good, she thinks. It is not good the way she is laughing and crying now and slapping at what she can reach of him as if he were a stinging insect coming at her again.

Like some pink rubber doll with the legs splayed and the central crease jimmied open with blunt instruments, she is inert beneath his rocking motion. A liquid runs down now between her legs and onto her thighs. He has put himself in her mouth and bowels and vagina again. There is a shaking in her limbs that seems convulsive. He'd spent the entire day in his boss's house, doing a job that should have taken a few hours, scraping it down to the bare plaster, peeling off paint and paper like scabs. *Will it never end? Will it never ever end?* But she is without words. And then it has.

Perhaps he has been in the bathroom now for a long while, she doesn't know. She feels no pity for herself. She is lying on the floor, on her face and belly, her arms and legs spread straight out, the fingertips lost somewhere. There is a dull ache inside of her. Every part of her has been slapped and hurt, and she is not sure whether any part of her will close on its own. Nor in which room she has finally found herself. She sees an unfamiliar fireplace, a lot of manuals, and books. A rivulet of spittle has run out the corner of her mouth. She feels herself split in two, and at the center is a new and unequivocal dark rural tunnel that runs straight up through her throat and out, in the place of human speech, as though she has been run through with a splintered post.

—⁂—

I have read that it is possible to drink and absorb more than one liter an hour while walking in the desert. In addition it is necessary to take in salt.

In dehydration, it is easy to experience debilitating heat cramps. One comes to understand the phrase, the salt of the earth.

Who wore this button? By choice? By command? Man? Or boy? A willful act? Who wielded the needle to stitch it into place, perhaps several times? Accompanied by what bodily tears?

I am thinking, the vertigo of the desert is barely anything at all. How do we even know any of it is going around? It is all so much the same. Yet I know it is pivoting. I walk in circles now around the only thing I can locate: an hysterical note—indeed I am all laughter now. I am glaring at my own two feet. Walking in a two-meter radius, round and round a single button. Here I am! And going around. The sun is most interesting now, how dependable it is. I take off all my clothes, but for my underwear, and cover myself with sand as best I can. Patting it down up to my armpits. Around one shoulder anyway. To get out of the sun. I prop my hat over my head. I did not want to find it. It is not what I came here to find. "Ancient armies are pure!" I shout into the button. "Ancient armies! Time purifies their intent! Ancient armies are pitiable and exotic!" I shout. "They were defenseless to wind! To solar glare! To the abrasions of flying sand! They had families! They had children! And parrots! And grannies!" I scream. "Their grannies had no weapons against wind! Granny was an ancient! Did you ever hear about that, antiquated grannies? No one cares for antiquated grannies anymore!" I lie down now and weep. Snuffling up the moisture already winging its way from Italy or perhaps some arctic front. On the cloud of a breath now, just under my hat, that might be my dream. I take a deep rest. Every once in a while I might raise up my cap, wave it feebly around, in the soon to be here-after, signaling for a little something or other, a fretful wish, tourniquet or tumbler, thimbleful or inward one and a half summersault pike.

—◊—

Finally Rose slips out of the apartment building unseen; she has no one to whom she could go, now that her sister and William have moved back home to be cared for by Freddy and Vivien. Rose lingers on the corner, watching the buses shuttling to and fro filled with strangers looking down on her. Eventually then, she moves to stand alone, in a dress clean and soft as a hospital gown, in an immaculate room—with shining floors. She is tipping a long thin and shaking brush, longer than her forearm, toward a broad white square. Here she has brought herself somehow to her own studio. The only place she and Alfie now have, the place where they will live on two cots in this one shining room. Others have had less, her grandmother would say. Here Rose will put the slightest touches to a blue droplet of paint on her canvas. Her arm trembles ever forward with the brush as she waits for her little son's return. The canvas is stretched tight and stuck to boards made square with heavy-duty staples shot into them with an electrical force. If only she could get enough perspective to see herself, and how she copes, perhaps then she could cope some more.

Soon, if she can gather her wits, Rose's voice may return to her. She dreams a request that she knows she will never ever be willing to make, a request that some unknown stranger might help her in some way, perhaps merely by sitting with her as she waits through that endless dinner hour when long ago Hibbie would have come home, or through those afternoons when the Lover would have laughed with her and watched her painting, all the while crying out, "More dunes, I say! Less water! More dunes!" But that is gone now, all of it. Already she has begun to grope her way across the broadening field as she waits for Alfie to come home again. She waits to take his little hands into hers. There is a peculiar light heaving over everything. If she could just know what exactly it is, or where the light is coming from, perhaps it would go away from her—or stay. Rose no longer knows which she might prefer.

—⁓—

Dunes are first formed when drifting sand is halted by a fixed or stationary object, for instance a plant. Average temperatures in the desert vary greatly between night and day. The Lover has said as much.

—◊—

CHAPTER VIII

I MUST REMEMBER TO WRITE THIS DOWN IN MY JOURNAL, how somewhere hidden are heaps of stone our guide found just last week and, in our group's wandering about, lost again. An effluvium of dust has hung over us for two months now, almost three, shielding us, or so the crew would hope perhaps, from excess of sun.

—⚬—

"My god," I say yet again. "What vertigo!" Or, has the horizon shifted again? Acres and acres of sand shift by in front of us.

—⚬—

"See that," I laugh. "You know you are going to get the wind knocked out of you when you see that. Probably for good. In ten minutes give or take a few." The wall is truly nine thousand feet tall, or so the manual says, as it looms above the dunes in a steely, carbonic-looking, bluish dirt. The wall, our newest hindrance, impenetrable dust.

—⚬—

My wife is sitting in a hole she's dug, looking at her fingers as if they ache.

"They're gone!"

"What's gone?" I ask.

"Everyone of them is gone! Can it be the heat?"

"What is gone, for Christ's sake, Isabella?"

"The moons in my fingernails. Every one of them is completely gone."

"That's very strange, Iz," I say. "Maybe the heat is getting to your eyesight. It's certainly done mine in, I must say. "

"Let me see your nails," she demands.

I hold out my encrusted hands. "Of course," I say. "Have a look at them— Look at any part of me you want, you're my wife. Even palm reading must be in the contract, fine print."

"Completely," she says, bewildered. For a moment I think her reddish hair is about to stand straight up. "Yours are completely gone, too!"

And they are. I look at them. I push the cuticles back a little bit. "You're right. The sun in abundance," I shrug, "but no moons." I can't bring myself to tell her what I think it means.

But there they are, my fingers baked completely brown and creased as though I were my own grandfather. And there's not one nail that has a moon in it.

"Call the others over here," she says.

They hold out their hands.

Anne, concerned, pretends to giggle but it comes out all wrong.

"You can't keep me in the house if I don't wanna stay here, Daddy," Piers screams, prancing, his arms behind his back, clowning around. "I'll go out my window, just you wait and see me, Birdy. You'll see the last of my tail feathers in this dirt, Big Daddy, if you're gonna put your nail cleanliness plan ahead of other truly important personal hygiene problems we're having here— Belly button odor stoppage, for one thing. I, for one, have grit just everywhere. And my toenails are not pared!" He rips his boots off. "Take your hands off my fingers, man! Look at your own goddamn nails. Let go, I say. I say, let go. I don't care if you are the Admiral or the

Commodore or whatever you claim to be. Get your freaking hands off me, right now!"

―〰―

We are working by night now under floodlight as long as the generator will hold out. Supplies should be dropped in the morning if Right-Reg, as we call him, can find us after the storm. Already camaraderie, purpose break down here.

"Come look—" I say. "See it rising up out of the dunes!" I have such vertigo I don't know.

"Come look at it, he said!" Piers mouths.

"We're not interested."

"Look at it anyway!" I say.

"It's not what we came here for."

"How can you not look at it?"

―〰―

I am alone, so far off from our base camp I'm not sure how to get back. A hull.

"Persians enslaving Central Africans?" Piers speculates, when in a moment he stumbles toward me just as I hoped he would, succumbing to his own nosiness.

Giant oars in their skeletal hands. So much is left of them, mummified by deep heat. On deck a shroud of skin and cloth reclines, ruby pendant sunken like a heart through the fallen sternum—into the violin case the ribs still make.

My wife shrugs up her shoulders, when we get back to camp. She mutters something behind my back. She sneers, as though I cannot hear.

"What did you say?"

Allan turns his camera on us.

"Go ahead knock me over, I said." Iz says again to me.

"Yeah, go ahead," Allan says. "We're rolling here. I'm recording."

"What did you say?" I say to her. I have never knocked her over, or even tapped her on the cheek. "Just tell me. What did you mean?"

"I can't remember the name now."

Allan groans. "Here we go again. Starving and thirsting to death with pseudo-archaeologists sent by shiny magazines—"

I know that I have lost all my former bearing in this unnatural atmosphere. I am so dehydrated, I am sure I hear myself whine. "Would you just come with me to shoot this one last thing, and then we'll all go home. That's what you're here for, isn't it? Would you just come look at what I've found? Piers saw it, too, didn't you, Piers?"

It takes almost a half-day to find our way back there after the next gale of sand. We go by compass, following the charts I made. The witch under the desert sucks us into her bosom. Rising and sinking, we hike.

"Yeah," Annie complains. "If only we had a really good gaffer we could hang onto the boom, skip over this sand pile for once."

"We're just about there," I say repeatedly to their recurring silence. "I've marked it on my map." No one answers, least of all Piers. Everything looks completely different today. The day is scorching suddenly, and windless. No one is saying that normally we would be in our tents readying ourselves for sleep, moving toward the kiln of day.

"You've really lost them now," Isabella ventures, trudging along beside me, stabbing her umbrella into the earth, her hair on fire with attraction as she unwittingly carries our disease. "Do you know? They've no respect for you, Bird. First you insist on this, and then you insist on that. Now you've really lost your crew."

Allan hands over the camera to the Kid. The young one aims, not at the boat. They are an eighth of a kilometer short of it. Now it's Piers.

Piers is dancing and chanting as though he were drunk. He looks like a goat in that rat-brown goatee he's managed to sprout. "Take off these clothes, this skin, my putrid flesh!" he yodels. "Just please oh pleasy, leave me my one good bone to make the music twang! One good thang to make me sang. Oh pleasy, pleasy, roast me, broil me, please don't pickle me, please—"

I don't need to say anything when we arrive at the site. Allan turns his camera on it. Even Piers is in awe of the fact that he has not dreamed the whole thing himself. "Mud. It's preserved, baked on, by mud," Piers ponders. "If the mud weren't here first, they would all have to have been exfoliated by sand down to their bones. There has to have been—but, am I wrong here?" Even before he can say it, everyone stares at him.

"Have we got evidence then of an immense, inland, desert, freaking flood here?" Anne asks out loud, just as we are all thinking it. Allan's camera emits its gritty, clicking, exuberant sound.

When finally, back at camp, I am aware of the daylight passing out from under the knobbed legs of Ramon's camel. So there, I tell myself, So there. I stretch out on a blanket under the stars, trying not to look into my wife's eyes. Yes, we may have, every one of us, lost our dignity for the last month or two, gone increasingly mad even, under the circumstances, but we haven't completely lost our sense of purpose. Oh yes, we are thinking, as the wind comes up rather fiercely again, and the sand begins to shift, there's no doubt about it: Even if we never get out of here, this tripped oasis truly lived.

CHAPTER IX

Gradually as the sky whitened a dark line lay on the horizon
dividing the sea from the sky and the grey cloth became barred
with thick strokes moving, one after another, beneath the surface,
following each other, pursuing each other, perpetually.

—*The Waves*
Virginia Woolf

WITH EACH SNOWDRIFT, THOSE SUMMERS SIFT BACK, as from the surface of a sugar snow. Sand dunes rise two hundred feet tall. Scattered over them, the roses are pungent still; there are no tourists here. Purple breakers crash onto the shore. Side by side on the white wool blanket, Georgia and Rose rest, the hems of their pastel skirts fluttering at their ankles, their sleeveless blouses icy with sweat-salt in the heat by the shore. Suddenly the whole scene is stifled in sand, the air too thick with dust, for an hour or so, for Rose to paint. Under the blanket, the four of them huddle telling stories in the dimly woven light. Finally up and down the empty beach William and Alfie ride their stick ponies again, leaping over rivulets. Again it has come, without effort. Everything changes from landscape to an irreversible luminosity.

Snow reels out in front of her.

Friends have returned, have insisted she come here. To paint. And paint again. Somehow. They say she must paint.

Sometimes at night she paints while carrying his ashes in a pillowcase pulled up in their urn, held tight to her belly and secured around her back. Try, just try, they say. She would not put him in the ground, his little bones. She is shriveled from weeping, moment to weeping moment. There seemed no way for anyone to ease his misery or pain, or vomiting. Alfie gone. Alfie gone. When she is tired, she wraps her body around the vase on the bed as though she were pregnant again. Pale blue flowers awash on the palest coverlet. The delicacy of them is so like his little warm hands brushing against her cheeks. "Don't worry, Mommy. It will be o.k. I'm so hot, Mommy. I'm so hot, Mommy. Mommy, I am viciously hot! Can't you understand? Please run the ice around my back again, Mommy, and a little one in my mouth. I love to suck on the cubes so much." She wraps her arms around the urn while she sleeps. She doesn't care what anyone thinks; no one will see her anyway. Her sister has gone back home, has never stayed around much during Alfie's illness, despite all her promises. And anyone who came to visit her, no matter how frequently, came only by telephone. Weeks, months went by without another human face. Canned goods dwindling. A strange woman came from an agency, left boxes on the step. She might have knocked.

When the television news comes on, Rose Reynolds must shut it off. She cannot bear to see little children suffering at the hands of grown men. In every child she has always seen her own. And always will. She has brought the urn with her to the artist's colony. She herself seems not yet ill enough to be declared so, though her laboratory tests say she is. She thinks she must have deserved to have more signs. Certainly before a child should suffer so. She has only had a few lovers in her life, but her child has died because of it. She names them off: the Student, the Sculptor, the Hit Man, the Husband, the Lover, and the Stranger after the fact, in that order. "That is patent nonsense," her sister says. "Your husband shot holes in his arms, between his toes, in every part of his body—sharing needles with whole unseen populations—and you blame yourself?"

Strangely Rose Reynolds is adamant in return. Even the Husband would never have done such a thing, even in his worst state, if he had known what would have happened to their little boy. He was only thinking that it might happen to himself. Or her. Impossible.

It is all a matter of time, as is everything in life; and time is something like space to her, foreground and background are often in reverse. The understanding of which has made for many great discoveries and artistic breakthroughs though comfort has never been one of them. Well, perhaps for a time the thought was comforting when she was very young; now it is not, and will never be again. She herself is not ill yet, she tells herself, though she certainly feels ill in the very core of herself. In her time she has seen grown men on the television news murdering small children in their mothers' arms. No one has deserved this thing. Certainly not an innocent child. And wasn't she herself once a child? A child still, her grandmother gently says.

Rose Reynolds sits at the piano in the great hall of the mansion that houses only artists here—where they may work uninterrupted on those things which may be salvaged from life itself, which may perhaps give reason or hope or relief. She is not sure about meaning anymore. She sits by the piano, or by the warmth at the large hearth, and listens to the others talking, though she does not distinguish individual words. She has no concern for individual words any longer. The urn is in her room in a corner. Safe from traffic, beside her bed. She has put her hands in and run them through the soft petals of dead flame. Sometimes she tries not to hear his voice. The little bundle of him pressed close up to her side, and saying her name. Mommy, she cries in her own sleep.

—m—

Over dinner they will sit at a long table in the library and hear how the director of the artists' colony must spend so much time fighting those local citizens who insist on poaching deer in their woods.

"Are they hungry?" Rose Reynolds asks.

"The deer? No, it's been a very good year."

"No, the poachers?" Rose asks meekly. She can almost hear Alfie asking for the word again—poaching? Mommy, is it deer, or eggs? Poaching, Mommy? You mean like Robin Hood?

Even Uncle Gideon has called her from the nursing home where he has gone to live, sequestered now and safe from himself. You just call me now, honey, he says, if you want to talk with your Uncle Giddy. Family doesn't turn away its own kind—no matter how far gone.

When Uncle Gideon dies, Rose Reynolds will sit down in the middle of the library, surrounded by books and painters and the feet of chairs, and cry to herself in a small squeaking voice, the letter in her hand and the clipping fluttering in the air that says he has had his services in the same funeral home where her grandfather's funeral occurred. Once her grandmother must have held Gideon in her arms, his little limbs wrapped around her neck, his sweet breath at her brow.

She has tried not to tell them, the musicians and writers and painters there, although she has come close to telling the painter who listens to country music. At night he draws her name sympathetically in the snow on the windows of her car. She has seen him in the moonlight, his tall, slightly sallow frame in the long parka, taking off his glove. The others know what troubles her; there is no concealing anything here.

She will not speak of it. Who needs to have it put into words? My little child has died. Why say it when his voice is so alive inside her head; he permeates the shell of her existence. Even his anger is still with her. Mommy, Mommy, can't you do anything right? She has spilled his medicine; she is trying so hard not to cry in front of him. Mommy, it hurts me in here. It hurts me in here. Please make it stop. She has doubled the dose of his painkiller just to the point before it will make him vomit again. She would give him too much and kill his pain and his little body, too; but she cannot, cannot stand the thought of being without him, anywhere. It would be so easy to help him stop hurting so. She is driving herself on in the attempt to kill his pain without causing him other misery. Now she has tripled it. No one who has not seen it, or had it, can possibly know the boundless ravages of pain, she thinks. If there is something that has no end, it is pain. *Implode,* a magnificent word. No, she must tell herself.

But, Rosie, her grandmother says, if you have nowhere to look, look up. There is an end; there is relief. She cannot bear to think of it. This is her greatest failing then, that she has not been able to help him through to a quicker death. And when, finally, his misery has ended, she will only know it when she wakes with him on her lap clinging to one small white button on the front of her, his little mouth drooling gently still against her shirt, his arm gone from the usual warmth into something too chilled to bear. Every day she forces herself to stop short, it takes all her strength. She must never, ever, relive that moment in her life.

There are deer in this field, behind the mammoth stone mansion with its fireplaces and row after row of portraits above the ascending staircase, old French and Italian portraiture. Some have been lent out to museums and replaced by a faded square of wallpaper and a tiny gold plaque saying where they are. And in the living room still, there are the sleds of the four little children who once lived here. All dead in a week to diphtheria, one after another in their mother's arms; their portraits hang still in each room. No one will take them down. Nor should they, though they have always haunted her. Now somehow they buoy her up on a sympathetic grievous wave.

Look up. She follows that deer now through the freshly fallen snow, out under the swaying pines where once she walked with Hibbie on her original stay when he came back to her cabin and made love to her on his knees, singing songs and phrases of affection he'd made up, shot through with legal phrases and tales of deeds by the universal barrister. There are so many things about him she will never know. To amuse her. He tried so hard to amuse her; without effort he had succeeded, it had seemed.

The pines are the serrated tips of ravens' wings overhead this day, sweeping back and forth on a brittle wind over the brilliance of snow. The sun cuts in, then out of clouds, its rays muted until only the dead white circle persists, and the biting cold. She will drive those feet of hers methodically through the woods, trundling in her long wool coat, past stables, past concealed rose gardens, iced grape arbors, and the blanketed summer cottages where once she paused. Deeper and deeper into the snowy woods, aiming for the fleecy lodge where once she sat with summer friends, even before she married, and watched the small white inconsequential ping pong balls sailing back and forth with mirth. She would sit there again right now, if she could, and dream to herself the hollow sound of the paddle hitting the ball, again and again, against the sound of her watch ticking on her wrist.

The doe, too, seems to have gone this way. One of them. Its hooves dancing in front of her. The other fields not pierced. The lodge itself is locked. She can see the familiar cement floor through the window. There the ball still flies back and forth across the room. One small, white sphere beneath the rotation of sun and moon. She forgets now who held the paddles. She only can recall the brilliance of their laughter, men and women calling out. Such camaraderie she had had never before, or afterwards. Their empty chairs are lined up and waiting against the wall.

Today she has turned on the television news and has caught quite by accident scenes of a child shot in Yugoslavia. How he has turned to clutch his mother, crying for his mother. The horror in this mother's helpless face as the blast went off. Rose has turned it off and wept in a heap on the floor. The total helplessness. Is there no comfort anywhere?

Occasionally she has found it as she sat and stared into the color at the bottom of a blue bowl perhaps. Even a dog's dish can have that color in it—so deep a Mediterranean blue that it speaks of an untouchable summer brilliance where children run careless with their rampant dogs along a beach. Yet, even a bit of lace is pristine enough now to bring collapse and fear. For sustenance she has a little incantation of prayer her mother taught her as a child. Some of the words do not even make sense; they are merely syllables. Still, it speaks to something within, and without.

The prints of the unseen doe lead her on again, out now in deeper drifts, passing right along the white-capped hill. Tiny forked hooves prance in a sprinkling of alternately blinding light. Here is an unusual knoll, and a metallic curvature, jutting out. Pine trees sway overhead whistling through gapped teeth. At first she thinks she is seeing the handlebars of a bicycle abandoned under the leavings of the blizzard last night. Feet and feet of snow have blanketed her life, it seems, since she went to bed.

The shock of it is thorough and unreal. There has been so much snow that this object has been almost completely concealed, a part of the never-ending field. Here in the midst of all this laden beauty, Rose has stumbled over the metal ladder to the diving board. But for the foresight of the doe, she might have run smack into it and fallen into the considerable depth of the snow-filled swimming pool. A chill from the sheer fright of it, disaster allayed, envelops her, boring deeper than the chill of the season through her cumbersome clothes.

Now Rose is crawling on hands and knees, curious as a winter creature while the weather, fluffy and light, continues to fall. Onto the end of the board, she creeps out toward the unseen end to look over the edge, feeling carefully with gloved fingertips lest she might fall straight in and fail to touch the bottom or even grasp an edge. She inches herself across the snow-packed ledge through the smothering particles that yesterday were merely droplets plunging through a changeful air.

On the end of the board, Rose has wrapped her arms around her legs now and buried her face in the wool of her coat. Her breath goes in and out, sobbing with the trees: *Alfie gone, Alfie gone, and nothing ever, ever to be done about it.*

It is as her own mother had always known. Somehow, so extremely far away, in that little town set down in the midst of the open plain, where the wind could sweep across the territory brushing aside identity, her mother had always known it: Rose has never been strong, she has never easily crossed over into anything. Only her vision has buoyed her up through all this time. And now it is meaningless—to her anyway.

Her arms and legs flail about, stirring air as she accidentally slips on the icy plank, and then throughout her sickening plunge. She is flapping about, or would be, in snow up to and now above her head, in substance not yet crusted or solidified. With all the weight of the moist new frost pressing into her arms and legs, against the collar of her coat, into the long glossy hairs above her forehead and at her scalp, against her nostrils and cheeks, sliding down her neck and calves into her boots, sucking her in, if only she could move. She cries as the snow falls in, powder infiltrating, as if shuffling into the secret entrances of a child's winter fort, even into her innermost ears.

In the whitened woods, in the depth of the pool, she feels it, more than hears it, in her own chest. Where is it coming from? A human voice. *Reach up, reach up, won't you please?* A jet of cold rushes down her lungs, wedging crystals into her with such solidity that she fears that she has so stupidly felled her own limbs, bones all going to putty now as if they could be manipulated under the cracks of windows and doors. As her feet touch down on the black drain she knows to be at the bottom of the pool, there is almost a foothold. She cannot see it; she can see nothing but glimmer now. Not the edges of the pool, or where the shallow end must be. Her eyes cannot completely close. They burn with the touch of a cold, soft, white grit that scratches her eyes.

And then, after a few odd jolts that seem to come from out of nowhere, there is hardly any use for struggling. There is nothing but to quietly think of someone passing by on a tiny sled perhaps, or in an automobile, reaching out across the front of the car to touch her knee and say wake up, wake up it's just been a bad dream, or someone to say, *Mommy, please stop screaming you're having a turrible bad dream.* Crystals shine throughout her lungs like powder laid out in two silver spoons. One for her, another for him. *Rose, get a grip on yourself! You're such a prude.* A tremendous explosion seems to fire her motionless limbs from within, like a spider's legs, to shake her hands and feet.

She dreams herself a Christmas rose, on this last holiday with strangers, in a woodland completely buried from the roofs to the tops of pines and hemlock, in a snow as fine as sand. At last she can stand on her own again, she tries to tell herself, to pry herself up by the bootstraps if necessary; she can will herself back through the Christmas woods, shakily moving over the deer's lost trail, veering almost drunkenly, stumbling from time to time, pressing her womanly imprints upon areas of virgin snow.

Then there it is! The house, almost around her now as she passes through the gate where it creaks. Up the porch she goes, in her little leather shoes inside her boots, stepping noisily through the squeaking snowflakes to the sound of someone calling to her. Her mittens rest on the icy handle, fumble to open the outer door, and then the other heavier one with the leaded pane at the top. Her woolen mittens bear clusters of hoary knots where she tries the door. She is pushing against it with her weight, trembling now in her hurry lest she in all her new weakness might fall down and freeze permanently in the road. But, the door swings open at last. A blast of warmth sears her face and the furniture falls from the ceiling into place. There they all sit around the table, just lifting up their cutlery. A peal of cold white fog calls from her mouth, and they turn to greet her, almost in fright:

At last you're here! they cry. *Don't let all that cold air in! Shut the door, Rose! Shut the door!*

There are still a few empty chairs. She takes off her rubber boots and sets them carefully by the door, takes off her mittens and lays them out like summer petals on the steaming radiator to dry. She looks all around the table in surprise. In the corner, a headless female statue towers from a metal pole, arms severed at the upper members, tipped in snow. Her breasts are broken, their delicate glazing shattered, the under structure of wires springing out like hair through the tips where her nipples must have been.

Sit down, sit down! Oh my darling! her grandmother says. She summons her again, wiping her hands on the familiar apron front.

Rose stands still, nearly disembodied by the sight of it: the radiance of their upturned joy. *Are you ready to sit down? Oh! My sweetie! At last you're here. Oh, don't worry so, my Rosie!* her grandmother clucks. *Life is so extraordinarily short to worry like that!*

Rose Reynolds is picking at her food again. Or so someone in the corner says. *Shush now, Giddy,* her grandmother says. *You remember how it is.*

Come now, her grandmother says, putting her arm around her again. *If you can't eat just now, why don't you go up on deck and see if you can see your little boy? We are so proud of him.*

Rose Reynolds steps up the planks and when her head comes out, the sky falls down. Constellations roar like luminous gnats around her head; and in their midst, the expansive square-rigged sails illuminate the dark under the intense and intricate light of stars and a fine moon rocking overhead.

Of a sudden, the cold weight of water pours over her, and then for a moment she is on her knees, blind with it, then released, and encompassed again, sliding down the deck nearly under someone's feet. A hand attaches itself, quick as a mother cat, to the back of her neck, jerking her free from her fall. If not for him, she might have washed entirely overboard and been lost in that boundless inland sea, she thinks. The ship pitches again with a sudden shift of winds. Waves wash over the gunwales and slop onto the bow before he has once let go his grip. The compass rose glows like a coal in front of her, as the wave takes them again and again, threatens to knock them entirely off their feet. She has never known such cold and damp, she thinks, such utter joyous fearsomeness. In the shelter of the binnacle, the compass rose grows its small flame yet.

There now, Big John laughs. *Best to keep the feet on deck, Young Rose, and not go dancing about.* He fixes her hands to the wheel, near his.

In a singular motion, the two of them lean to port. And, to port again, pulling down the belaying pins, guiding the ship through the tunnel of sleet this night has become. No, she has never felt so cold. If her sister or her brother were to ask her that, she would say, No, never, in all my life, Georgie, Freddie, have I ever felt like that. *It is the nature of water to come alive when least you thought it so.* Up and down, the wooden ship pitches like a cork. Up and down, up and down, she rocks, bow to stern, port to starboard, port, port, port, to starboard, and then everything at once. Rain has begun to drain over them in sheets from side to side, to drizzle along her skin.

Look up, the Helmsman laughs. His eyes are black as a wrought iron latch, his beard as well. Somewhere near the mizzen top, a friend carols, black hair and gleaming teeth in moonlight overhead,

Through the midnight hours, snow has begun its drifter's journey toward their earth. Even higher now, the waves; relentless, they seem. With all the torque and motion of their bounty—the luminous crystals are as stationary as stars, as though the fragile flakes had been hung before her eyes on wires, or plunged beneath her lids. Ahead of them, raindrops crack open into globes mid-air, careen into the feathered scene as though waiting for discovery in a distant spring. She hears the repeated impact then, like the slapping together of wet green boards, or wooden footsteps overhead, first the snap, then the shudder of wet sails being loosed and furled. The silhouetted crew is strung like holiday ornaments, working, in the rig.

Weather comes down in flurries, sweeps into the torrent behind them, goes windward, and slams back again as she tries to breathe.

A shout on deck as if from dreams. High and low, another and then another from the top. *Reef that mizzen top! Reef yer mizzen top! Reefing yer mizzen top! Reefing that mizzen top! Reef yer mizzen main!*

"I'm so sorry, Rose. I'm so very, very sorry to tell you about yourself and your darling little boy."

South by Southwest! Running away now before the storm. Light is off the starboard bow, Alfie. I can see the moonlight on your little face. Fog without moisture or solar magnificence, space without stars.

—⋙— —⋙— —⋙—

About the Author

 **Meredith Steinbach** is the author of *To be Sung on the Water, Village with Blue Doors, Beata Rustica: The Tale of the Would-Be Saint, The Charmed Life of Flowers: Field Notes from Provence, The Birth of the World as We Know It; or, Teiresias, Zara, Here Lies The Water, Reliable Light.*

She has written numerous short stories, and one play about the newly homeless, entitled *In the Realm Of Which There Is No Sign.* Prizes and honors have included Winner of the International General Fiction Category in the 2013 Paris Book Festival and Honorable Mention in the 2012 New England Book Festival for *The Charmed Life of Flowers;* the O. Henry Award for the Short Story; the Pushcart Prize, the Bunting Fellowship of Radcliffe College at Harvard University; Thomas J. Watson Institute for International Exchange Travel Grant for research in France and Greece; inclusion in 100 Distinguished Stories, *Best American Short Stories;* National Endowment for the Arts Creative Writing Fellowship; the University of Iowa Fairall Scholarship for a Fiction Writer; Rhode Island State Artist's Grants; among others.

She lives in Rhode Island in a sea captain's cottage with her family, and a Great Pyrenees Mountain Dog and a rescued Welsh Corgi known for spin dancing. She is Professor of Literary Arts at Brown University.

Accolades for Meredith Steinbach's Books

VILLAGE WITH BLUE DOORS

Howard Norman: "Meredith Steinbach is a brilliant writer. Like all of her previous novels, *Village With Blue Doors* is provocative, haunting, a little other-worldly. Page by page offers such vivid immediacy, it is like walking through the Louvre alone by moonlight. Life is illuminated as well as written."

Robert F. Pope: "Meredith Steinbach's *Village with Blue Doors* is a piece of magic, the conjuration of a modern French village in terms of the past, rich in literary allusiveness. With Pere Martin in recovery from near drowning—from which he has been saved by the stone arms of the blue virgin—the aging giant cannot marry his beloved albino sweetheart. In a world both idyllic and terrifying, a village seeks its fulfillment in its people and traditions, in its faith in themselves and each other, in food and music and love. This is a book of pure madness—the kind of madness we might live with every day. . . . The writing is just brilliant. "

BEATA RUSTICA

Meredith Steinbach, lauded for her 'gorgeous prose' by the N.Y. Times Book Review, and by Publisher's Weekly for being 'a writer of sensitivity and grace,' Meredith Steinbach presents in her new novel BEATA RUSTICA an elegant and disturbing view of the inequities of our time as seen through the eyes of a beautiful, young dwarf. Confined not only to living at home with her family, but also to living in a basket when both she and her family forget that she can walk, Beatrice sets out to record all she remembers while on her self-imposed hunger strike toward sainthood. She fails to foresee the arrival of a mammoth cousin, the devotion of villagers, the designs of an uncle, the mercenary nature of her own mother, and the amorous wiles of the owner of the local egg factory. Wryly comic, at times appropriately dark, BEATA RUSTICA is a modern day Canterbury Tale set under the boundless open skies of the rustic midlands.

Edmund White: "I so enjoyed Beata Rustica! It's just the right blend of fantasy and realism and the writing is beautiful."

THE CHARMED LIFE OF FLOWERS: FIELD NOTES FROM PROVENCE

a novel by Meredith Steinbach

THE CHARMED LIFE OF FLOWERS is award-winning novelist Meredith Steinbach's magical tale of camaraderie and delight in the face of adversity. Professor Steinbach reconsiders and reconstructs the components of an old-fashioned fairy tale in this modern day novel set off the beaten path in the vineyards and olive groves of Southern France. When Pearl Queneau, the little albino schoolteacher, seeks refuge in the village of St. X, even the plants and animals transcend their days as textbook entries and come to life for her. Here she falls in love with the proverbial Woodcutter and raises her son in an atmosphere of increasing tolerance and generosity---but for the ill will of a few miscreants who would try to cause them irreparable harm.

REVIEWS & ACCOLADES:

Winner, 2013 Paris Book Festival, international general fiction category

Honorable Mention, 2013 New England Book Festival, general fiction category

CAROL LOEB SHLOSS, Carol Loeb Shloss, author of *Lucia Joyce: To Dance in the Wake*): "This book is as improbable as it is delicious, as dark as it is full of rapture. Above all, it is a meditation on the delightful colors of all growing things: adolescent sons, surviving mothers, and the eels and hedgehogs and plane trees and flowers that inhabit the small villages of our imagination. An amazing read... so scary and yet so incantatory."

JOE W. HALDEMAN: "*The Charmed Life of Flowers* is a love-letter to Provence and to the lives that are intertwined there, animal kingdom and the vegetable one, as well as the charmed and charm-less humans who drift through and observe, and know a little. The writing is evocative and accurate and hard to put down."

THE BIRTH OF THE WORLD AS WE KNOW IT;
OR, TEIRESIAS,

by Meredith Steinbach

 "In her fourth book of fiction, award-winning American novelist Meredith Steinbach reimagines the life of the Greek seer Teiresias. Having outlived everyone he ever knew, the seer looks back at the most significant episodes in his life--a visit to the Delphic oracle, mediating arguments between Hera and Zeus, his experiences as both man and woman--as he confronts the traveler Odysseus in the Underworld. Narrated from shifting points of view with tremendous psychological acuity, Steinbach's novel intertwines time, event, and narrative."

Reviews:

Publisher's Weekly: "…a metaphysical tour de force. Steinbach's writing is as elegant as a neoclassical column."

St. Louis Post Dispatch: "Her latest work of fiction, *'The Birth of the World as We Know It,'* [is] a witty cross-breeding of Greek tragedy and contemporary fiction. Think James Joyce and Homer in a running conversation."

Marjorie Garber, Harvard University, Vice Versa:
"I take the liberty of quoting at length because Steinbach's work is not as familiar as Eliot's or Joyce's, and also because Steinbach does something they do not. She imagines Teiresias in the moment that will answer the gods' question."

Chicago Tribune: "The source of the considerable strength of *Teiresias* resides not only in the vividness with which Steinbach imagines each event of her narrator's life, but in her willingness to let those episodes collect and cumulatively resonate in her reader's imagination…narrated with an extraordinary and just passion."

Harvard Review: "Superbly orchestrated, ornate, convoluted retelling, one in which she has spiced up, ad-libbed, and otherwise domesticated, re-routed, authenticated, and tampered with the archetypes. Steinbach seems to be following no other voice than her own; the result is a shamanistic meditation on the telling of time, the telling of history."

Boston Review: "She is like Joyce, mingling an ironic undertone with sensuous descriptions of vintage cosmetics, sexual sporting, war, and grief. Plot is shiftily dispersed throughout the book, playfully revising the natural sequence of events, so that the novel reads rather like a long, accelerating prose poem borne forward by its rhythms."

ZARA, by Meredith Steinbach

"'Zara Montgomery has not had an easy time of it in this town,' the housekeeper tells us. In moments as close as dreams, as impersonal as newspaper accounts, Meredith Steinbach gives us the life of Zara Montgomery—the precocious only child of a successful Midwestern physician and a failed British lieder singer. In *Zara*, Steinbach has given us fiction as it was meant to be—exacting, compelling, and enduring. The lucidity of this writing, the intricate craft of her structural designs, the richness and humanity of her characters, all point toward Meredith Steinbach as a novelist of exceptional power."

Reviews:

JOHN HAWKES: "Rich, horrific, beautiful, *Zara* is about the life of a woman extraordinary in every way, and is written in prose as strong and fabulous as Zara herself. I could not admire more this profound and exhilarating novel."

HILMA WOLITZER: "Zara is a beautifully realized character whose story is constantly engaging and moving. Ms. Steinbach is gifted and nervy and her book is very accomplished."

BOSTON REVIEW: "She's a critic of myth who also chooses to re-dream and brilliantly reinvent it. In *Zara*, . . . she considers the challenge of heroism in an American setting."

Los Angeles Times Book Review: "Steinbach probes vulnerability, futility in a style interlaced with quality and power."

Chicago Tribune: "The completely written quality of *Zara* marks an author page by page discovering the giddy limits of her talent. . . . I doubt a finer first novel will be published this year."

Chicago Magazine: "A rare, invaluable prize."

Boston Magazine: "A masterpiece."

HERE LIES THE WATER

by Meredith Steinbach

 "Steinbach's intense novel of a circle of friends in rural New England addresses the misunderstandings and lies that destroy people by depriving them of 'the human will to love and learn.'"

Reviews:

Hungry Mind Review: "There's far more metaphor in *Here Lies the Water* than plot or character. Let's read it like a poem. The descriptive language is remarkable. . . . We are sustained by loss, memory, and the order and beauty of art. . . . Steinbach's prose is opulent, musical, disconcerting."

The New York Times Book Review: "Meredith Steinbach would probably cringe at the comparison, but her second novel is the spookiest tale of life gone wrong in suburbia since Ira Levin's *Stepford Wives*... As these revelations mount, ... its gorgeous but sometimes soporific prose becomes its strength, for it makes the wallop that's packed at the end even more powerful."

RELIABLE LIGHT by Meredith Steinbach

 "In this collection of seven stories, Steinbach again distinguishes herself as a writer of sensitivity and grace. The effect is of real voices and real situations, portrayed with scrupulous fidelity to human nature. In robustly simple and direct prose, Steinbach introduces characters who range from an old woman in a nursing home to a black doctor in a New England village. In 'To Be Sung on the Water,' a woman visiting her mother's grave with her sister and young nephew is dismayed to find it sunken and filled with water. The boy's question, 'Why is your mama sleeping in that little lake?' helps bring the protagonist to a moment of transcendent understanding. 'In Recent History' observes the people whose lives have been profoundly affected by one man's experience in Vietnam, which he is tragically compelled to recreate. In the aftermath, the narrator occasionally glimpses the man and thinks, 'How strange and painful to see his face, as if he had not one terrible secret moment in his heart.' Constructed with a quiet and effective craftsmanship, these tales range in tone from comic to tragic, displaying the diversity of Steinbach's interests and themes."

Reviews:

Publishers' Weekly: "In this collection of seven stories, Steinbach again distinguishes herself as a writer of sensitivity and grace."

The New York Times Book Review: "Meredith Steinbach has won both a Pushcart Prize and an O. Henry Award for short fiction, and it's easy to see why. At her best, she gives us what we want from stories: root emotion recognized through someone else's consciousness.

www.ingramcontent.com/pod-product-compliance
Lightning Source LLC
Chambersburg PA
CBHW071232250626
47163CB00001B/149